Acclaim for Graham Swift's

TOMORROW

"A writer of great range, vigor and acuity."
      —*The New York Times Book Review*

"Emotionally piercing."   —*The Boston Globe*

"A continually interesting writer. The secret lies in his story-
teller's gift of tongues, his flair for creating voices that
seem to be talking directly, intimately in your ear."
      —*The New York Review of Books*

"A compelling meditation on family relations."
      —*The Washington Post*

"Seeks out the extraordinary in ordinary events."

"Swift has proved himself
Evocative."

"Builds toward the emotional truths of everyday life. . . . Deftly written." —*Courier-Journal* (Louisville)

"Reminiscent of Harold Pinter's brilliant *Betrayal*."
—*Palm Beach Post*

"Will keep you guessing. . . . The urgent question for the reader is not what will happen next but what has happened in the first place." —*The Guardian* (London)

"An elegant exploration of the fragility of love and the bonds that hold families together." —*Bookreporter*

"Swift once again gives us a book full of characters to care about, and worry for." —*PopMatters*

"Very good indeed. . . . [Swift] is a writer of easy subtlety, who specializes in the sidelong illumination of ordinary details." —*The Independent* (London)

Graham Swift

TOMORROW

Graham Swift lives in London and is the author of seven previous novels: *The Sweet-Shop Owner*; *Shuttlecock*, which received the Geoffrey Faber Memorial Prize; *Waterland*, which was shortlisted for the Booker Prize and won the *Guardian* Fiction Award, the Winifred Holtby Memorial Prize, and the Italian Premio Grinzane Cavour; *Out of This World*; *Ever After*, which won the French Prix du Meilleur Livre Étranger; *Last Orders*, which was awarded the Booker Prize; and, most recently, *The Light of Day*. He is also the author of *Learning to Swim*, a collection of short stories. His work has been translated into more than thirty languages.

INTERNATIONAL

TOMORROW

TOMORROW

Graham Swift

Vintage International
Vintage Books
A Division of Random House, Inc.
New York

FIRST VINTAGE INTERNATIONAL EDITION, SEPTEMBER 2008

Copyright © 2007 by Graham Swift

All rights reserved. Published in the United States by Vintage Books,
a division of Random House, Inc., New York. Originally published in
Great Britain by Picador, an imprint of Pan Macmillan Ltd., London, and
subsequently published in hardcover in the United States by Alfred A. Knopf,
a division of Random House, Inc., New York, in 2007.

Vintage is a registered trademark and Vintage International and colophon are
trademarks of Random House, Inc.

The Library of Congress has cataloged the Knopf edition as follows:
Swift, Graham.
Tomorrow / by Graham Swift. —1st American ed.
p. cm.
1. Family secrets—Fiction. 2. Twins—Fiction. I. Title.
PR6069.W47T66 2007
823'.914—dc22
2007018684

Vintage ISBN: 978-0-307-38643-4

Book design by M. Kristen Bearse

www.vintagebooks.com

Printed in the United States of America
10 9 8 7 6 5 4 3 2 1

FOR TIM

Were we not wean'd till then?

—JOHN DONNE,
The Good-Morrow

TOMORROW

1

YOU'RE ASLEEP, my angels, I assume. So, to my amazement and relief, is your father, like a man finding it in him to sleep on the eve of his execution. He'll need all he can muster tomorrow. I'm the only one awake in this house on this night before the day that will change all our lives. Though it's already that day: the little luminous hands on my alarm clock (which I haven't set) show just gone one in the morning. And the nights are short. It's almost midsummer, 1995. It's a week past your sixteenth birthday. By a fluke that's become something of an embarrassment and that some people will say wasn't a fluke at all, you were born in Gemini. I'm not an especially superstitious woman. I married a scientist. But one little thing I'll do tomorrow—today, I mean, but for a little while still I can keep up the illusion—is cross my fingers.

Everything's quiet, the house is still. Mike and I have anticipated this moment, we've talked about it and rehearsed it in our heads so many times that recently it's sometimes seemed like a relief: it's actually come. On the other hand, it's monstrous, it's outrageous—and it's in our power to postpone it. But "after their sixteenth birthday," we said, and let's be strict about it. Perhaps you may even appreciate our discipline and tact. Let's be strict, but let's not be cruel. Give them a week. Let them have their birthday, their last birthday of that old life.

You're sleeping the deep sleep of teenagers. I just about remember it. I wonder how you'll sleep tomorrow.

Sixteen was old enough, sixteen was about right. You're not kids any more, you'd be the first to endorse that. And even in the last sixteen years, you could say, sixteen's become older. Sixteen now is like eighteen was, sixteen years ago. There's an acceleration, an upgrading to things that scare me, but seem hardly to touch you. 1995—already. I'll be fifty in August, I'll have done my annual catching up with your father. What a year of big numbers. Fifty, of course, is nothing now, it's last season's forty. Life's getting longer, more elastic. But that doesn't stop the years getting quicker, this feeling that the world is hurtling.

Perhaps you don't feel it, in your becalmed teenage sleep. Perhaps you *want* the world to hurtle. Come on, can't it go any *faster*? Perhaps what all parents want from their children is to feel again that deep, long, almost stationary slowness of time. Another sweet taste of it, please.

But sixteen years have passed and sixteen's like eighteen once was, maybe. But that doesn't matter. To me, tonight, you're still little kids, you're tiny babies, as if you might be sleeping now, not in your separate dens of rooms, but together as you once did in a single cot at Davenport Road. Our Nick and Kate. And what I'm feeling now is simply the most awful thing: that we might be wrenching you for ever from your childhood, in the same way as if you might have been wrenched once prematurely and dangerously from my womb. But you were right on time: the tenth of June 1979. And at two, as it happens, in the morning.

Mike will do the talking. He knows, he accepts that it's up to him. On a Saturday, knowing you both, the morning will be half gone before you even appear for breakfast, and you'll need your breakfast. Then Mike will say that we need to talk to you. He'll say it in an odd, uncasual way, and you'll think twice about answering back. No, right now, please. Whatever other plans you had, drop them. There'll be something in his voice. He'll ask you to sit in the living room. I'll make some fresh coffee. You'll wonder what the hell is going on. You'll think your father's looking rather strange. But then you might have noticed that already, you might have noticed it all this week. What's up with Dad? What's up with the *pair* of them?

As he asks you to sit, side by side, on the sofa (we've even discussed such minor details), you'll do a quick run-through in your minds of all those stories that friends at school have shared with you: inside stories, little bulletins on domestic crisis. It's your turn now, perhaps. It has the feeling of catastrophe. He's about to tell you (despite, I hope, your strongest suppositions) that he and I are *splitting up*. Something's been going on now for a little while. He's been having an affair with one of those (young and picked by him) women at his office. An Emma or a Charlotte. God forbid. Or I've been having an affair (God forbid indeed) with Simon at Walker's, or with one of our esteemed but importunate clients. Married life here in Rutherford Road is not all it seems. Success and money, they do funny things. So does being fifty.

You're in tune with such under-the-surface stuff from your between-lessons gossip. It's part of your education: the hidden life of Putney.

But then—you're sixteen. Do you notice, these days, that much about *us* at all? Do you pick up on *our* moods and secrecies? We've had a few rows in recent weeks, have you actually noticed? And we don't often row. But then, so have you. You're at a stage—don't think *I* haven't noticed—when that cord, that invisible rope that runs between you has been stretched to its limit. It's been yanked and tugged this way and that. You have your own worlds to deal with.

And you've only just finished your exams. Ordeal enough. This should have been a weekend of recuperation. And if you'd still had more exams to go we'd have stretched our timetable to accommodate them. Let's not ruin their chances, let's not spoil their concentration. Bad enough that your birthday, last weekend, should have been subject to your last bouts of revision. As it is, we've been tempted. Let's wait—till after the results perhaps, till after one more precious summer. But we came back to our firm ruling: one week's cushion only. And since your birthday fell this year, handily, on a Saturday . . . Forgive us, there's more revision. Exams can affect your life. So can this.

Mike will do the talking. I'll add my bits. And, of course, when he's finished he'll make himself open to questions, as many as you wish. To cross-examination, might be the better expression. It all just might, conceivably, go to plan, though I'm not sure what the "plan" really is, apart from our rigorous timing. It might all be like some meeting that smoothly and efficiently accomplishes its purpose, but it can hardly be like one of your dad's board meetings or one of our cursory get-togethers at Walker's: "That was all dealt with at the meeting . . ."

I think, anyway, you'll want to know everything, the full, complete and intricate story. And you deserve it, as a matter of record.

Your father is gently snoring.

I remember once you said to me, Kate: "Tell me about before I was born." Such simply uttered and innocent words: they sent a shiver through me. I should have been delighted, charmed, even a little flattered. You actually had a concept of a time before you were around, a dawning interest in it. You saw it had some magic connection with you, if you still thought of it, maybe, like life on another planet.

How old were you then—eight? We were on the beach in Cornwall, at Carrack Cove, we had those three summers there, this must have been the second. I'd wrapped you in the big faded-blue beach towel and was rubbing you gently dry, and I remember thinking that the towel was no longer like something inside which you could get lost and smothered, you were so much bigger now. And a whole year had passed since the time when, off that same beach, you both quite suddenly learnt to swim. First you, then Nick almost immediately afterwards, like clockwork. One of those first-time and once-only moments of life. But I'd suddenly called you "a pair of shrimps." Why not "fish?" Or "heroes?" I suppose it was the pinkness and littleness. I suppose it was the way you just jerked and scudded around furiously but ecstatically in the shallows, hardly fish-like at all. I didn't want to think of you yet swimming out to sea. Shrimps.

Did you notice the odd look in my eye? A perfectly innocent question, but there was something strange about it. You
said, "Before I was born," not "we." Nick was still down at
the water's edge with Mike. He came up so much higher
against Mike now, and Mike's always been a good, lean
height. Did you notice my little teeter? But I would have
quickly smiled, I hope. I would have quickly got all wistful
and girl-to-girl, if still motherly. I kept on rubbing you and
I told you, you'll remember, about another beach, far away
in Scotland, where, I said, your daddy "proposed" to me. In
a sand dune, in fact.

That was eight years ago. Half your life. I could still dare
to wear a bikini. It was one of those many panicky but
smoothed-over moments—you'll understand soon what I
mean—which have sometimes brought Mike and me to a
sort of brink. Why not *now*? Oh, we've had our jitters. But
we've kept to our schedule. It will be up to you, tomorrow,
to judge, to tell us if, in the circumstances, you'd have done
the same. But what a stupid idea: if *you*'d have done the
same!

You said you'd like to propose to Nick—to practise proposing to Nick. I said it didn't tend to work that way round,
and it was a thing, anyway, that belonged to "those old
days." And suppose, I said, Nick should say no? My bikini
was dark brown, your little costume was tangerine. It's men,
I said, if it happens at all now, who do the proposing.

And sometimes the explaining. But I think you both
deserve the full story from me, your mother. Mike will give
you his story, his version. I mean, it won't be a story, it will
be the facts, a story is what you've had so far. All the same, it

will be a sort of version of something real. One thing we've learnt in these sixteen years is how hard it can be to tell what's true and what's false, what's real and what's pretend. It's one thing you'll have to decide, unfortunately. Which version is it to be?

At two o'clock in the morning. Of course, we let you know that. A charming little gloss on those facts of life that were bound to get raised sooner or later and can sometimes be (or they could be in those "old days") a cause of awkward Saturday mornings. Though hardly when you were barely three and first put the innocent question and were both completely enchanted, it seemed, to learn that you both came out of my tummy, that you'd both once been there together. And that seemed to be the bit—do you even remember?—that really tickled you pink, that you'd been there *together.* So much so that though you'd moved by then to your first little separate beds, it seemed to reinforce your obstinate habit of ending up nonetheless in the same one.

One morning I found you like that, trying to form a positive little *single* ball of clinging, squirming, not to say giggling flesh. And you said you were practising "not being born yet." And making, if it's possible to say so, a pretty good fist of it.

I should have said that it had tickled me pink once that you'd been there together inside me.

As to that other, critical question: how did you get there?—it never came up then. A stage *before* the stage of not being born yet, that was beyond your reckoning. But you should know that it was our first, unsteady, provisional position: that when it did come up it should be our guide, our testing of the way ahead for the other thing we had to tell you. It should even be, perhaps, the one and the same occasion. Except that when it did come up it was all at my rushing instigation, and you, Kate—this you'll surely remember—took the wind clean out of my sails.

Another girl-to-girl moment like that one about "proposing," and it can't have been so long after. I was the one, not your dad, who suddenly pushed myself to the fore of doing all the explaining. Though I would have started with the standard biology lesson. "Kate, there are some things you need to know . . . about how babies are really born . . ."

God knows what prompted it. Some little look in your eye, which I took as a challenge? Just that speed at which you were growing? What had we been talking about? And you might have let me just stumble on, even topple, still clutching you, over a precipice you were entirely unaware of. And if the truth be known, a sort of gong was banging in my head: Come on, get it over with! But you took the wind from my sails.

"You mean *periods* and stuff, Mum? You mean what boys have to do with their willies? It's all right, I already know all about that stuff. And don't worry, I've told Nick all about it as well."

How old were you? You seemed so blithely, safely sure of your ground that I no longer wanted to risk mine. And I'm not sure, to this day, if I ever want to intrude on those early biology lessons *you* would have given Nick. Your eyes met mine perfectly sunnily. Well, that takes care of that, I thought, that takes care of the facts of life and, until further notice, of the other facts that go with them.

It should all, perhaps, have worked the other way round. That happy well-informedness, apparently, of both of you, should only have let Mike and me press on with our full— agenda. But the fact is it was really then that we fell back on our default position: when they are sixteen. You were surely *too* young, then, for the full agenda. And, on the other hand, if those facts of life really were taken care of and weren't any more like some flashpoint still in store, did we need to hurry towards trouble?

Okay, you'll grasp this, I'm sure: it was to protect us, as well as you, to extend our sweet lease as much as yours. Will you be able to sympathise? Will you blame us—a minor issue, perhaps—for leaving it so long? Or will you understand, at a ripe sixteen, that the timing could never have been perfect and is perhaps academic anyway? At least we'll have kept faithfully and truly to the date we set ourselves.

Outside I can hear rain just starting, softly plopping on leaves. For some idiotic reason, I checked the weather forecast before we came to bed, as if we had some major journey planned. We won't be going anywhere, the last thing that matters is the weather. But they promised rain, steady, persistent rain from dawn till late afternoon. Well, it's started early. Pattering summer rain. I can't say I'm sorry. Good weather for staying indoors. I can't say I'm sorry that tomorrow this house will be curtained and cordoned off by a veil of rain.

What can I do but tell you how it was? What can I do but give you your mother's version of that time before you were born? You're sixteen and the night's not young, but here's a bedtime story.

2

I MET YOUR FATHER when I was twenty and he was twenty-one, in Brighton, in 1966, when we were both at Sussex University. When I say "met" I really mean "went to bed with," "slept with," if there wasn't, that night, that much sleeping. I should be as frank at the start as I mean to carry on. I'd met him, *merely* met him already, and when I met him in the full sense, he'd already met in the full or nearly full sense my two flat-mates, Linda Page and Judy Morrison.

This is your dad, this man fast asleep beside me now, I'm talking about. And that was how things could be in 1966. They couldn't have been like it in 1956, but they could ten years later, particularly at a new university like Sussex. They weren't like it all the time, maybe, but for your dad and me, in the early months of 1966, they were. Whenever we mention "the Sixties" both of you yawn or glaze over as if things are so much more nonchalantly free-for-all and uninhibited now. But I'm not so sure they really are. What are you actually up to, my darlings, at the advanced age of sixteen? You tell me. At least we had the excitement of the new—the "liberated" as we sometimes called it. And it wasn't so amateurish, or so aimless. Your father slept around. He slept with Linda and (possibly) Judy in fairly quick succession, then he slept with me. Then he never slept with anyone else. He's sleeping with me now. These are the simple and basic facts which I've never doubted and I hope, so far as the last part goes, nor have you. And they add up to something that I hope will count for a lot when he speaks to you tomorrow.

At Sussex there was a university doctor who had the happy name, in the circumstances, of Doctor Pope. Every so often, along with a regular queue of other girls, I'd go along to get my dispensation. I remember another, less eager queue when I was small, to get a polio vaccination. What made that age so new, so different from previous ages, was a little pill: once a day for twenty-one days, then a week off. A bit of science, a bit of social sorcery. It was called the permissive age, but was it the pill that produced the age or the age the pill? Sex must always have been around, our parents must have known how to get it. But had there ever been such a rush of it, a glut of it—as if it had just been discovered specially for us, like gold in the Klondike, in the South Downs? Of course, it hadn't just been discovered. But we were children of our time, as you are of yours. Though we only understand afterwards, perhaps, what time it is we're children of.

Doctor Pope was one of those young, fresh doctors, not so long out of medical school, who was only too happy, I think, to have this flow of largely healthy patients, not so much younger than himself and predominantly female, passing through his door. I still see his unpapal, even mock-priestly face. Dark hair, dark eyes, a taste in brightly coloured, unphysicianly ties. Half the girls who went along to him fancied him just a little. He's one of those minor and incidental figures from the past—one day you'll find this too—who suddenly float into your head, so that you wonder, where are they now, what are they doing right now? Do they still have that dark hair? Though this same thing can happen, this same sudden looming out of nowhere, with people who can't be called incidental at all.

Your father slept around and so, thanks to Doctor Pope, did I. Let's not be exact about who did the most, but let's give the edge to your father. I was the younger, if only by six months. And, just for the candid record, your father, before he met me and even in those pill-blessed times, always carried a traditional stand-by: the packet of three. You may think this is information that doesn't particularly concern you. I said to him, "You won't be needing these." But your dad had always been—careful.

How it is for you I don't know. In these mid-1990s, when sixteen is eighteen and when, from all I can tell, what once went on at university now sometimes goes on at school, you'd think you might already be beginners at least. What with all that early knowledge you seemed so glad once to advertise. The facts of life? They've simply been in the air you've breathed, the common small talk (apparently) of infants, they don't need special elucidation.

But on the other hand, for all the all-around-you of it these days, schoolgirl pregnancies by the dozen (yes, Kate, I worry), I think there's sometimes too a weirdly opposite reaction. Why rush into something so patently available? A sort of sex-fatigue before it's even started, a sort of purity or just stubborn sensibleness. Abstention is the new liberation: is that the way the tide is turning? Sometimes when we refer to those oh-so-wonderful, oh-so-yawn-making 1960s, it's not just that you make a show of boredom. Sometimes in your eyes there's the faint hint of a tut-tut. As if you might be about to say to us, a little too late in the day, perhaps: "Oh, grow up."

There's a gap of quite a few years between us, as you may have noticed. You're sixteen, your father's fifty. But that's another shift that's become unremarkable these days. Thirty, thirty-five: that's no longer a cliff-edge for a woman. Mike says—you're familiar with his ironical and slightly professorial mode, though it's not, I'm sure, how he'll address you tomorrow—that the whole thing is changing, there's no longer the pressure of brevity, we'll all reach a hundred, one day, and procreate when we're fifty. Well. "All other things being equal," he adds. If there isn't by then anyway, he says, "some completely new system." The slightly prophetical mode as well. Once anyway, as we all know, people were lucky to get to forty and there were brides of fourteen. (If not, Kate, of eight.)

I don't know. The world doesn't feel to me more relaxed and better adjusted, it has this way of suddenly racing. I don't know how it feels to you. But what I do know is that at sixteen you're both virgins. I don't have the proof and I don't have your direct confirmations, just intuition. And I don't think this has anything to do with the world around you and how there's more time at your disposal and how you can just be cool and calm about everything. It has to do with you, with what you are: Nick and Kate, with that invisible rope straining, and sometimes catching painfully, between you. Little upsets and outbursts, not helped by recent symptoms of parental tension. Now and then a door gets slammed.

I don't know how tomorrow will affect it. A big snapping of all our ropes? You're sixteen, you're eighteen, you're grown-up and able to handle anything? We'll find out. Right now it seems to me that you're as changeable, as suddenly mature then as suddenly childish, as suddenly moody and tetchy then as suddenly brimming with verve and sparkle, as any teenagers. And you're virgins. It's a sweet thing, from the outside. Like the sweetness, from the outside, of your inescapable togetherness. And thank God, for the time being, you have each other. You're virgins, you could say, in another way too.

3

SUSSEX IN THE SIXTIES: the very phrase like some glisten-
ing salad. And Sussex was the place to be, the best, the cool-
est university in the land. And *of course* it was the place to be:
it was where I met your dad.

I was reading English with history of art. Your father was
a student of biology—or biological science, as they called it
there. Now I'm one of the directors at Walker and Fitch, and
your father's more than a director, he mainly owns and runs
Living World Books, which includes *Living World Magazine.* How far we've come. He's still in science, in a manner
of speaking. That is, he sells it. And now and then, as you
may have noticed, he'll still come over all self-searching and
conscience-stricken about having deserted "real" science to
become a money-maker. As if there weren't all those lean
years before you arrived when he hardly made any money
out of science at all. As if it wasn't his own decision. And
now the irony anyway is that times have changed again,
there are big fish around poised to swallow up Living World
and your dad's on the verge of selling up completely. Something else he's yet to announce.

We had you late in life—with shrewd foresight it may
now seem—but the fact is we weren't to know. Science only

became lucrative, it only turned into "popular science," in your lifetime and your father only emerged as a successful publisher when you were too young to notice.

Was it something to do with you? Quite possibly. It was arguably to do with you that he gave up true science, abandoned biology in the first place. Since that happened long before you were born, you may wonder how you can have affected it either way.

Your dad likes to maintain that his latter-day success is all down to luck, to just happening to be in the right place at the right time. To luck and to his "Uncle" Tim—I'll come to him later. But I think it was all a little like that contraceptive pill. Which came first: the pill and the science that produced it, or the change in the air that went with it? Science might never have become popular if your dad, among others, hadn't discovered a gift, a marketing gift, for making it so. And he didn't just "happen" to be there. He was there for a long and dubious time (I was one of the doubters) before the time was ever right.

He still likes to deny this and to have those moments of wistful, scientific regret. But this is at least fifty per cent tosh—trust me—or it's really about something else altogether. Selling isn't the same as disowning, or we'd all have nothing to our names. I buy and sell art. For many years, as I remind your father, it was our bread and butter. But I can still *like* it. I can still love Tintoretto. This usually shuts him up. Your dad appreciates a good picture too. Over the years he's developed quite an eye. He'll even admit, if you push him, that the art department at Living World is a major factor in its success. "Uncle" Tim was simply never visual.

And I certainly appreciate, as does your dad, the pictures, if they're not Tintorettos, that we can buy now and hang on our own walls. This house, as you've grown older, has become full of pictures, full, as you like to call it, of "stuff." And large enough house though it is, you might have wondered—teenagers, these days, seem wised-up on these things—why we haven't moved yet to an even bigger house that can contain yet more stuff, on a grander scale. Especially as not so long ago we quite casually bought a farmhouse in France—your father called it a "bolt hole"—still being worked on. Selling up, and buying up. All things being equal, to use your dad's phrase, we might be over there right now for the weekend, checking up on progress and staying at the Hôtel des Deux Églises. I think he wishes it *were* ready, right now, for immediate refuge.

But all things aren't equal, though we're all here in this house tonight, as is only proper. All your memories, just about, are in this house. All your life, just about, is within these walls. "After your sixteenth birthday," we said. How could we possibly have moved anywhere beforehand, how could we have told you what we'll tell you tomorrow anywhere else but here?

Once upon a time your dad and I used to share a basement in Earl's Court. Tatty posters, reproductions only, on the walls. And in those days, yes, your dad was a real scientist, working in a lab. His special field, as you know, was molluscs, and within that special field, his special area was snails. And his special area within that special area, which he would say wasn't at all small, was the construction and significance, the whole evolutionary and ecological import, of their shells. How is it done? Why doesn't a snail just remain a slug? A question that you and I might never think to ask. But it was one of the many instances, your dad might say in his best professorial mode, of biology's skill in chemistry, in sub-organic ingenuity.

I'm referring now, of course, to his own article, years ago now, in *Living World*. (A very wishy-washy and barely scientific article, he would say, but I know it meant a lot to him, I know it was a gesture to his long since aborted PhD.) Not just chemistry, but in time and by a long, slow process far beyond the needs of molluscs, mineralogy, geology, the very composition of the world. Or, as he once put it to me when we were still at Sussex: a limpet will never know it, but without the ability of its ancient ancestor to make a shell, there simply wouldn't be *any South Downs*.

Just think, he might have studied limpets. But I don't think your father has ever really given up science. And he can still say things, still give the little lectures that almost stop you in your tracks.

Snails, not limpets. One moves, just about: the other just clings. Mike went for snails. And what a fitting choice, I've sometimes thought, but never, of course, ever said, for a man who'd arrive late in life. Your dad, and his snails.

They'll be out there now, it occurs to me: a whole crop of them in this summer rain. Rain always brings them on, or brings them out. This house is being surrounded, perhaps fittingly and even with a delicate, nostalgic empathy, by snails. We treat them now like the regular garden pests they are, despatch them casually and mercilessly. But once your father was an expert on snails. And once upon a time, in Sussex, he was a genuine student of biology, though I might have said then that his special field in biology was his own.

Linda Page and Judy Morrison might have said the same. I shared an upper flat with them in Osborne Street, Brighton. They became our "bridesmaids." You've met Linda some years ago. She married a nice plump lawyer in the end and now lives in Highgate. What you've never known is that once she slept with your dad. Judy's become less in touch. I mustn't let her get like Doctor Pope, like one of those people you just wonder about. We used to have our regular get-togethers, the three of us, our lunches or girls' nights out. Sometimes these would be in Piero's in Jermyn Street, just up the road from Walker's (Simon, eyebrow ever cocked, wanted to be introduced). Linda and Judy: if there were ever two people to whom I might have just blabbed the whole story. When we got on to our third, unneeded bottle. But I never have.

The Three Sisters of Osborne Street. We shared most things. We may even have shared your dad. I'm still not sure if it actually happened with Judy. Your dad is good, and he's needed to be, at being cryptic. But however far the previous sharing had gone, after I'd had my first share there was definitely no more sharing. This you should know, if only for the straightness of the record. It was Linda your dad visited first, or it would be more correct to say, it was Linda who first brought him home. And your dad and Linda didn't last so long. It's an unresolved question who ditched whom. I think they ditched each other, gently. Then, putatively, it was Judy. But then it was me.

Number thirty-three Osborne Street, Brighton. A stone's throw, as they like to say ambitiously in Brighton, from the sea. But on a still night, if the tide was in, you might sometimes just hear the soft crash of waves, like far-off cymbals I always thought, and on a wild, wet night you'd have the feeling that the rain on the window might be spray.

We had the top two floors: three bedrooms and a kitchen. It all had its own front door and separate stairs: not so much a flat as a "maisonette." A word of its time. As well as the Three Sisters we were the Three Maisonettes. Linda had the front bedroom, I had the one next to hers, Judy had the room at the top. And we all had our visitors.

Mike has maintained ever since, which may be complete tosh too, but I've never not gone along with it since it would hardly behove me to disagree, that he had to sleep with Linda and Judy first in order to get to me. Fair's fair: all of us right there under the same roof. As if he were some knight in armour and Linda and Judy were just challenges, obstacles who popped up to waylay him on his otherwise unswerving quest.

In any case, the result was the same, and I have my own simple summary of it all, from which I've never wavered. I can't really remember if at the time I was actually jealous or impatient, or just desperate, as he worked his way, according to him, to me. Or if I actually thought—or hoped—that contriving to be third in line might give me some precarious advantage. But what I've always simply told your father and now I'll tell you is that I was lucky, oh so lucky, third-time lucky.

Luck which stayed. The incontestable and lasting truth is

he never went on to anyone else. Our auditioning days, so to speak, were over. We'd each found the one. Your father got into bed with me one night in Brighton nearly thirty years ago and, though the place and the room and the bed have changed from time to time, he's never got out.

4

"SLEEPING WITH": it's a funny expression. It doesn't mean what it says, though sometimes it just does. As if the closest you can ever get to another human being is to lie beside them, unconscious that they're even there. I've slept with your father for nearly thirty years. That's nearly ten years, if you think about it, of mutual oblivion. Though look at me here, wide awake. I'm not sleeping with him tonight.

And we didn't do that much sleeping that night, thirty years ago. Though it's not the sleeping (of either kind) that counts, right at the start, take your mother's word for it. It's the pillow talk. You'll find that out one day, I hope, though you haven't even begun the process, so far as I can tell, of finding someone to sleep with. It's hardly for me, your own mother, to say: time to get going, it's 1995, time to start sleeping around, time to follow your mother's hardly commendable example. You've only ever slept with each other, long ago when you were babies and again, rather subversively, when you were toddlers, which you won't want reminding of anyway.

But listen to your mother, pillow-talking to herself.

I knew it wasn't the same with Linda at least: no pillow talk there. Her room was next to mine, the wall wasn't discreet. Plenty of *noise,* plenty of bed sound. And I heard—it's a very strange thing to remember now—Linda's rather high-pitched, hurrying gasps. But I didn't hear many *words,* I didn't hear much conversation. And after not so very long I didn't hear anything: just the sound of two people asleep while I lay awake, the sound of two people sleeping together and doing, really, just that.

But Linda, if she were awake, when it was the other way round, if she were listening with some special device, a glass to the wall perhaps, would have heard *us* whispering and murmuring away long into the night. Heard our thrustings and thrashings-about certainly, and later on heard something softer, slower, just a lovely, steady undulation, I recall, the merest gentle creaking of my bed. But, in between and afterwards again, she'd have heard, if she listened hard, the sound of us swapping the stories of our lives. Though I'm not so sure, if I'm honest, and knowing Linda, if she'd have cared that much or been so free to listen, having moved on from your dad, a thing I find hard to comprehend, though I have to thank her for it utterly.

Pillow talk. It's how you know, it's how you tell, that something different, something special is happening: that this might even be the most important night of your life. Some day—some night—I hope you both may know it, with whoever it may be: the wish, stealing up on you, not just to merge bodies, but all you have, all your years, all your memories up to that point. And why should you wish to do that, if you haven't already guessed that your future, too, will be shared?

I was twenty, he was twenty-one. At some point, deep in

the middle of that night, he told me that when his dad had been twenty-one, he'd been a prisoner of war, somewhere in Germany. Why did he say that then? I didn't really want to *know* about his dad, not quite yet. He was talking, of course, about your Grandpa Pete. But I suppose it only made me want to squeeze him a bit more—your dad, I mean. Should I be telling you this? I suppose, on that very first night, I was squeezing your dad's dad in him. I imagined your dad as a prisoner of war, who'd just made it back. Thank God! As if my legs were wrapped round your Grandpa Pete. Who's dead now. What a thought.

We'd both been born in 1945—Mike in January, me in August—and each of us, we discovered, was an only child. In January 1945, when Mike was born, his dad had been in some freezing prison camp. Now here we were, by the sea-side, with the run of a fashionable campus on the South Downs, having the time—having the night—of our lives.

It's all in the luck of your birth.

I hate to think how remote and historical that year 1945 must seem to you. It starts to look pretty remote and histor-ical to me. You never think your own life is going to include the feeling "that was another age, another time, another world." But it does, it will for you. Even sooner, perhaps, than you think. And I suppose it's a feeling we're all going to have more of, if we all start living to a hundred.

He said his parents lived in Orpington. His dad had a small factory in Sidcup—"Dean and Hook Laminates," as you know. But these were things I hardly wished to dwell on as we lay there together at Osborne Street. So: he lived in Orpington and I lived in Kensington. Did it matter? We both lived in Sussex now—we would soon be *living,* not just sleeping, together. And Mike, it turned out, was a sort of Sussex boy anyway.

"And *your* dad?" your father said to me.

A fair exchange and a reasonable question, if I didn't entirely welcome it and I needed to take a deep breath. One of our first conversations was about fathers. My dad—your Grandpa Dougie, whom you never knew—was sixty-six even then. He had me (and it was only me) even later, much later, than Mike and I had you. My father was forty-five when I was born: he was almost, but for a few months, as old as the century. And in 1944 he'd married a woman twenty years younger than he was, my mother, Fiona, who's now still only seventy-five. I don't know why I say "only." She's also, of course, your Grannie Fiona, whom you've also, for different reasons, never met. I don't think being called "Grannie" was ever one of her chief aims in life. My father sometimes used to call her Fifi.

Family life—*my* family's life, I mean—it's all now a matter of history, but at the time I met your father it was still in the process of unravelling. It was like one of those things you gossip about at school. My parents had separated, they were getting divorced. Fiona had someone else, my future stepfather, Alex. And, not to be outdone, so did my dad. That's to say, to be accurate, someone was hovering around him, ready to swoop: my future stepmother, Margaret, a mere thirty-six.

I was younger than you are now when I first got wind of all this. If it's not the same thing, I can offer you my early experience, in solidarity. In 1966 I'd been living with the familiar ache of it for several years, but I wasn't keen to unload these unappealing complications on to your dad and, as it seemed to me, his straightforward little Orpington threesome.

But that wasn't quite the only problem on that otherwise (believe me) truly blissful night.

Come back to that bedroom in Osborne Street. The bed had a slatted wooden bedhead, of common and unbeguiling design, like a section of polished fence. There was a bedside light with a parchment shade and, across the room, a standard lamp. On the floor were three giant-sized red cushions, my three-piece suite. A lot of that room was on the floor. But on one wall, watching over your dad and me, though since both those lamps were off they may not have been able to see very much, were the faces of Manfred Mann. *Five-four-three-two-one*.

I won't forget that room. I don't know if that night you could hear, we weren't specially listening, the sound of the not so distant sea. On the other hand we were engaged in a wonderful, slow, wave-like motion that neither of us wanted to stop. We were making love, but we were also falling, falling in love. It's possible, I assure you, for the two things to happen at once. I'm the proof. Once it used to be the case, or it was supposed to be, that you fell in love and then, after being patient and chaste for perhaps a long and excruciating time, you got to make it. Now, I sometimes think, it may be all the other way round. You make love and then, maybe and maybe only rarely, you fall in it. But on a March night thirty years ago it happened at the same time. Though it may be a shade more honest to say to you now, since I'd never have made the mistake of saying it then, that I'd fallen in love with your father—who'd been around the house after all—just a little bit, before.

We were undulating anyway. Not just pillow talk, you might say, but billow talk, and what with this and all the sharing of our earlier years, I may even have had a fleeting picture of the long, rhythmic waves that used to roll and spill, not onto Brighton beach, but onto the sandy crescent bay at Craiginish in Scotland, where I'd spent summers as an unsuspecting girl and where one day, yes, Kate—I certainly wouldn't have suspected this on that night in Osborne Street—your father would propose to me, actually if not exactly formally propose to me, in the dunes.

I'd already broached the Scottish thing. Yes, I was a Campbell, Paula Campbell, though in fact I came from Kensington. And here I was anyway in Sussex, on the south coast, about as far from Scotland as you could get.

But the undulating, for a moment, had its obstacle, its impending, unavoidable difficulty. There was no way I could break it gently to your father. He would form the wrong impression, he would take alarm, he might even feel he was caught (please not) in some kind of punishable act.

I didn't want to interrupt your daddy's sweet and gathering rhythm, so I said it as softly as I could.

"He's a High Court judge."

5

WHEN YOUR FATHER was twenty-one, he didn't wear prisoner-of-war clothes. He wore, just for the embarrassing record, purple trousers with huge flares and a cracked leather jacket over a rotation (turquoise, muddy orange, salmon pink) of those T-shirts with buttons at the top which used to be called, and I never thought it funny then, granddad T-shirts. He had black hair almost to his shoulders, which was a bit curly and gypsyish at the ends. (Let's not delve into my student wardrobe.) He looked pretty good, pretty unembarrassing to me.

And to Linda and to Judy, with differing consequences, beforehand. One way or the other, they'd relinquished their claims. There was no competition. All the same, since they were both in the house and were certainly *interested*, it was an open question exactly how things would proceed on the morning after that night.

We must have got *some* sleep. After dawn, perhaps, as the light came seeping in and the Brighton gulls began their morning mewing and squawking. It was a March night, a Friday to a Saturday night—like this night. It's permanently inscribed in my mental almanac, and I've mentally placed an indelible plaque on the front wall of 33 Osborne Street:

"Paula Campbell and Michael Hook first slept together here."

I suppose it was still technically possible when we finally emerged, at some time approaching midday, that that night might have proved to be just another visit. No, your dad hadn't come to stay, to spend the rest of his life with me. But I didn't think I had to ask the question, and Linda and Judy at least weren't going to deny what they could see with their eyes. All students get up late, but the two of them had been loitering for some time in the kitchen, clearly not intent on going anywhere. They were waiting to check us out. I still see their slightly glassy stares. Well, well, they might have said. Well, well, what have we here? But their silences and fidgety displays of matter-of-factness were perhaps more eloquent still.

And could this all have happened—it's an entirely theoretical question, of course—if he hadn't slept (or had some kind of turn) with the two of them first?

It was a mild, moist morning, the sun just trying to break through pearly clouds. The kitchen window was open to let in the air, or to let out the smell of burnt toast. All four of us were grouped round the table, all of us in various states of undress—but then didn't we all know each other, just about? Wasn't there now a pretty thorough familiarity, in fact?

But then again, was this quite the same kitchen, quite the same Brighton even, its relaxed weekend sounds wafting through the window, as only last night?

I suppose it was still technically possible that your father might have crunched his toast, downed his coffee, smacked his lips and said, "Well, nice knowing you, girls, must be off." Three more notches (if that's how it really was), a full house, so to speak, to his score. The purple-trousered bastard.

But he definitely didn't.

And let's call it two and a half. In Osborne Street, that is. I've never known precisely what his *overall* score was. One doesn't ask. I think it can be assumed that this is a number no man is honest about. But, take it from me, your dad did his sleeping around before he came to a halt with me. I don't say that to boast, to claim surrogate points. Perhaps I do. With me, it was six. Honest. To some that may seem quite a few, in two years, to some not so many. It was enough for me: to be able to say I'd slept around. And to sort out the Mikeys from the rest. What are women programmed to do? Biologists will tell you, and Mike was one: to select a mate.

But take it from me too, the formal study of biology, in your father's final year at Sussex University, was of secondary, temporarily receding interest. He'd branched out. Whatever his score was, before me, he *scored.* Scoring wasn't his problem: this fifty-year-old man, comatose now at my side.

But before he fell asleep tonight we made love in a special, a poignant, a farewell way. You'll understand this soon.

It's possible that in that never to be forgotten kitchen in Osborne Street your father might have taken his leave of my life, of Linda's and Judy's. And of yours. I might have become just a sad addition to his score. But I don't think it was ever on the cards, and what he actually did was something marvellous. I fell in love with him, if that was possible, *more*. And, given our nocturnal conversation, I could just about feel, too, how it must have felt for him. Sometimes a woman can feel like a man feels. I'd already begun, you see, to feel your dad's feelings. To be twenty-one and not to be a prisoner of war. To be centre-stage of life and not to put a foot wrong.

He finished his coffee. He looked levelly at all of us, but his hand, I remember, under the table, was surely placed on my thigh. The granddad T-shirt, that weekend, was a gruesome shade of magenta, his hair could probably have done with a wash, but he spoke like a lord. These days, as you know, it's your father's business to command. He has to address those board meetings, give little rallying speeches at conferences, generally come up with the right message—he'll need all his skills tomorrow. I could never have predicted it, all those years ago. But perhaps that little quorum round the kitchen table at Osborne Street was an early glimpse.

"Ladies," he said. Ladies! The three maisonettes. "Ladies, thank you for breakfast. Lunch will be on me. On the beach, with champagne. You're all invited."

Undoubtedly one of your father's finest moments—not counting the whole of that preceding night. I was amazed at his chivalrous presence of mind. Even I could see that Linda and Judy couldn't have been expected just to clear off. They were part of this unique occasion, they had to be honoured—thanked. In any case, they weren't going to decline such an offer. I was amazed by how your father masterminded that day. As he spoke the sun came peeping through those pale clouds. It would be starting to dry and warm the pebbles already. And what do people do on a warm, sunny Saturday in Brighton, the first such Saturday of the spring?

But *champagne.* That was really impressive, in a student kitchen, in 1966. Champagne for four. Even when I found out that your father already *had* that champagne, it hadn't cost him anything, I was still impressed by his ingenuity, his quick thinking. I was impressed, in a different way, by the fact that he still had three bottles left.

He said, could we give him twenty minutes, while he went to "fetch" some champagne? We had no reason to suppose he didn't mean "buy." My first thought, in any case, was that I didn't want to be separated from your father even for twenty minutes. Twenty minutes was suddenly like a chasm. I would have offered to go with him, foolishly insisting, perhaps, on sharing the bill, but something in his eyes was telling me, gently, not to. Linda and Judy, meanwhile, for their own reasons, were clearly determined I should stay right where I was. Twenty minutes! They couldn't wait: to round on me as soon as your father was gone and say: "*Well?*"

Your dad had a bicycle, chained to the railings between us and next door. The Mike-bike, which came to be there quite a lot. He used to ride it in a crazy, splayed-kneed way to stop his flares getting caught in the chain. He disdained cycle clips, like a true man. That Saturday he rode it not to the nearest off-licence, but, as fast as he could, to his room across town, where there were still, remarkably, three bottles left from the whole case his dad had sent him for his twenty-first birthday in January, two months before. Dean and Hook must have been doing well. With those three bottles dangling dangerously in a duffel bag from his handlebars, he came whizzing back—I still picture his furious purple legs—true to his word.

That day on Brighton beach we drank champagne provided by your father. Though it had really come from his dad, your Grandpa Pete. I've often wondered if he ever knew. Did Mike tell him? For some delicate reason, I've never asked. It would have been a bit tricky, perhaps, for Mike to have given the full and complete details, but he might have glossed a bit, just given the gist.

I even thought once of telling your Grandpa Pete myself—or of checking if he knew. This was at our wedding, or at the little reception afterwards in the back garden in Kensington: another occasion when champagne flowed. My dad had assured me that it would be "nothing too grand, just like you want." But the champagne was vintage Taittinger. Mike's dad's champagne had been Mumm, Cordon Rouge. Though it had been a whole case and it had meant he could make a neat little joke—Mike kept the card: "And Love from Mumm."

I'm sure that wasn't what stopped me: some fastidiousness that your Grandpa Pete might feel outclassed in his choice of champagne. He was looking mellow and tipsy enough, as I was, on my father's stuff, and this might have been the perfect moment for some slightly daring daughter-in-law and father-in-law bonding. I was the blushing bride and I might have made your Grandpa Pete blush. For whatever reason, the moment passed. And I think he never did know. A minor secret.

Grandpa Pete would have been not yet fifty then—at our wedding. How weird. You'll remember how back in January, on your dad's fiftieth, we all felt a bit sorry for him. Just a year on from *his* dad's death, which had been so badly, and suddenly, timed: less than two weeks before Mike turned forty-nine. No birthday for him that year, though not a big number at least. But now with every successive birthday, he'd have to cross that sad ditch first, the anniversary of his father's death. And this year was his fiftieth, and his dad wouldn't be around to see it.

Your Grandpa Pete: your first death. You thought, quite reasonably, that on his fiftieth birthday your dad was a little subdued, not so much because of the growing-old factor (is fifty *old*?), but because he was thinking of his dad. True. But I know he was thinking of something else too, something still to come. It was a quiet fiftieth, anyway. And your dad rather likes to celebrate, I'll say that for him, he's good at celebrating. He loves nothing better than to pop the champagne, and in these last few years, courtesy of Living World, he's been able to do it quite a lot. That day in Brighton was a precedent, perhaps.

But here's a complication. There's a cause for celebration coming up, as you know, very soon, in just a week's time. It's our wedding anniversary. Not just that, it's our twenty-fifth. We're about to turn silver. You may already have bought us (it troubles me to think about it) some special silvery present, and you may also have been wondering why nothing's

been said on the subject so far, and surmised that your dad
has been keeping some surprise up his sleeve.

Well, he has, but not for me. It's just how it's come about:
it's a year of big numbers, and of bad timings. And you'll
understand in a little while why it's been a thorny question
between us: our anniversary, I mean. What to *do*?

Your dad's all for celebrating it, that's his natural instinct.
It's about *us,* he says, there's *us* anyway. He wants us to go
away for the weekend, as couples often do on these occa-
sions, to celebrate us. That, of course, would mean leaving
you here by yourselves. No problem, you may think, what
would be the big deal? Except, this year, you might not actually agree.

Your dad says it would be a good thing nonetheless. It
would give you time to think, to talk things through, to be
by yourselves. I'm not so sure. To me it feels like absconding,
it feels like deserting my babies. And I know, I know: you're
sixteen.

But not so long ago Mike told me he'd booked us into
a hotel anyway. He actually did it months ago—it's that
kind of place, a five-star country hotel. The Gifford Park.
We had a bit of a row. I suppose it was mean of me, it was
pretty foul of me, arguing with my husband about his
generous arrangement for our special wedding anniversary.
But it could be mean to *you,* you'll realise—our just waltz-
ing off.

He said, well, we could always cancel, any time. A little
soft touch of blackmail. And, oh, I could see where he was
coming from: an escape plan, a safety net—not having that

bolt hole ready in France. He said, well, let's just see, let's leave the booking standing and let's see.

I'm not sure he should even have made that booking without telling me first. It could never have been, this year, like some straightforward, happy surprise. But that's how he is, he likes the big and generous gesture. You'll understand.

6

HE MADE A GESTURE even about today—by which now I mean yesterday, Friday. He called me at work to say we should meet for lunch in town. We hadn't made any prior plans, but he called me to say we couldn't just let it pass unmarked: our "last day." His last day, your last day, I'm not sure what to call it. And I'm not sure it was a case of "marking," more of nerves and solidarity, but I had to allow him his prerogative. The condemned man's choice of supper. I think my notion of our "last day" had been of something entirely indistinguishable from any other: a Friday, a working day, the more workaday and busier, perhaps, the better.

But the truth is I was glad of your dad's last-minute call. I can't say my own nerves have been steady. And I too had begun to feel there should be some—gesture. Though I didn't think it should come from me, like an offering of pity.

But I was glad of your dad's call in another way. You'll think this absurd of me, I'm not your age, after all. It was like that call you get when you think you may not *get* a call, when you even think that something may be ending. That simple word in my ear: "Paulie?"

The only small problem was that I had to cancel, abruptly, my lunch with Simon. I had to stand up my boss.

And all week long, I think, Simon, who notices things, had been noticing my nervousness, my not quite sparkling form. Everything okay, Paula?

Every month or so Simon likes to have a one-to-one lunch with one of his directors, and this was my turn. All part, as he sees it, of his caring and counselling and not merely boss-like role. He nearly always begins, after the first sip of wine, with a: "Now—tell me all your troubles." A wry joke by now, since I never seem to have any to tell him. Though I have a hunch that nothing would do more for Simon's sense of his own worth than if I were to grasp his wrist across the table and pour out some tale of woe, even show signs of wanting to cry on his shoulder. And perhaps this week he'd been scenting the possibility.

A complicated soul, my boss. The soul of sweetness, charm and urbanity, but a discontented soul who, since he has no envy or spite and no obvious cause for them ("unhappily married art dealer with a house in Holland Park" doesn't quite get the sympathy vote), rumbles not with anger but with a strange thwarted charity.

And a world expert on Piazetta. And in more than thirty years of buying and selling, he hasn't lost the love which is my love too. No disrespect meant to your father. It's not a case of one thing or the other, and it's not confessing to anything treacherous to say that when I was starting at Walker's, in the years after I'd married your dad, before you were born, it was Simon who really brought out in me the second passion of my life. No disrespect, either, to you.

Art's not for the very young? For you it's just "stuff." You have to have grown up and had a taste of loss. I'll explain that later. Art's just compensation? I'm not saying that either. And I'm definitely not saying I could imagine an alternative life for myself with—God forbid—Simon Fitch. But two people who in most other respects may be entirely mismatched can still thrill together to a third thing, a passion shared. The light falling round people in a painting which is like the light falling round real people too, except it can't go out. What do you care for such things? The light which fell today (yesterday, I mean), just sunny June light shafting into the narrow streets between Jermyn Street and Pall Mall. What was so special about it?

But "better at art than life," that's what I think Simon would confess of himself, if you ever dared to press his rawest nerve, to prod his art dealer's solar plexus. He'd like some compensation the other way round. At sixty-one, the light, in that respect, is starting to look a little thin.

I know he's fond of me. More than that, possibly. It's he, perhaps, who at one of our lunches should grasp my wrist and unburden his breast, but it hasn't happened in over twenty years and I think my job is safe.

I think Simon thinks—if we set aside the "Walker and Fitch wouldn't be Walker and Fitch without you" and other such tripe he talks—that what's lying here now, under this roof, may be a sort of perfection, as good as it gets. Art and life. If only he'd found the same recipe. And I can't disillusion him. I love my husband. I love you, my precious ones, I love this home. And Simon's been here, of course, and seen it and you, and you've seen him. You treated him, the first time at least—paraded in your jimjams before bedtime—like some visiting crown prince. You almost bowed and curtsied (but I won't remind you). Simon Fitch and his stately wife, Veronica, for dinner.

But he was enchanted by you, always asks after you. And to cap it all, I think he's always been enchanted by what we'll call the "Living World Story"—by how his indispensable junior colleague became in time and in turn rather outshone, professionally speaking, by her once obscurely occupied and poorly paid husband. He once proclaimed, like some minister who'd personally blessed our union, that your dad and I were "Science and Art." Now look at that splendid pairing.

If I were to tell Simon the little truth behind that splendour—that even you don't know about yet—I don't think he'd adjust his appraisal. I don't think he'd suck thoughtfully at his half-rims, step back and (as he can do) declare the picture not to be genuine after all. I think he'd just relish the entrusting and the opportunity to protect.

But the thought that I might have spilled out to Simon at lunch today, over a plate of crab linguini, the full facts of this imminent weekend is—unthinkable. Poor Simon. But unthinkable.

And anyway now I'd had, abruptly, to cancel and, in the secret circumstances, to be blunt about my reasons. Though I was a little mean and sly.

"Another lunch date, Paula? Who is this special client?"

"It's Mike."

"Ah. Well—far be it from me . . ."

The sunshine fell too into Simon's office, onto his crisp striped (Jermyn Street) shirt.

It wasn't lost on Simon, of course, that it was very odd

that Michael Hook, head of Living World and a busy man, should want or feel it proper to phone his wife in her busy office at ten-thirty on a Friday to press her to lunch.

"Well, of course. Of course, Paula." He looked suddenly solicitous—and intrigued. "You must have—something important, I dare say, to discuss."

"Yes," I said, being tactful.

But not discuss actually. Just mark, just observe what day it was, which Simon couldn't possibly have guessed. And it was a fine one in June and your dad had a simple plan. Not even a restaurant. A restaurant seemed ceremonious and conspicuous. Mark, not celebrate. And this was lunch, not quite yet that actual terminal supper, which we'd already agreed had to be simply at home, and absolutely without any attempt at ceremony, with you.

I can say now that that would have been a tricky undertaking, I'm not sure how we'd have managed it, and I should thank you for getting us out of it. Since what, in the event, did we find? You were both out celebrating, your recent release from exams. There were separate, dutiful phone messages from each of you to say you had your separate Friday-evening plans, hastily fixed up, it seemed, like our lunch. The days have long gone for asking permission: "Fine. Have fun. Home by midnight." This was hardly a night anyway for taking you to task.

And in fact you were both home before eleven. They can't have been such riotous celebrations. Neither of you seemed especially worse for wear, and neither of you had been aware till you came in that you'd both been doing similar things. Of course, you were immediately and automatically uninterested in that fact. These days you don't like anything that smacks of synchronicity. Your lack of enquiry after each other meant that your dad and I couldn't do much enquiring either. It turned out, this last day, to be one of those not so uncommon days which pass with our exchanging barely a handful of words with you. How different tomorrow will be.

After some fridge-raiding, you both seemed ready to go to bed, or at least to your rooms. They're tired, we said condoningly, clearing up after you, those exams have caught up with them. Ordinary parental concession. Soon afterwards we came up too.

I hope you had fun anyway. If you think they were not particularly memorable evenings, you may find that you'll always remember them nonetheless. You weren't to know there was something else—to mark. Conceivably, on this of all nights, I might still be waiting up for you, listening out for you, in this rain. By now, I'd be seriously worried. But you're safely tucked up and I'm telling you this story.

I left my office a little after twelve-thirty and walked towards Lower Regent Street. Your dad left his office in a cab. I met him at the top of the Duke of York's Steps. I'd called in, on my way, at the sandwich bar in Crown Passage. We walked down the steps and across the Mall to the park.

That simple thing: a picnic, lunch in the park. Not celebratory, nor on the other hand so solemn. Once upon a time, before you were around, your dad and I quite often used to meet "under the Duke of York"—it was one of our places—and walking to meet him today I had the feeling, though you won't especially want to know this, that I was twenty years younger.

Your dad was there first, his jacket hooked in one finger, patrolling that odd stage of a place like an actor silently rehearsing. I saw him first, then he saw me. The strange little quivering interval when that happens. I remembered that too. He smiled and waved. I smiled and waved and I lifted up my sandwich bag like a trophy.

We had lunch today rather like you did, I imagine, sprawled with your friends on the grass, in a state of post-exam languor, in some corner of the playing fields at your respective schools. Perhaps you'll always remember doing that. The warm grass under your bellies. You'll see yourselves locked in the sunny amber of one exam-taking June.

But your dad and I allowed ourselves the dignity of two deckchairs, our exams are still to come.

I said, "I stood up Simon for this," handing your dad a baguette. He said, "I hope you'd have stood up anyone." Sunshine poured through the plane trees. The deckchairs and the lunchtime crowds around us made me think, despite the greenness, of Brighton beach, and I wondered if he was having the same thought. I'm all in favour of synchronicity. He said, almost with a little catch of apology, "I just needed to see you." As if we hadn't been married for twenty-five years and sleeping together for nearly thirty, as if we'd met only last week and still couldn't bear to be out of each other's sight for more than two hours. But I remembered that feeling too.

7

HE CAME CLEAN about the champagne. It hadn't cost him a penny. I didn't think any the less of him, nor, I think, did Linda and Judy. It even made the day go better (*could* it have gone better?), since it was rapidly and unanimously agreed that if it was his birthday champagne, then it must be his birthday. His birthday had been in January, but it was still his birthday or it was his birthday all over again. Or rather, if no one said this at the time, it was *our* birthday, it was your dad's and my birthday, if such a thing can be, which I'll confirm it can. You two aren't the only ones to have had a joint inauguration. That day—March 19th, 1966—was our birthday, it was our launch party, celebrated, appropriately enough, by the edge of the sea. The ship of our future, which now includes sixteen years of your past, was launched that day and was christened, of course, with champagne.

Will you have such days in your life, will each of you have such days? I hope so. Nothing could make me happier than the knowledge that you will. It's a stupid and a superstitious thought—a very stupid one to be having tonight—but there must be stored up for us all only so many possible happy days, and my fear is that your dad and I will have taken more than our share, we haven't left enough for you.

"A bottle for each of you," your father said, having sped through the streets of Brighton on his bicycle. By now, Linda, Judy and I were fully dressed, even a little over-dressed it could be said (a great deal of Biba) for a Saturday lunchtime. But what do you wear exactly for such an unexpected party? We stood in a row like prize winners while your dad unloaded his duffel bag onto the kitchen table.

"Spare some for me," he said.

He could do no wrong. Outside, the clouds had dissolved and the sun shone approvingly. Second birthdays definitely occur, lives begin all over again. I was a little in love with Doctor Pope? I admit it. No disrespect to your father. And I was a little in love, as every female student of English was, with John Donne. The words had begun to echo in my head: "And now good morrow . . ." And now good morrow.

But your dad did the honourable thing. With his bag empty and those bottles on the table he looked a bit like a man who'd been stopped at customs.

"Actually," he said, "they're from my dad."

From his *dad*? How could his dad possibly have known about or felt so generously towards the three sisters of Osborne Street?

And then your father, who'd already explained to me, in the small hours of the morning, quite a lot about *his* father, explained to all three of us about his twenty-first birthday back in January.

We felt like honorary daughters. That doesn't quite work, I know—it would have been to construct the most bizarre family. But for a moment your Grandpa Pete was the talking point, as he'd soon become the toast of three girls in

Brighton. If only he'd known. Each of us with our bottle. He must be quite a dad, Mike's dad, we agreed, we would definitely drink to him.

Quite a dad, I privately thought, champagne apart, just to have produced Mike. And quite something that he'd sent a whole case. This was the 1960s, not the 1980s, champagne wasn't like fruit juice. Most dads would have settled in those days for sending their son a single bottle, on grounds of expense, on grounds of sheer sense of proportion. Let's not go overboard. What would your Grandpa Pete have got, after all, for his own twenty-first birthday? A food parcel?

This must all seem so far away to you. As if that "maisonette" in Brighton—but it must still be there—is as distant, in its own way, as some awful camp in Germany. Your dad told me, later, that he'd been overwhelmed to get those twelve bottles. It was like receiving an inheritance. The truth was he wouldn't even have said he was particularly close to his father, and here was this sudden bounty. That accompanying note, apart from the joke about "Mumm" and wishing him happy birthday, had simply said, "Have fun." Your dad showed it to me. And he still has it. Your dad and me, we're sentimental that way. He got it out and looked at it again after Grandpa Pete died.

But he was so moved by those twelve bottles that he couldn't simply regard them as bottles of fun, he couldn't just knock them back at the first chance. He even had the thought, since there were twelve of them, that he should broach only one bottle a month for the whole of his year of being twenty-one—a resolution that soon got broken. But it was still a miracle that he had those three bottles left in March.

I think your father, in January 1966, underwent a moment of historical, of filial humbling. Twenty-one: it's the real ripe age, perhaps, and you're only sixteen. I think he paused to appreciate, not to take for granted, his own good fortune. Remember, we hadn't even met yet. And maybe that's why he invoked, on our first night together, his own once-captive dad. What kind of fun was there to be had then? I think your father, a scientist by vocation and therefore surely not prone to superstition, may have said to himself: but put three bottles by just in case, as safeguards. Save three bottles for a rainy day.

Tomorrow looks like being a rainy day, my darlings.

But that March day, years ago, was anything but a rainy day: a day in March that was more like a day in May.

And what I couldn't quite tell him yet, in the circumstances, was that my dad, the very awkwardly mentioned and very nearly coitus-interruptive High Court judge, had a whole cellar in Kensington of magnificent and expensive wines, including, of course, a fine range of champagne. It had become in recent years his favourite room in the house. The fact is that in those days before Fiona and then Margaret siphoned off their share, your mother (who's scarcely hard-up now) was something of a little rich girl. But I didn't want to scare or prejudice your dad, and certainly not upstage him.

And anyway that champagne we drank on Brighton beach was the best I've ever tasted. I can still see the little dull-red chain of roses round the rim of the hastily shop-bought waxed-paper cups. Champagne glasses? You'd have had to be joking. Lunch that day—and here I can report that your dad really did pay for everything—was the standard stuff of the beach-front caffs, an emphasis on greasy chips. But it was washed down with bubbly. We had no ice bucket, but that was no problem: the English Channel in March, a pocket of pebbles at the water's edge, and the tide was almost full. How everything came together. We agreed on ten minutes' chilling time, then settled for five.

And there is that great advantage of champagne, that you don't need to remember a corkscrew. But I didn't forget to keep one of the corks. The other two, I decided, were Linda's and Judy's business, perhaps they just floated out to sea. But I kept my cork. It's precious beyond reckoning. Did I say I can be sentimental? It's in a special box I have where I've kept all kinds of stuff. I'm a foolish old mother in that respect. Pressed flowers from Craiginish. Your primary-school artistic triumphs, as valuable to me—and your mother knows about art—as Tintorettos. Then there's a little collar, also now a dull red, with a small bell on it and a name tag. More of that later.

Brighton beach in the middle of March: not always inviting. But it turned as warm as summer. The sea was calm and compliant and grew bluer by the minute, and the waves, lapping gently in and breaking with a silver flash then turning to creamy foam round first three, then two and then a single bottle of champagne, might as well have been champagne themselves.

By that third bottle, if your father had told me that he'd

planned that day long in advance, foreseen it and planned it in every detail—as he'd planned, all along, those special transitory roles for Linda and Judy—I would, of course, have utterly believed him. But how could he or either of us have known that day would unfold as it did, so perfectly? Some days are just gifts, some things are just gifts. He'd planned the weather? He'd planned that the tide would be so co-operatively full and then—but it's only what tides do— slowly, respectfully creep away? That the afternoon would turn gold and dreamy, and that as the light deepened and the tide slipped further out, Linda and Judy, without any prompting but with immaculate, if drunken, timing, would get up and slip away too, guests at our feast who knew nonetheless when they ought to be going? As if they weren't leaving us where everyone could see, on the pebbles of Brighton beach, but in some special, private, garlanded bed.

But we hardly noticed them going or heard their softly crunching, retreating footsteps, since, nestled up to each other in a sort of gauzy blanket of champagne, and not having had much sleep the night before, we'd drifted away ourselves.

8

WE WERE BOTH "only" children. Do "onlies" attract "onlies?" And we were both "war babies"—your fearsome parents—me in the sense that I was conceived in the war, Mike in the true and classic sense that he was born in it, and hurriedly produced, like armies of other little war babies, to be what was left of his dad should his dad soon not be there. For a little while that's exactly how it must have looked. Your Grandpa Pete and Grannie Helen acted only just in the nick of time, since shortly after she became pregnant Grandpa Pete went "missing," a word which often meant the most dreadful thing possible.

1945: how weird it sounds now to give it as your date of birth, like saying 1789 or 1492.

When your dad was born, in January 1945, his dad wasn't there and wouldn't be there for another five months. It was the son, in theory, who was waiting for his father's arrival, not the other way round. Not that your dad would have known what was going on or had any idea how significant his own arrival was, even before it had quite occurred. It's just as well, perhaps, that memory waits for us further down the road from our birth. But do these things somehow filter through anyway? I've often tried to put myself in the position of Grannie Helen in that brief period when your father would have been the unborn consolation in her womb.

I was waiting, further down the road, for your father. I know it sounds silly. I was waiting, too, for him to be born.

Was there always a little gap, a discrepancy, between your dad and his dad? You've noticed it too? Was it just the gap, the edgy stand-off that exists between any son and father, or was it that niggling gap of around five months? His dad had tried to close it, perhaps, with those twelve bottles of champagne. Perhaps for a while he succeeded. I think your dad may have wept a little when he read that message: "Have Fun." What an odd reaction to such a message. And he certainly wept, as you yourselves saw, at his father's funeral, in Birle churchyard, eighteen months ago. It was the first time you'd seen your father weeping, and they say it's not good for children to see their father in tears. I'm not so sure. And I'm not so sure your father wasn't weeping for a different sort of gap.

As it happened, it wasn't until the year I met your dad that Grannie Helen ever really spoke to him about that time before and just after he was born. Did that have something to do with me? Your dad told me, anyway, that he'd had this chat with his mum, at Christmas. He let me in on a private conversation with his mum.

And you told me, Kate, that he brought it all up again with you *last* Christmas—the first one without Grandpa Pete. Grannie Helen was dozing in our living room. You and Mike had volunteered to do the washing-up. Nick and I decided to take a walk round the block. I can see how all the circumstances would have primed your dad. You told me, Kate, that he told you about a Christmas years ago when Grannie Helen had told him about that time when Grandpa Pete wasn't around.

I may have looked at you rather oddly—as I did that time at Carrack Cove—and you may have wondered why. But you just said to me, "Dad's really missing Grandpa Pete, isn't he?" Good, sweet, daughterly words. And true.

"Yes," I said. "The first Christmas, it's tough."

I didn't say, though I might easily have done, that I could remember the first Christmas without *my* dad. I'd had a major consolation, a double consolation: you and Nick were in my womb.

I just said—as if it needed to be said—that Grandma Helen would be missing him too. Your dad and Grandpa Pete always used to do the washing-up at Christmas. They'd roll up their sleeves and put on aprons, a ritual, two-man chore. Now, this year, for whatever reason, your dad had chosen you. It was another wobbly moment.

You may both have noticed that there's a bit of a gap too, these days, between your Grannie Helen and me. I mean, there's always been a bit of a gap: she's my mother-in-law, it's a ritual thing too. I always got on better with Grandpa Pete, I think I get on better with men all round. But now there's an extra gap between Grannie Helen and me, just when, perhaps, there shouldn't be. I ought to be offering her comfort and support, and I've done my best. But I'm afraid of her, if I'm honest, I've become a bit afraid of her.

Is she lying awake too right now, just like me, but by herself, listening to the rain?

It seemed just a touch romantic, I'll admit, when I first heard it from your dad: that his dad had once been "missing," then returned as if from the dead, to lift his son in his arms. If it never really quite squared with the man I'd get to know who ran a factory in Sidcup, or the man who'd sometimes do those strange little comic double-acts with his old pal, Charlie Dean—"Uncle Charlie" to you. Grannie Helen always said they should have gone on the stage. Charlie and Pete, "Dean and Hook"—it could have worked. Charlie the little bouncy joker and Pete, like some older brother, the tall, slightly solemn straight man. Have fun, have fun.

My dad had never had to fly off to his highly possible death, he'd had a rather different war. He'd spent it cracking codes in the safe and cosy depths of the English countryside, pleasantly surrounded, so far as I can glean, by lots of young female clerks, typists and telephonists, some of whom came from far from lowly backgrounds, but were doing their humble bit.

And among them was my mother, Fiona McKay. The Scottish thing may have been entirely coincidental or it may have been the clincher. Do Scots attract Scots?

How do our parents get together? Do we need to know? You once seemed pretty keen, Kate. Here are *my* speculations, anyway. I think my father's war was, in fact, a bit of a holiday from his earnest and industrious dedication, up till then, to the law. I think it was his version of Sussex in 1966—if he was a good deal older than twenty-one. He would have been over forty. Life hits you at different times.

It had been a rather monkish dedication, perhaps. He'd never before been thrown so strategically among the girls. He'd never before discovered his own seductive talents. That is, in my father's untall, unhandsome, but short and cuddly yet high-powered case, his talent for being ever so seducible. It amounts to the same thing, perhaps, if you can generally keep an eye on what's going on. And a man who'd become a High Court judge ought to have been able to do that. A big "ought" as it proved.

It's a lasting sadness to me, and it will have its extra stab tomorrow, that you never knew your Grandpa Dougie. But, of course, I never knew him *then*. Those days before we were born.

When I was in a state of less than imminence I think, or I hope, my father was having the time of his life. I think he was having fun. All because of the war. I wouldn't dare to estimate *his* score, and perhaps it was never like that. But I know that it was Fiona McKay who in 1944 became his young war bride—twenty years his junior. Some fifteen or so years later, when I was a schoolgirl and she was approaching forty, she'd show the first undisguised signs of wanting to move on (was it so unpredictable?), but not without taking a good deal of what had really been his with her. War bride and future mercenary. And this, I'd realise, would make him vulnerable, even amenable, to the same process happening all over again.

Your Grandpa Dougie died in 1978, over a year before you were born. His funeral, unlike your Grandpa Pete's, was attended by three ex-wives. Fiona was number one. You've never met her and, for the record, Mike's only met her once—at that funeral. You know I don't see my own mother: these things happen. When you were very small we used to call her, expediently, your "fairy grandmother," as if this gave her an ethereal status beyond mere ordinary grand-motherness. She's one of the never fully explained mysteries of your lives, though, believe me, not the only one.

9

YOUR DAD HASN'T lost his looks. I think he's even gained some. I'm biased, of course. Under that tree in St. James's Park, at least, the summer light did him proud. Or is it that his midlife success has given him a new lift, a new lease? Where do you separate handsomeness and success in men, handsomeness and achievement? Any thoughts, Kate? How the passing of time can be kind to them anyway. But perhaps I shouldn't be thinking that right now.

It wasn't always so. I mean, he was just handsome once, he was just Mike. The success wasn't there. And should you demand it? Isn't love more than enough? Professor Mike—I mean, a real true accredited Professor Mike—was waiting a long way down the road (it has to be said he'll go on waiting) while your dad toiled away, a third, a fourth year, at his PhD. Those snails of his were supposed to be his stepping stones—an unfortunate phrase—to his brilliant future in science.

It may be hard for you to imagine that your dad and mum, who now own this house and do all that we do, once shared a rented basement in Earl's Court. Your dad was "researching" at Imperial, I was a trainee at Christie's in the Old Brompton Road. Our bed then (compare this barge of

a bed we're in right now) was a mattress on the floor. Not
so much an economy, though that was needed, as a gesture
to sprawling decadence. We never invested in a real bed,
though we did invest, one impulsive and salacious day in
the Portobello Road, in a vast, crimson, slinky-thin bedspread beneath which, immersed in its ruby glow, we'd often
flail and tussle, like people caught in a happy ballooning
accident.

In those days—forgive me—you were very far from our
thoughts, you weren't even on our radar.

My lunch with your dad in the park today didn't just
make me think of Brighton. It made me think of those
trainee days and of a happy month I once spent as a menial
at the Dulwich Gallery, a place I'm still very fond of. Some
lovely Poussins, a gorgeous Watteau. I'd mooch about in my
lunch break in the park just across the road—it had a lake
with ducks—and think about Mike, across town, at Imperial, and think how sweet and treasurable even the most
unambitious moments of life can be. Our "careers" were in
place anyway, in reassuring embryo, Mike's perhaps a little
more latently than mine. But there was no rush, there was
even the argument that the slower the incubation, the more
glorious the outcome. I'm sounding like some biologist
myself.

But I was even, in those days, still a little enchanted, a
little seduced by your dad's devotion to snails. I was devoted
to his devotion. Who cares about snails? Some people find
them repellent. But if Mike cared about them . . . That's
how it worked. Under our red bedspread I willingly learnt a
good deal about snails, about their natural history and life

cycle, not least about their extraordinary reproductive system and method of performing the sexual act (you'd think those shells would be a major encumbrance), though now's not the time to be going into that.

Your dad used to say that the simple joy of biology was the sheer peculiarity of things. What makes anything special? And I used to think that for me the question "What made Mikey special?" was a question that required no answer, let alone a scientific one. Nor did it occur to me especially to ask: what makes anyone, who might, after all, do all sorts of things, become a specialist in snails?

In the park with your dad today I saw myself in that other park in Dulwich. It was spring. The rhododendrons were out, the ducks clucked. There were little scudding flotillas of chicks. I didn't imagine then that one day I'd ever want to say to this man here, this special specialist: "Perhaps there's been enough of snails now, Mikey. Where are their silvery trails leading us?" I didn't imagine that one day I'd want to make this man—my husband as he'd then become—reconsider his own sticky trail in life.

His work involved breeding the things, long-term, patient cycles of experiment. It didn't seem to involve sudden, life-changing discoveries.

I've never been a fan of Seurat, but in the park today I thought of those lounging, sprinkled figures, made up of dots themselves, as if people are really just clouds of atoms, which your dad would no doubt say is exactly what they are. I had that strange feeling that I was meeting him all over again, as though, if I'd never known him and had gone down to St. James's Park to choose from the crowds, I'd still have picked him out. I should have told him perhaps. I should have said, "It would have been the same even now, Mikey, no question. Even at fifty."

Except I had the sudden, panicky *opposite* feeling: that I was meeting him for the *last* time. I'd got it all wrong. "I just needed to see you," he said. It wasn't a meeting, it was a last look. People do that too, they meet one last honourable time, just in order to part. Your dad was already staging his *disappearance*.

How stupid of me. When we climbed up the Duke of York's Steps again all the breath went out of me. He said, standing in that old place, "I'm glad we did this. I won't forget that we did this." Two sandwiches in the park! I didn't dare say anything foolish. He hailed a cab at the corner of Pall Mall and kissed me before stepping into it. I watched it weave its way, its black roof glinting, up Lower Regent Street. And fifteen minutes later Simon, who I think was vaguely on the lookout, would have seen me return and shut my office door behind me in the way that people shut even office doors when they want to cry.

But, look, he's still here, isn't he? How absurd of me. Your dad's still here.

And he can still talk, as you know, in a special way about snails. As he can talk about all kinds of creepy-crawlies and barely considered life forms, as if passing on some marvellous secret. His business these days may be, so to speak, the whole range of available products, but he can still do a good pitch on the little individual item.

You know not to yawn when your dad talks about snails. A look comes into his eye. You know not to push the mollusc jokes. What you don't know is that there came a time, after we'd moved to Davenport Road, when your dad announced to me that he had to go one last time to the labs at Imperial. He had to make one last visit. He didn't elaborate, and I should have guessed perhaps. But he told me afterwards. He said he'd gone there personally to exterminate his remaining working stock of snails. He said he wanted to do it himself, efficiently and "humanely"—a strange word to use about snails. He hadn't wanted to leave it to "some technician."

10

BUT COME BACK to when he was twenty-one, and to another visit. To one day in May when I stood with your father outside the front door of number seven Napier Street, Kensington, waiting for my father to open it.

I'd never seen your dad look so scared. He was quaking in his Chelsea boots. Ever since I'd told him, in that unfortunately timed way, that my father was a High Court judge, your dad was convinced that *his* moment of judgement must come. On that May afternoon he was about to be condemned.

No amount of soft-pedalling on my part would reassure him: it's a wonder I got him to that doorstep. In the Queen's Bench Division they didn't sentence criminals—not that your dad was one—or send anyone to the gallows. Not that, by 1966, *anyone* was sent to the gallows. Though it's a rather chilly historical fact that not so long before, they still were. And an even chillier fact which I don't like to dwell on and didn't like to dwell on then, that if my father had chosen criminal law he might, for a brief period at least of his judge's career, have been one of those who sent them there. How far we've come since before you were born.

In any case, as I tried to persuade your father, my father was a complete sweetie, a lamb. He wore lambs-wool cardigans from Harrods. He was not Judge Jeffreys. You'd never even guess he was a judge. But none of this washed with your dad, it even gave him more cause to quake. A sweetie—yes, of course he'd be, with his *own daughter*. Your dad knew the situation well enough by then: that my father was about to divorce his wayward wife. Which left this mutually devoted and clinging household of two, father and daughter. The more fondly I spoke of my father, the more Mike was sure he was going to be Mr. Interloper, Mr. Rival. My dad was going to cut him dead.

Pity your poor father, if it makes sense to pity retrospectively, standing outside my father's front door. Picture him then, when you look at him tomorrow. He really had nothing to fear. And if only he'd known his real moment of judgement was to come much later in life.

It was useless to explain to him that the Kensington situation was not as simple as it seemed. My father was not quite the wronged and wounded party, taking his only comfort in me, meanwhile seething with unvented spite. He was magnanimously—or soft-headedly—anxious that the divorce shouldn't be punitively framed. Fiona was still the mother of his only child (and knew how to milk his better nature). There'd still been the good years. I remember them. The three of us outside "Craiginish Croft" waiting idiotically for the time-release shutter (the photo's in that box): Dougie, Fifi and Paulie, as we called ourselves then, like a litter of puppies. My mother stood to get a good deal more than most lawyers—not acting for a judge—would have advised. She'd get Craiginish, for a start. If I hadn't, that spring, been busy tumbling into bed and into love with your father, I might have argued more fiercely with my poor daddy about that.

Then again, there was the potentially ruinous factor of Margaret Gould, my stepmother-to-be, already staking her place. He had to be very careful this didn't give Fiona grounds for extracting even more. I'd already begun to hate Margaret—*that* interloper. So couldn't I understand your dad's qualms? I'd already begun the unbecoming process of outlawing my own mother. Perhaps it's me you should really be judging tomorrow.

It would have been better, in some ways, if my father had actually gone out and, in a spirit of reckless and conspicuous revenge, "picked up" Margaret. But he was sixty-six and it might have wrecked his judge's career. Judges don't "go out," they don't "pick up." And judges, perhaps by definition, should be fair to all parties and free from all vindictiveness. In any case, that wouldn't have been him. He *had* "picked up" Margaret, but in his normal, helpless, passive-but-effective way, like a burr that had stuck insistently to one of his cardigans. A sweetie and a softie: though I couldn't convince your father, going through agonies, outside his front door.

The door was a glossy, implacable, judgemental black, the standard livery of Kensington, but that didn't help your dad. It stood at the top of steps inside a porch supported by two glossy white pillars. On one of them would have been a large, finely serifed black "7."

Adding to your dad's unease, I can't deny it, was the sudden palpable tang of wealth in his nostrils. At Sussex there was the general levelling of student existence. Now he was the boy from Orpington, about to be put in his place by a Kensington your-lordship. Not that he'd minded, I'd noticed, having a "bird" (don't laugh, it was the word then) from just up from the King's Road. Those Chelsea boots he was quaking in were the genuine article, in the sense that we'd bought them, in the King's Road, not so very long before.

Before your Grandpa Dougie's divorce the wealth was probably at its peak. From then on the depredations began. But, more and more, I think my father somehow, strangely, connived in them: not depredations so much as some gradual, stumbling process of divestment. He was sixty-six, even then. He would marry again twice, and both failed experiments. It was as if he was really, circuitously but slyly, working his way back to being an unencumbered bachelor, a bachelor of law, though, now, of course, a judge. Whatever else might be taken from him, no one could take from him those robes and authority of office.

It's not just snails who need those shells, Mikey.

And whether or not those depredations were part of some weird plan, I can't deny that your dad and I helped significantly to deplete the stock. In 1970, when Mike and I married, my father effectively bought us a house. His argument then, when I rather weakly protested, was that it would be so much less for Margaret "to get her hands on" (things were already approaching *that* stage), an argument that was hard to resist, setting aside the more basic one of gift horses and mouths. But like most of my father's kindhearted impulses, this wedding gift of a house—or the money to buy one with—caused all sorts of ructions and tensions.

It embarrassed your father and only made him wish, I think, to persist all the more in being the penniless post-graduate and servant of pure science. And it embarrassed *his* father who, though by then Dean and Hook were prospering and though he'd sent your dad that champagne, certainly wasn't in the business of making presents of houses. We should stand on our own feet. Young people today—they don't know the half. All the standard phrases. But how they catch you out much later, my darlings, how they sidle through my head right now, about you.

I think that gap between your dad and his dad widened again around this time. I think your Grandpa Pete was rather confused, and I can understand. A son who worked with *snails,* in a state of near-pauperdom, while receiving preposterous handouts from a High Court judge who, if he had to be bowed and scraped to, was plainly a fool: more money than sense. Not to mention his flighty wife.

In the war, as you know, Grandpa Pete was a navigator.

But thank God he always liked *me,* if I say so myself (and I'd once done my own bit of quaking, in Orpington). Thank God he seemed not to fault his son on that point. At our wedding, as it turned out, he shook hands with my father and they embraced like long-lost friends. Weddings can do this. My father came up only to your Grandpa Pete's nose, though he was the senior by nearly twenty-five years.

And thank God it was a house in never-fashionable, even obscure Herne Hill. It wasn't a bijou gift-house in a

Kensington mews. Nor was it a dive in Earl's Court. It was leafy but affordable, sensible and child-rearing suburbia. It was Dulwich, as the estate agents said, at two-thirds the price, and the area would soon "come up," though it never really did. It was a house which, in all the circumstances, your Grandpa Pete could approve of, not that he had any real say. And the truth is I was the one, with some help from my father, who'd mainly steered your dad and me towards it.

I'm talking, of course, though I'm talking of twenty-five years ago, of your first house. You were there for three years of your life. You can dimly remember it: 27 Davenport Road.

But *this* house, which we're all in now, is the real house of your life: your life until now. And you could say that this too came from your Grandpa Dougie. Or rather from his death. We couldn't have bought it otherwise and though we needed somewhere bigger—you were growing fast—this house, if it hadn't all begun to happen for Mike, would have been a big and risky jump beyond our real means. Now it's come into its own, it's even started to look like a staging post itself from which we might move on.

But there was never any question of that, before tomorrow. And it was never, even at the outset, for ourselves. It was for *you*. You were three years old when we left Davenport Road. Your memories were meeting up with you. There were thirteen years to go—or that was our working plan. We wanted to offer you the best we could get, the best we could provide. We wanted to put those thirteen years of precious memory in the best possible box. Though you have your Grandpa Dougie, who you never saw, mostly to thank.

Rutherford Road, Putney, on the fringe of the Heath—now one of the most "sought-after" streets in the area. I've always thought it should be called "Rectory Row," since each broad-fronted semi looks as if it's really aching to be in its own sub-rural island of gentility. Your Grandpa Dougie, who died aged seventy-seven, was just a little older than this house we're in. We once told you, years ago, that it was "Edwardian," and you told me, Nick, not so long ago, that your sister used to think of it as "Edward," as if it was a person, a secret friend, a being. Though I'm not so sure you weren't really in on it too, the Edward thing.

"Kate can be a real dope, can't she, Mum?"

Well, if it was a person, if Edward had kept his eyes and ears open, he might have whispered to both of you a secret or two.

And what doubly struck me about this little fancy was that Edward was the name of your great-uncle, Edward Hook, usually known, in fact, as Eddie, your Grandpa Pete's older brother, who can't have meant much more to you than a gravestone in Birle churchyard you'd been shown once when you were small. But perhaps it made an impression, a connection. And Eddie had once owned Coombe Cottage, outside Birle, which despite its name was actually more like some (mid-Victorian) rectory.

But come back—all these houses!—to Napier Street, Kensington. Come back to when my father was a mere sixty-six and your dad, who was twenty-one, was quaking on that white-pillared porch. Poor man, he's been there quite a while.

And now my father is opening that black door . . .

They got on like a house on fire. I knew, I'd promised, I would have bet your father that they would. Mike may have thought that when he stood there, face to face with Justice Campbell, he was being rigorously sized up. And so he was. But I was being sized up too. I saw the little glances that bounced off your dad onto me. My father was sizing us up as a pair.

Your dad at this time was just my boyfriend of two months. What a word: *boyfriend*. But I think my father knew—a true judge, in some things—even before he ushered us into his house, that your dad would be a permanent fixture in my life. There was even a little dart of a look in his eye just for me, that made me think, for the first time: perhaps I should try and get to like this Margaret.

Your dad was wearing, apart from the Chelsea boots, his best black flares and his best cream round-collared shirt. And my dad was wearing—what else?—a cardigan. A rather chunky cardigan, in fact, for a warmish day in May, with those buttons like little footballs: navy blue, over a pale-pink shirt. Blue cord trousers, suede loafers. Mr. Justice Campbell in Saturday clothes.

Though I had every faith your father would pass with flying colours, I knew there would be two principal tests. One was that first clapping of eyes on the front porch—already sailed through. The other was the wine cellar. I'd already told your dad that it was the hub, the nerve centre, and that if he was asked down there, as he almost certainly would be, then it was best not to venture any opinions, but simply to be guided, boggle and agree. Not a difficult thing to do. I couldn't believe Mike *wouldn't* be invited—the only question was how long the invitation would take.

It seemed to me it took rather less than a minute. I didn't mind at all that I was summarily deserted, and I absolutely knew I shouldn't tag along. This was a critical moment. Never mind the opening chit-chat, never mind the rest of the house. Your Grandpa Dougie felt we needed something decent to drink.

"Er, Michael—come with me, would you?"

I waited upstairs while subterranean bonding occurred. A judge of men, a judge of wine. It was perhaps five minutes. I looked round the room: the padded-leather fireguard, the tall gilt mirror over the fireplace, the Staffordshire dogs on the mantelpiece, the De Brant still-life in the alcove (we have it now). I thought: this is my *former* home.

Your father told me later that after a memorable guided tour my father had picked out a bottle and said (though it was three in the afternoon and more like tea-time) that we should drink it now, right away—by way of welcome. Your father had concurred. My father had patted the bottle. Then, with his non-dusty hand, he'd patted Mike on the shoulder and said, "Call me Dougie."

By the time they reappeared I could see that your father had lost all traces of his recent trepidation. The only uncertainty left in his mind, I could tell, was the question of how this sixty-six-year-old teddy bear of a man could ever actually have become a judge. A question that had once puzzled me.

That evening, now that your dad had met my dad and so

plainly hit it off, I told your father something that in all our two months, so far, of pillow-talking, I'd never whispered to him. Something, in fact, I'd never shared with anyone before. Now I'm sharing it with you.

I waited till we were on the train back to Brighton from Victoria. Then I told him how when I was only thirteen I'd gone, all by myself, in the school holidays, to Court Number Six, Royal Courts of Justice, where I knew my father would be presiding, precisely in order to solve that baffling question. It still seems to me an intrepid thing for a thirteen-year-old to have done.

I'd sat in the public gallery, no one had stopped me, and I'd received a small, unforgettable shock. Because there before me—below me—was a man in scarlet robes and a grey wig, who, though I unquestionably knew him, I wouldn't have recognised as my father. A man who was fearsomely, awesomely in his element, who ruthlessly, I could see, if I hardly understood a word of what was going on, cut through the quibbles and chicaneries of lesser, if important, wigged men and left no one in any doubt who was in charge in that courtroom. Podgy of stature though he familiarly was, he dominated, he towered.

I'd felt suddenly terrified, I told your father. Worse, I'd felt suddenly guilty—and it seemed the right place for guilt—to be watching at all in this way, on the sly. Suppose he were to look up and spot me there, small as I was and now trying desperately to look smaller and to keep my head down, in the back row.

Maybe he had seen me. I didn't think so. But then how would I have known? Since I'd felt suddenly, unnervingly sure that if he had, he wouldn't have let the recognition upset for a moment his superlative act. There would have been no sudden fluster, no sudden, inexplicable and unjudgelike smile. He was Mr. Justice Campbell. I was just a child in the gallery.

Had he seen me? I still wonder now. I'll never know. But surely, if he had seen me, he would have told me, at some time at least, when I was grown up. Before he died. Paulie, I saw you, that day.

I told your father all this—not that last part, of course—as we clacked back to Sussex through that May evening, and I told him not to tell anyone. As if he would have done, as if he was going to broadcast it. But it was a measure of my thirteen-year-old's fear, even then. And I think I scared Mike just a bit—mellow and sedated as he still was from my dad's wine. Yes, it had been that same man.

We've never even talked about it again since, though I've certainly thought about it, and I think so has Mike. In fact, I think he may have been thinking about it quite a lot recently. I think he may have been thinking about that smaller version of me, seeing a man I did and didn't know.

The bottle my father brought up from the cellar was a Clos du Roi, '55. Some bottles, some vintages you never forget. (Mumm non-vintage—but for all time.) When we moved in here to Rutherford Road, we moved in with you, of course, but also with some eight or nine cases of extremely fine wine. It was all that was left by then. My father may have had to do some selling up. On the other hand, if you want to divest yourself of liquid property, there's a simple way of going about it.

He died aged seventy-seven, a single man with a great deal less than what he'd once had. But he died, I think, with what he wanted at the time. He died a Justice. And he died a Campbell—that was the disconcerting bit. He also had me, his only child (of three marriages), and he knew I had the man I loved. There was just one thing, which he never mentioned, that he didn't have.

He opened that bottle in front of Mike and me in his familiarly unceremonious way and sniffed it. "Spot on—after a breathe." Thirty seconds later, after fetching three glasses, he said, "It's breathed." He poured. He said to Mike, but as if specially for my ear: "I drank this wine in August 1944. All kinds of wine was getting back to England then, care of Special Operations. It was the evening I proposed to Paulie's mother. Do they still do that these days? Welcome, Michael, to my somewhat depleted home."

I could tell that your dad was letting slip down his throat something unlike anything that had slipped down it before. Later he said it was well named, it made you feel like a king. We moved out with our glasses into the sunshine in the little walled garden, where four years later (Taittinger '61) our wedding would be celebrated.

I wish you could have seen him. Not your dad when he was twenty-one in his cream shirt (though I wish that too): your Grandpa Dougie. I wish you still could see him—I wish I could—from some special gallery. And not, I mean, the man I once saw in the wig and robe, whom you've seen anyway, in a sense, in the silver-framed photo in the hall. New visitors to this house sometimes pause and say, "My God—who's that?" And I say, a little sternly, in keeping with the photo, "It's my father, actually, it's Mr. Justice Campbell."

No, I wish you could have seen that other man, that out-of-court man, my one-time daddy, pouring wine for Mikey and me at Napier Street. He'd have loved to have seen you.

11

I CRIED WHEN HE DIED. I was just like Mike, I cried at my dad's funeral, at Invercullen, when there was rain, at least, to prompt me and to screen me—not like this soft, midsummer stuff falling now: an icy Caledonian onslaught. But I cried, anyway, afterwards. For weeks I was like a wet sponge, one touch would set me going, in spite of my saying to myself: come on, you're over thirty, stop blubbing like a girl. But that's what all my tears were really, I think, my childhood finally seeping out of me.

And I thought I'd parted with my childhood, finally and formally and even rather beautifully, that year I met your father and he met mine. I thought I'd said goodbye to it with Mike. Our childhoods aren't so easily discarded, it seems. At thirty-plus—at forty-plus—they can still pop up and claim us. And why should we want to part with them anyway, like friends who've begun to embarrass us? Perhaps you'll tell us tomorrow. Sixteen is really like eighteen now? Childhood is a smaller and smaller luxury? And I've seen you, my pets, trying to leap out of your childhoods, like fish onto land, long before now. It's made my heart leap into my mouth.

I can still see Mike's childhood in him—summers at his

Uncle Eddie's—though I was never there with him. It's a sort of privilege I have, another special gallery. And I told him, on that train back to Brighton, about that time when I was thirteen. Was I still a child then? Dimming green fields slipped by the window, clumps of ghostly-white may blossom. It would have been one of those old, vanished, plumply upholstered train compartments. String luggage racks, wooden-framed invitations to south-coast beauty spots. Another world. Another sort of childhood too, it seems now. We had it to ourselves. Your dad had taken off his Chelsea boots, his socked feet were between my thighs. The Clos du Roi was still in our veins.

"We must go to Craiginish," I said, "this summer. It's our last chance." Perhaps I really meant "my." "Before my mum gets it."

I could still say "mum." She hadn't yet become just "Fiona"—with now and then an emphasis on that first, already hissy "F."

What a time to be talking about Scotland, while we sped back to the Sussex coast. Your dad might have thought, if he wasn't so happily mollified by top-notch burgundy, that he was really being put through the hoops. First my father—so far, so good—now a trip to the bloody Highlands. And what a prospect: some windswept beach, as he must have seen it, in the frozen north. A "croft." A *croft*? I had to do some serious talking up.

But we went that July. The sleeper from King's Cross, then a hire car from Fort William. My father blessed and subsidised the trip. When he handed me the keys, which he'd soon have to surrender for good, he said rather solemnly,

"Say goodbye to the place for me, won't you?" And all the way up I hoped it wouldn't be one of *those* Scottish summers—grey, wet and squally, clouds charging in over the islands. That the Gulf Stream would do one of its timely tricks and bring a touch of the Caribbean to northern Argyll.

But so it was. It was actually hot. And the "Croft," your dad could see now with his own eyes, wasn't a croft but a substantial, if eccentric and isolated, summer house, even with an air about it of some misplaced Riviera villa. What's more, as we opened it up, and skimpily furnished though it was, it released an impregnation, a bouquet of former occupation. Even your dad, who'd never been there before, could recognise the corky, trapped-in-a-bottle smell.

I wish we could have gone there with you. But don't you remember—won't you always—the smell of Gull Cottage in Cornwall?

We opened windows. They yawned and sighed. When you add fresh oxygen to that bottled-up stuff a heady chemistry occurs. And they opened up to a view below of a white crescent beach, backed by dunes and washed by long, slow, rolling breakers—on which there wasn't a soul. My Brighton-train rhapsody, fondling your father's feet, hadn't all been sales talk. I didn't have to say, "I told you so."

And so it was there, at Craiginish—but this I really hadn't premeditated or prefigured, it was never part of my idyll-painting—that the "proposal," as I would later call it, took place. "Proposal" really isn't the right word. Your dad even likes to quip that it was a slip of the tongue. But what else to call it? It was there, in the high summer of 1966, that your

dad and I became—an even more exotically antique word—
"betrothed." Though having betrothed ourselves, in a decid-
edly impetuous and breathless way, we didn't actually get
married for another four years.

What was stopping us, you may well ask. And isn't it the
point, or one of the points, of this bedtime story, you must
be thinking, to underscore the proposition, never mind pro-
posals, that this man lying here and me were always meant
for each other, made for each other, as they say? We were
meant to be. And would you yourselves, who have such
an intimate interest in the matter, have written the story
differently?

Forgive that last question, it's unfair and foolish. Especially tonight. You hardly had any option. It's like saying
that you were *meant* to be born in Gemini. Forgive your
foolish mother. What would have happened if your dad and
I had never "found" each other? We'd have been lost souls
for the rest of our lives, for ever searching for our missing
other halves? By an incredible stroke of cosmic luck, we just
happened to cross paths in Brighton?

Of course I know it wouldn't have been so. I'd have found
someone else. I'd have found another Mikey. He'd have
found another Paulie. And what would you have cared who
it was, so long as there was *someone,* two someones, to produce you? I married, as it happens, a biologist, but I don't
need a biologist to tell me that it's a rough old game, the
mating game, a game of chance and scramble. There's no
sweet bedtime story in biology.

But forgive me for thinking that's unthinkable. Forgive
me for thinking I've proved it otherwise. Another Mikey:

not *this* one? Another me? Forgive me for thinking, even back then, at Craiginish, at the mature age of twenty: why had it taken so *long*? All those missed-out years. What kept you, Mikey, what kept us?

Nothing was stopping us, except that awkward fact of being children of our time, children of the Sixties, obliged to scoff at the very idea of marriage. How embarrassing. When your father "proposed" to me I was, of course, on the pill. He couldn't have done it, in fact, or done it so passionately, if I wasn't. It was that magic pill, principally, that had made marriage so unobligatory, or so unpressing. Otherwise, if there was just the two of you, and you were only twenty . . .

You see the way—the unfortunate way for you—this is heading?

When your Grandma Helen met Grandpa Pete, in the war, it was rather different. They got married quickly and went on a brief and urgent honeymoon. They had their special reasons. None of which, of course, can have been to conceive expressly for me my future husband. But forgive me.

You've seen the photos, like archive material, of Pete and Helen's wedding. For all the haste, it was the full ceremony. A church, of course. It was in Dartford. Grandpa Pete in his uniform, Grandma Helen, considering it was wartime, in amazing bridal flow. Is that long train really a parachute? April 1944. Two months later Grandpa Pete was in a prison camp.

We finally got married, as you know, in Chelsea Registry Office (where else but the King's Road?), on the twenty-fourth of June, twenty-five years ago. But that four-year gap before we made things formal can't all be ascribed to the issue, if you'll pardon the pun, of children. If that were so, why did we wait another *nine* years before having you? I've sometimes wondered if that nine-year gap has ever vaguely hurt you. We left it so long, till our critical thirties, because we might, in fact, have been entirely happy without you? But then it's perfectly common these days, almost the standard thing, women happily wait till they're past thirty. What's the big rush? How different from Helen and Pete.

But come back to that "betrothal." Come back to the white, bridal sand of Craiginish. Though this is one of those moments when perhaps you really *shouldn't* be listening. On the other hand, I can't believe you didn't work it out between the two of you long ago. What were we *doing* in those dunes? And what a prim, archaic word I'd chosen: "proposed." It conjures up a man on bended knee with a bunch of flowers. It conjures up an Edward.

But a principal detail you don't know. Your father is a biologist. And, yes, we were being biological. But he'd been being biological beforehand. He'd been telling me, at some length in fact, about marram grass—that wind-blown stuff that grows exclusively on the brows of sand dunes and that right then was gently waving and whispering, conspiratorially I have to believe, just above our heads. Apparently, it has, among the grasses, unique and extraordinary properties, not least of which is its stubborn desire to cling and take root where no other plant will, on bare and barren sand. It's the grassy equivalent of limpets.

An early and incongruous instance of one of Professor Mike's lectures. I can't say I was concentrating. Though I

can't say that before that day I even knew it was *called* marram grass. Just think, he might have been a grass expert.
Soon afterwards, anyway, we were engaged in other things,
and in a short while this man who I'd known then for just
four months was crying out to me in a state of high but pur-
poseful excitement, "Marry me! Marry me!"

A slip of the tongue? A likely story.

And what did I say? Well, the answer's obvious. Here I
am, married to your father. For twenty-five years now,
nearly. And you may think, Kate—I don't know if you've
put it to the test, though I rather think you haven't—that
you may be the only woman who'll never gasp out the word,
but I bet you aren't or won't be.

"Yes," I said. "Oh yes, yes, yes!"

12

I MARRIED A HOOK. The jokes work both ways: I was hooked, or I was the lucky girl who hooked a Hook. Twenty-five years ago, in any case, I changed my name from Campbell to Hook, a simple, then-customary procedure which, if you think about it, can seem just a little outrageous.

But what's in a name? I've always liked, anyway, the simple, no-nonsense, Anglo-Saxon sound of it. And it's your name, my two little Hooks, the name you were born with, have grown up with and, so far as I know, have never resented: your dad's name, since that's the custom too.

Kate Hook, Nick Hook: two neat, quick syllables for each of you. Even if you'd never met them, you'd think: "Kate Hook," "Nick Hook," well, they're going to be two bright, sharp, good-to-know people, they're not going to be a pair of drips. I suppose you might also think: "Hook?"— never trust anyone with a name like that. But I even like that little hint of crookedness.

When I started at Walker and Fitch (good names too, at least in the art world), not long after I got married, I made a decision: to be Paula Hook, at work, not Paula Campbell. It was my decision and it went against the grain again, for 1970. But it really wasn't a decision at all. I was happy to wear your dad's name, to settle the debate permanently and openly: Okay, Mikey, *you* hooked *me*. It's another debate whether you'd rather buy a picture from a Paula Hook than a Paula Campbell. I know, there was always a joke or two there. That's the picture, I'm the Hook. I'm a senior director now, anyway. I can turn down lunch with my boss.

And all this made me the crooked and treacherous one, I suppose, trading-in my proud Scottish name to this family from the deepest south. Hook being a Sussex name. But that's where we'd met—in Sussex, at Sussex. We even told you when you were small that we'd met on Brighton beach, a little myth or half-myth we had to modify later. And in those days it had just been Paulie and Mikey. What's in a name? What's even in a family?

But two years after we were married I found out what it really meant to have changed my name. And by then (if you've been wondering) we were certainly thinking, more than thinking, of starting a family. One evening your father came off the phone and said, "That was my dad. My Uncle Eddie's died." Then he went very silent for a while, and a little later shed some tears—something I'd never seen before then, and which you saw for the first time not so long ago when we were all standing, as it happened, not so very far from Uncle Eddie's well-weathered grave.

Grandpa Pete was your first death. That had been ours: Uncle Eddie, when we were a good deal older than you were last year. When I saw your dad cry, I thought: it's only an *uncle*, it's not his mum or dad. What's with the tears? Though I'd met Uncle Eddie myself, two or three times, and I had some idea of the story. And wasn't I now a Hook?

A few days later, on a beautiful spring morning, I found myself standing in that churchyard at Birle, my first visit there for a funeral. It's a picture-book country churchyard, as you know, it's pure Gray's *Elegy*. Though I'm not sure if such things mean anything to you, in 1995, plugged as you are so much of the time into one kind of electronic life-support system or another. Kids these days—this was your dad's joke when we bought you your first computers—they don't ask for the *world*, do they, they don't even *want* it. For you, perhaps, it's all the other way round. I'm not so sure you don't think that churchyards and villages like Birle and country cottages and the country itself don't really *belong* in some old-fashioned picture-book. I'm not sure you've read Gray's *Elegy*.

Anyway, once when you were small you were taken, for the possible interest of it, to that churchyard at Birle and shown those gravestones, a century or two old some of them. Look, that's your name: Hook. And the most recent one of them was Uncle Eddie's: Edward Hook. Look, he was born in 1915. Which seems to have struck a little chord with you, to have made a strange, mutated impression.

And there you were again, early last year, for Grandpa Pete. Your first taste of death. Dank January weather to go with it. I was quietly proud of your fourteen-year-old dignity, so was Grannie Helen. You both seemed so calm. Perhaps you were just numbed and dazed, it was all just washing over you. Then, of course, the memory suddenly flooded over me, making my heart thump in the middle of that funeral: this *wasn't* your first dealing with death, was it?

But perhaps you were just aching to get back to your CD players, your teenage agendas, whatever they were at the time. Sometimes it's as though there's a wall of plate glass between us and you. We haven't noticed it, we think we can just walk through. Can I really remember any more how it actually *feels*—to be fourteen, to be sixteen?

Back in 1972, in that churchyard, when I was twenty-six, my range of emotions was rather different. I thought: well, who wouldn't want to be buried in such a place, if they could choose? Death tasted, that day, of April sunshine and new, juicy grass. Lucky Hooks. Who wouldn't want to be a Hook? Then, of course, it hit me: I *was* one. And then that other thought hit me: that I might, one day, be one of these stones.

It hit me like some almost-actual bolt from that blue and fluffy-white April sky. It travelled right through me. There's that expression which I fully understood that day: to be "rooted to the spot, to the ground." And then, I can't explain it, but perhaps it had to do with being rooted, I felt— well, sappy and juicy. I'd never known quite such rampant *sappiness*.

I suddenly felt, I have to confess it, a great lust for your father, for your father's body—definitely not a new thing, as I must have made plain, but never before in a graveyard. For the body of this man I'd known then for six years. For the body of this man, lying sleeping here, with whom, as it happens, I made the tenderest of sweetest love just two hours ago.

Lust in a churchyard, at a *funeral*: that's worse than mere randiness in church. Even as your father stood, in his dark suit, mourning his Uncle Eddie. Red-bedspread lust. But lust with a will, a determination, it wouldn't leave me. Don't be ashamed of your mother. All through the gathering that followed at Coombe Cottage, in that home of Hooks, while sherries were served on the lawn by Mrs. Sinden, Uncle Eddie's bravely smiling old housekeeper, I was really thinking: couldn't there be some magic time-warp in these proceedings so that, without anyone noticing, I could take Mikey off and satisfy my lust with him, then return with him, not a stitch out of place, as if we'd never gone anywhere?

It was April all around, greenly lusting anyway. If only it had been—perhaps I shouldn't have had the thought— January. From the end of that garden, as you know, you can see, beyond a field or two, the South Downs suddenly swelling up to their bosomy skyline. I'd never felt so much the truth of what your dad had once said about them (Sussex University, after all, was plonked down right in their midst), that they were the most libidinous landscape he knew. All those curves and dips, those little pubic clumps of trees. When you saw them, you wanted, he said, to run your hand over them, like you wanted to run your hand . . .

Well, Mikey, I thought, let me be your South Downs.

It's usually men, we're given to believe, who go through these torments of disguised, of intolerably postponed rapacity. When they do they try to think, apparently, of chastening and chilly things, like funerals and coffins.

At least by the time we got home to Herne Hill that evening the lust had become plainly mutual. I'd infected your father, despite his April grief? Or it's just how death can work anyway, even on the grieving? Biology talking. Lust, but with a will and a purpose to it. No guesses what it was. I really believed—does this sound strange to you? It sounds now even a little strange to me—that on that April night we would conceive you.

Uncle Eddie died when he was only fifty-seven. That gravestone would have told you. For his twenty-first birthday, Grandpa Pete sent your dad that case of champagne, but his Uncle Eddie sent him a beautiful, leather-bound Victorian book, with some lovely, hand-tinted illustrations: on molluscs. At that point in his life, I think your dad appreciated the champagne more than the book, and he was more interested in girls than snails. But the champagne got drunk and the book got kept. It's still here, right now, in this house, with Uncle Eddie's austerely calligraphic inscription inside. "To M.H. from E.H. . . ." Wilkinson's *British Terrestrial and Freshwater Molluscs*: what a mouthful, what a present. Four years later we got married, two years after that, Uncle Eddie died.

How quick and rushing life can sometimes seem, when at the same time it's so slow and sweet and everlasting. How soon you start to count the numbers. I was twenty-six— *already?*—nearer twenty-seven. One moment it's just life, life, nothing but life, and though you're in a state of higher education, you know nothing really, you're just kids really, still at play. Then along come the announcements and reckonings and understandings. You know a bit about death. Even about birth.

When my father died, just a few years later, it turned out that, though he'd lived in Kensington most of his life, he wanted to be buried at Invercullen, in Argyllshire, among his ancestors: gravestones with the name "Campbell." It meant a long and rather ghastly journey north for your dad and me—not at all like our earlier journey to Craiginish. It meant rather a lot of things. I said to your dad, "I think you're going to have to meet Fiona."

But one of the things it meant to me, amid a great inundation of grief, was that little prickle of treachery: that I was a Hook now, not a Campbell. It might even have occurred to the two of you, last year, that though Grandpa Pete had lived most of his life in Orpington, there he was now in that churchyard at Birle, just yards from his brother Eddie. It seemed he'd reserved the plot even before he and Grannie Helen retired permanently to Coombe Cottage. More significantly still, he'd booked a double plot. So Grannie Helen must have agreed, though her maiden name was Kingsley, and the Kingsleys came from Dartford.

What weird things families are. How weird that we all sit somewhere in the branches of a family tree.

When I stood with your father at your Great-uncle Eddie's funeral, I'd been off the pill for a while, if nothing yet had happened. But that sudden, highly awkward surge of lust was like some extra confirmation, an endorsement. I "wanted his children." And what a strange phrase that is, "his children," another dubious bow to custom. I wanted *my* children too. (I wanted that dark suit off him.)

Quite clearly it *wasn't* that night you were conceived, though it had everything going for it, even the time of the month. All the same, perhaps you could say it was where you really "began," seven years before you were actually born: at Uncle Eddie's funeral. How canny you were, Kate, when you secretly christened this house.

I was twenty-six, Mike was twenty-seven. We were in that seven-month period of every year—we're in it now—when your dad has the edge on me. I haven't finished yet with that crucial year of 1972. This year, on his fiftieth birthday, Nick, you needled your father—I suppose every son has to—about what it felt like to be an old man of half a century. As if being forty or even thirty isn't already ancient to you.

You did it jokingly and gently enough, and your dad took it in the same spirit. It didn't seem to rattle him, I think he was prepared for something like it. And you'll both of you remember what he said. He said that fifty was nothing these days, it was the prime of life. I was glad to hear it. But in any case, he said, he wasn't bothered, because after a certain point in his life he'd always really felt the same age inside, the age at which he'd sort of stopped. Remember? And you said, Nick, still a tender fifteen yourself, "Oh yeah, and what age was that then?" And he said, "Twenty-seven."

13

YOU NEVER KNEW your Grandpa Dougie. You've never even seen his grave, on a hillside in Argyll. And you've never met your Grannie Fiona, last locatable even further north, amid the oil and twinkling granite of Aberdeen.

The Campbell side of things, disappearing into Scottish mist, was always the remote and fairy-tale side of things, not to mention those complicating and never-seen step-parents of mine, somewhere in between. But the truth is it was the Hook side, with which you've had close and familiar dealings, which was really the fairy-tale side. And it's time you were told—you're sixteen now, after all—the full, unexpurgated fairy tale.

Which includes the fairy tale of how your father's legendary snails, which you also never met but with which he once worked very closely, eventually turned into this thing which, along with some lucrative art dealing, has kept us now very comfortably indeed for years. I mean, of course, Living World Publishing. You can't complain that you've ever gone without. In fact, you've even been a little spoilt. But I hope you'll agree that, contrary to another kind of moralising fairy tale, this has been at no cost to happiness.

This has been a happy home. And nothing has made it happier, for us, than that you're in it.

Once upon a time, as you know, there was your Grandpa Pete and your Grandma Helen—Grandpa and Grannie Hook—in Orpington, when we were all still in Herne Hill. You might just about remember number nineteen Hathaway Drive (also known as The Firs), when Grandpa Pete was still running his business in Sidcup with Charlie Dean. You got taken there once, to the factory, and you didn't like the artificial-resin smell. As a matter of fact, though I have a little professional knowledge of resins, nor did I. But you knew your grandparents better from Coombe Cottage, just outside Birle, where they'd go at weekends and where we used to go and stay. Then they retired there permanently, when Grandpa Pete was sixty and you were not quite five.

But before Grandpa Pete owned Coombe Cottage, it had belonged to his older brother, Edward, your great-uncle, whose grave, at least, you'd been introduced to. There was a gap of nine years between Pete and Eddie and not much love lost between them, as far as I could tell. Grandpa Pete must have been one of those children who sometimes get called "accidents" or who, at least, were late-in-the-day afterthoughts. It can hardly help sibling relations. A nine-year gap must seem crazy and unimaginable to the two of you.

Uncle Eddie was a schoolmaster in one of those country schools hidden away up drives, among trees. "Birle School." He was thin and softly spoken and had a droopy moustache. He smoked a pipe and rode a bicycle and, since he lived in the country, he had a library of books on natural history, which he knew a lot about anyway. He was the sort of man who collected butterflies and beetles and birds' eggs (all of which would be frowned upon now, of course) and he passed some of his enthusiasm on to your dad. He was a bachelor who lived alone, apart from Mrs. Sinden, who came in every day from the village to cook and clean. Even when I met him those few times, he was like a man from another age. Yes, he seemed Edwardian, like his name. This was in the late 1960s and, yes, they're ages ago now.

But in the even more distant 1950s, your dad used to stay with his Uncle Eddie, whole summers long, when he was a boy and Grandpa Pete was working hard to get his business off the ground. He'd be dropped off in July and picked up again at the end of August. This is why your dad could call himself a "Sussex boy," even though he was brought up in commuter-belt Kent.

Those summers in Sussex proved a boon for your dad, but they didn't help relations with *his* dad or between his dad and Uncle Eddie. Grandpa Pete got it very wrong if he thought he was neatly solving the problem of summer holidays while exploiting his older brother at the same time. It was always pretty obvious to me that there'd been plenty of love lost between your dad, when he was a boy, and his Uncle Eddie. That Uncle Eddie had been like a second father, a sort of summer father, to him.

It was also pretty obvious, to go back further, that during that time when Grandpa Pete was a prisoner of war and your dad was born—during that time, Kate, he got talking to you about last Christmas—it must have been Uncle Eddie who first saw your dad, first picked him up and held him. I can picture him putting aside his pipe carefully first. Picturing your dad here as a baby dangling from his uncle's arms is a little trickier, but it's a nice trickiness.

Uncle Eddie had a heart condition—which didn't seem to stop him puffing away at that pipe. He'd never had to serve in the war, and that was another source of resentment for his younger brother. Eddie had just sat out the war in that far from pokey cottage of his, while Grandpa Pete had gone off to fight. Oddly enough, according to your father, that was the very phrase that Grandpa Pete liked to use about the war: that he'd "sat it out." Your dad never really knew if he was referring to being a prisoner of war or just to being in the air force. Airmen, after all, go to war sitting down. And Grandpa Pete, as a navigator, used to have his own little desk, with a desk lamp, up in the sky, though I don't think it made him any safer.

But perhaps it was just his formula for having been a prisoner, or for stopping his son asking any more questions. I remember you, Nick, once asking Grandpa Pete about the war and saying, "But didn't you try to escape?" He just looked at you apologetically, as if he was sorry he wasn't Steve McQueen.

Uncle Eddie died because of his heart condition years before you were born, and I went with your dad, who was pretty upset, to the funeral. Then Grandpa Pete got the cottage and eventually moved there with Grannie Helen. Now, of course, he's in Birle churchyard too, just a few steps from Eddie.

Mike and I have never really talked about it (I'm not *that* much of a Hook, perhaps), but it always seemed to me that in his last years at Birle, at Coombe Cottage, Grandpa Pete got more and more like his brother—or like his brother as I'd remembered him, or like his brother might have been if he'd lived beyond sixty. Grandpa Pete must have always thought that Eddie was the main item, destined to be, but for a little glitch of family planning, an only child like me and your dad. Could that even be why your dad was so fond of him? Eddie was nine when Grandpa Pete was just a baby, the same age your dad was when he spent his first summer at Birle. These things count maybe.

Anyway, it seemed to me that your Grandpa Pete in his later years got more like Uncle Eddie. Grandpa Pete never smoked a pipe or rode a bicycle and Uncle Eddie never had a dog, but the differences got less and the similarities got more. Grandpa Pete even died of a heart attack too, if not at fifty-seven. It could be just a coincidence or it could be one of those things that runs in the family. Ever since your Grandpa Pete died, I've wanted your dad to go and have his heart checked.

I think his heart might come under a bit of strain tomorrow.

But at Uncle Eddie's funeral, years before you were born, there was another "uncle," called Tim. Tim Harvey. He was pretty upset too. He wasn't your dad's real uncle. He was another of those pretend uncles, like your "Uncle" Charlie. "Uncle Tim" was Uncle Eddie's oldest friend, they'd been at college together, and he used sometimes to come and stay at Coombe Cottage when your dad was there as a boy. You would never have met him, though he was still alive when you were small. If we could call Fiona your "fairy grand-mother," then we might have called Tim Harvey your "fairy godfather" or your "fairy great-uncle," though it might have given the wrong impression.

I asked your father when he first mentioned "Uncle Tim" to me: had there been anything—you know—between him and Uncle Eddie? Two bachelors in a country cottage . . . But your dad said not a bachelor, actually, in Uncle Tim's case, a widower, a confirmed widower. His wife had been killed in a flying-bomb raid at the end of the war. Which rather stopped me doing any more teasing.

He'd lost his wife all those years ago, but he was devotedly married now, you could say, to a science journal called *The Living World,* which he'd kept going all through the war and which had become his life. Your dad said the dead wife's name had been Eleanor. She'd been wealthy, a sort of patroness, and when she'd died she'd left Uncle Tim a lot of money. Though more to the point, perhaps, when she'd died she'd been pregnant.

A struggling science journal—I'd certainly never heard of it—and when I met him it was clearly Uncle Tim's standard joke, a little awkward at a funeral, that he'd kept the living world alive.

He scared me just a bit. He scared me like Grannie Helen scares me now. He looked as if he was very familiar with being at a funeral. But I liked him, I felt sorry for him— saying goodbye now to his oldest friend. He was a bit like some struggling, persevering science journal himself: tall, silvery-haired, abstracted—professorial. I was nice to him. In fact, I think I even flirted with him just a little, if that's possible at a funeral, and only in the way that you can flirt with silvery-haired men you're both scared of and sorry for. Though I've flirted with quite a few silvery-haired men, of all kinds, at Walker's. It can sometimes help to make a sale.

Perhaps I just mean that while I was being nice to Uncle Tim, I was smouldering for your father. It was a sort of over-spill, perhaps. I was being particularly attentive to Uncle Tim in order to curb my lust for your father. I don't know quite how he took it or if, in his grief for his friend, it even registered, but he didn't discourage me: "So, you're Mike's lovely young wife. I remember him in short trousers, you know." Perhaps he was flirting with me or just accidentally pressing buttons.

We got on, anyway. We warmed to each other, in that April sunshine. So when he offered your dad a job a few months later, I could hardly object. Not, that is, to Uncle Tim himself, if I could object on just about every other score. I could even blame myself for having been, perhaps, a little instrumental.

But on the other hand, Tim Harvey could hardly have known how uncannily perfect his timing was—in just what a vulnerable condition your dad would be, setting aside his Uncle Eddie's death, by the time he made his offer. Setting aside, too, that question I'd begun now to ask: how much longer, with those snails?

But then this was surely crazy. A struggling science peri-odical that hardly anyone seemed to read—run from an attic in Bloomsbury? And only its *deputy* editor? It was just as well, I said to Mike, they seemed to like me at Walker's. It was just as well we had just the two of us to feed. I might have been a little crueller, if I hadn't also had to consider your dad's "condition," and if it wasn't for my own complicity, so far as it went, on that back lawn at Coombe Cottage.

In a nutshell, Tim wanted your dad to be not just his deputy but his heir, if I don't think he ever quite used the word. It was as if your dad had been earmarked, even from those short-trousered days perhaps, and now Tim was thinking of the future. He wanted your dad, in the fullness of time, to take over his baby. Though, again, that's my word not his.

And, in a nutshell, I yielded. Partly for those back-lawn reasons, and partly for intimate and sensitive reasons I've yet to come to. A temporary phase, I thought. Be flexible. A passing aberration. A year or two . . .

It's lasted over twenty.

Now, of course, I'm not sorry. Now, of course, I even shamelessly like to make out that I knew all along, I kept the faith. Our ship (no more, in those days, than a rather leaky boat) would one day come in. Your dad likes to say it was all Uncle Tim's doing, really. That right-place and right-time theory. And Tim had always told him (he says now) that one day there'd be a bonanza. In *science*? I think that's just your dad being modest. It doesn't sound like Tim Harvey. The "fairy godfather" factor only goes so far. Tim may have had the money and even his wishful thinking, but he had his limitations. And your dad had his hidden talents. I think they were even rather hidden from your dad.

But you're familiar with the story now, you're part of it—its real heirs. Things began to come good for us in the end, not so long after you arrived. Tim stepped aside when I was on maternity leave, dealing with the insomniac havoc you wreaked on Davenport Road (forgive me) and wondering if I ever really *had* worked in art dealing. Meanwhile, your dad's talents had begun to blossom. Don't ask me where he got the energy. Then Tim died, in 1981, leaving most of what was left of his private wealth to what he liked to call "*LW.*" Then it was the Eighties and there was a publishing boom.

You know the rest: *Living World Magazine,* Living World Publishing, Living World Books. A whole new image. That now familiar logo, the little button-sized, blue and green Yin-and-Yang biosphere. It more or less just got better and better. But, most importantly—and who can say if *you* didn't actually bring out that other entrepreneurial man in your father and give him all that drive?—there was the bonanza of you.

I remember how in what I'll call now the "in-between" years—I mean, before there was you, in the mid-Seventies—when I was starting to do well (and just as well) at Walker's, I'd sometimes find myself saying, at art-gatherings I had to go to: "My husband? He's deputy editor of *The Living World.*" Or, later: "My husband? He's editor of *The Living World.*" It *sounded* good, of course, it sounded important: what could be bigger than the living world? People in the art world aren't necessarily clued up on science. And it was certainly better than saying, however confidently and breezily, "My husband works on snails."

All the same, I'd wait for the vacant stare or the bluffing, knowing nod—keeping up a sort of bluff myself. Or I'd prepare for the embarrassed and embarrassing, "I'm not sure that I've ever heard . . ."

But once, at least, it made a big, even a startlingly strong impression. It was with our vet—who would, of course, have been a scientific man. He actually said, "I'm impressed." It turned out he was a regular subscriber, one of the very few I'd ever knowingly met.

"Your husband's editor of *The Living World*? Well, I'm impressed."

And, naturally, I told your dad. I said, "I had this interesting chat with our new vet."

But you'll be thinking: vet? What vet? How does a vet come into the story?

14

I'M JUMPING AHEAD. Come back to Davenport Road in the year that Uncle Eddie died. I need to explain now some difficult and delicate things. I need to explain in my own words what your father will explain in his tomorrow. It's one thing we've agreed on: your father will do the talking. Who else, in the circumstances? But he's asleep now, amazingly, before the biggest speech of his life. And I want him to sleep. Sleep on, Mikey, as long as you can. And what is your mother supposed to do, while these last vigilant hours slip away? Simply keep silent?

This bedroom, in the dark, with the rain outside, feels like some temporary refuge.

I need to explain that there might never have been you. There was Mike and me, the two of us, but there might never have been you. The world, our lives, this house might never have contained you. Big stuff. But then not so remarkable, you're already thinking. We all have the flicker of the thought, then brush it aside as superfluous: I might never have been born. Gosh, but here I am.

Some people can wish—I hope you never will, I sincerely hope you never will—that they'd never been born. But it's not as though any of us could ever have asked, chosen. We always have that little retort to throw back at our parents. Though, speaking for myself—but I think I speak for Mike too—I can't suppress the quite illogical but painful thought that if you weren't there, if we hadn't allowed you into the world, we'd have committed a crime, we'd have done something terrible *to you.*

Have I ever told you? Have we ever told you? How beautiful you are.

Professor Mike here will point out that nature is colossally wasteful. For every life that makes it, a staggering number of potential lives are lost. There may be millions of us walking around, but we are all extraordinary little exceptions. The same is true of ants or centipedes—think of all those never-to-wriggle legs—or, I'm sure, snails.

But then, if we didn't ask or choose, but we just arrived against all the odds, how many of us can say that we were really *meant*? Another thing to throw at our long-suffering parents who've done so much to make a home for us. Though even *that*, of course, isn't always true. Sometimes there isn't much of a home to speak of. Sometimes our parents aren't there or have parted. Sometimes we don't even know who they are.

It's another notion we all have, perhaps, then dismiss it, leaving it surprisingly unpursued, considering how totally relevant it is: the notion of tracing ourselves back to our actual moment of conception. It involves a taboo, an intrusion, like entering unasked the parental bedroom. Or it just involves a risk. Who knows in what chancy and sordid circumstances we might have first come about? Perhaps best not to find out. And were our parents, anyway, at the time actually thinking of *us*?

How wonderful, though, if in following that route back, we were to come to some marvellous chamber, to be guided to it even by our smiling parents themselves—to some glorious bed, a tapestried four-poster, say. There you are, you see, for you we wanted only the very best. Though how many of us might arrive at the back seat of a Ford?

I honestly don't know where my dad and Fiona . . . Or if they were particularly intending. I just think, I hope, they were happy at the time. It would have been in the autumn of 1944. And how terribly far off that sounds. Your dad strikes me as exceptional not just in being able to pinpoint the circumstances, but in being pretty confident of the hundred-per-cent intention. Helen and Pete married, then honeymooned—in the Cotswolds—in the limited time that was granted, on special leave. Your dad might even have been conceived precisely on his parents' wedding night, like a perfect little old-fashioned, recipe-book procedure. The act and the intention were perfectly joined.

But I can honestly say that you were truly and wholly intended. You could not have been more deliberately *meant*, both at the time and before. You're doubly exceptional in that respect. You're double, anyway. You were born, as it happens, in Gemini, but there was nothing fluky about your *being* born. As for that Gemini thing—which I know rather bugs you—don't blame us, at least, for that. We used to say to you, when you were smaller, that you'd have been two stars anyway.

I can honestly say too that I'd never intended you more, never wanted to conceive you more—if, hot with lust for your father, I'd never have quite put it to myself in such cool terms—as on the evening after Uncle Eddie was buried. I really *thought* it was going to happen. In which case, it would have been our bedroom in Herne Hill. Or, very nearly, the upstairs landing. Did your father have the same sense of propitiousness too? He was grieving for his Uncle Eddie. On the other hand, he was definitely up for it.

But, obviously, it didn't work. Just think, if it had, you'd have been born in 1973. You'd have been January babies, just like your dad. A tough month, on the purse, for me. By now (just think) you'd be twenty-two. Though why am I assuming—it's simply a habit I can't ever get out of—that you would always have been *two*?

It plainly didn't work, then or for another six years: things you must surely have considered. Four years until we married, starting from that fabled meeting on Brighton beach, then another period, twice as long, before we got round to having you. But we didn't leave it *too* late, clearly, and parents like to have a little time before they enslave themselves to the next generation. All the same, you must know—which puts a very different colour on it—that we were very much meaning and intending and trying, at least as long ago as that spring of 1972.

We were definitely *trying*. I wouldn't like to say for exactly how long. I would have kept a note, at least a mental one, of when exactly we went "ex-contraception," but it's gone. It had been a long while anyway. You don't expect that it will be bingo, first time, you try again, but how long is a trial period? Or periods?

What was significant about that year of Uncle Eddie's death, even for your lives, even right back then, was that it was the year, the summer, in which we made a solemn, slightly shamefaced, but apparently necessary agreement that we would each go to the appropriate clinical facility, to have ourselves tested. We looked sadly and sympathetically at each other, as if one of us might have to choose, heads or tails, and one of us might have to lose. At this stage we still hoped.

But I have to say—and you must both be starting to muster an intense interest—that this was, in all we'd known so far, the worst moment of our lives. Little war babies to whom nothing especially dreadful, let alone warlike, had happened. The divorce of your parents, the death of an uncle—these things, for God's sake, aren't the end of the world. But this little crisis, even before we knew it was insuperable, was like a not so small end of the world. In one, strictly procreative sense, it might be exactly that.

You yourselves may think, before you think any further: hey, come on, what was the great tragedy? Had some terrible accident occurred? You yourselves, putting yourselves in our position (though how exactly do you do that?), may think: but what had so drastically changed? Wasn't life, weren't *we,* just the same? Though wouldn't that be—forgive me for thinking the next thought for you—only to cancel out yourselves?

These are the 1990s, I know, not the primitive Seventies.

Sometimes I think you live in some cool and remedied world where every glitch has its fix, every shock its shrug. But we'll see tomorrow.

It was a blow, my darlings, a true blow. And where it truly hurts. It turned out there *was* a problem and that the problem was your dad's, not mine. To make matters worse, I got my all-clear first. I was reproductively A1. Your dad had been slower about things or he'd just got a later appointment. I think he'd assumed that, what with all the gynaecological complexities . . . Let's see what they say about Paulie first. I think he was being a typical bloke. It surely couldn't be anything so simple, so simple and deflating, as you know what. But now he had to go down to the clinic for some further testing and double-checking and to receive his final judgement.

If only he'd known—when he was screwing around at Sussex, before he met me, and being careful or, apparently, lucky. If only *I*'d known. All those years on the pill. But, of course, that wasn't the point. There were no real jokes to be made along those lines, none at all. If I'd known—well, I'd have known. And if he'd known, before he met me, then by some bizarre process of honourable self-sacrifice that is hard to imagine, he'd have had to tell me, wouldn't he? Wouldn't he? By all that's fair and right, he'd have had to tell me, pretty soon. And I'd have had to respond, wouldn't I? Pity your poor mum. And that moment in the sand dunes at Craiginish perhaps would never have happened. Mikey and me would never have been Mikey and me.

We didn't use, we carefully avoided, the word "fault."

And if it was your dad's problem, it was still, at least for a little while, not beyond all possible reprieve. It still might, depending on that final double-checking—depend. An unfortunate word, perhaps. My tests were at least just tests, passive tests. Poor Mike must have felt that his tests, even if he knew scientifically it wasn't so, were tests at which he had to *try* harder, his very hardest, to *do* his upmost best.

One has to count so many things in life. Days, hours, minutes. Years, birthdays. Money. The miles between places. How many metres you'll need for those new curtains. Calories, pounds, blood pressure, heart rate. Days since your last period. Your dad spends a lot of time, these days, counting sales figures. Once he counted baby snails. Is there a word for them: snailets?

But there's one thing in my life I never thought I would be concerned with counting. You can't *see* them, after all, though there are millions and millions of them, apparently, in any given—I don't know what the right word is either—sample. It must be like counting shoals of herring, or hordes of frantic lemmings, but worse. How *do* you count them? I still don't know. Ask your dad. And you'd think that if they were there by the million, you wouldn't really have to count them all. You'd think that just one million or a good deal fewer than a million might be enough. Five, say.

But life is based, it seems, on this extraordinary percentage of waste. It would be like trying to count all these individual raindrops pattering down now outside, but blending into just one soft, continuous, murmuring gush. How many drops in just a minute, say, on just this house, on just its slippery roof and gurgling gutters, or on just the lawn below and the dripping garden leaves? And any given drop, potentially, life or death for some flower.

No, I've counted lots of things, but I never thought I'd become so keenly involved in counting sperm.

15

HE WENT TO SEE a man called Chivers. I don't suppose he'll give you these intimate details tomorrow. I never met Doctor Chivers. He made me think, inevitably, of jam jars. He made me think of Doctor Pope: all those visits for the opposite reason. Doctor Chivers said your dad was "less than two million per millilitre," which still sounded like an awful lot to me. But your dad, who was a biologist and didn't need a doctor to tell him, said, "Or about one chance every blue moon."

So, there you are. You were a chance—two chances—in a blue moon.

Nothing changes, of course, nothing is outwardly different. When a man is given this news, nobody hangs a sign round his neck, or anywhere else, saying "Out of Order." It's true of so many things in life, perhaps. It was like, I couldn't help thinking at the time, when a woman first becomes pregnant. No one would know, she may not even know herself, but no sign lights up for other people, even if it does for her. No one can tell if the girl or boy who was a virgin yesterday is no longer a virgin today. That's an unfair example, perhaps. There are all kinds of ways in which life just carries on and no one would know.

But now you know. Now you know what the score was for us, over twenty years ago. It was under two million, but call it zero. Which doesn't explain one very obvious fact, does it? Your dad will explain tomorrow, your dad will talk you through it. But there's still a lot more of the story left which he won't or can't go into. And he can't explain anything without explaining that for six years—it's a strange way of putting it perhaps, but it's how you yourselves might look at it, and it's only fair you should know—we decided against you.

It was the option that won out, of the limited options that were available. Try not to blame us. Other options were discussed, and there was one that very nearly succeeded— and remained, as it happened, on the shelf. But the option that prevailed was to do nothing. No further action required. To be and to stay just as we were, a couple, a childless couple. It's only a sad expression if you choose to see it that way. And anyone else, such as your grandparents-in-waiting, might have thought, impatient as they may have been getting: well, they're just biding their time, they're not "ready" yet. And then had the second, non-interfering thought: or perhaps—they're just happy without.

Happy without. Isn't that possible? Weren't we happy with each other? That was surely, with us, a given. And isn't one sorry reason for having children to make up for a deficiency of happiness, for something that doesn't seem to be there any more? If happiness is a completeness, then what does it matter how many components go to make the whole? If two can complete the circle. Let it be just us.

We never thought of you, you'll be pleased to know, as little remedies.

But first you must know that for a little while after Doctor Chivers's pronouncement—Mike's not going to tell you this and perhaps your mother shouldn't—we simply couldn't do it. Complete the circle. Make love, I mean. The very thing that should have been our comfort and mainstay, the very thing we'd always done a lot of and, recently, with a good deal of application. *That* had never been our problem.

They say this is a common reaction, and Doctor Chivers may even have touched, gently, with your father on such possible repercussions. But I don't mean *just* your father, for whom, I could see, there was a question of "manhood." I had my own disinclination. There was a question of "womanhood" too. There's a time for such big words. For quite a few nights we slept together, to use that ever ambiguous phrase, as if seized by sudden chastity. There was a gap between us, just a little gap of inches in our bed, but it might have widened like a crevasse—and what would you have ever known? I think Mike feared it would. I think he feared *me*. Judgement day. Marching orders. Cruel biology speaking.

But, look, he's still here. Fast asleep.

Just us? But enough of that "just." We came out of this period of quarantine. Let's not be so feeble—or so ungrateful. Not the end of the world: this world that had been so kind to us and that can be a lot more terrible. We started to make love again, and with a new—I don't think it's the wrong word—potency. And that's just what it was now, making love, since it wouldn't be making anything else.

Love without any dues to pay to reproduction. And I think we became better at it and more ardent. Just love. But enough of *that* "just."

This was the time when we started to appreciate, since it was to be just the two of us, going away for weekends. The era of hotel rooms. A time when we were not exactly rolling in it, but we could afford, not having other commitments, these occasional gifts to ourselves, which sometimes came, anyway, courtesy of Walker and Fitch: art-dealing assignments to which we'd attach our private pleasure trips. Venice, Rome, Paris . . . We made just love in some fine places.

Art and sex, there's never been a clash for me or (though I'll never ultimately know how it works with Simon Fitch) any question of an either-or. Paint's sexy stuff, and isn't so much of painting to do with the rendering of flesh? Doesn't paint sometimes ache to *be* flesh? Art's not so artificial.

And these were weekends, in case you're now feeling a little left out, that, with or without the help of art, weren't just consumingly sexual. I think we both felt it: as if in our brave undertaking to be just us we'd left a small corner for magic. This was our last thin unscientific but fervent hope. How silly, but how sustaining. If we just made love keenly, resourcefully enough. If we just made it *enough*. As if Doctor Chivers had offered it as his final unofficial nose-tapping advice. Try going away for the weekend—if you know what I mean. A change of scene, a special room, a special bed . . .

And as if we'd only followed his recommendation. Let's see if that room in Florence, with the shutters closed, bright-slitted, against the hot afternoon, won't swing it. Or if that place in the crisp, autumnal English countryside, with the oak panels and the log fires—October swelling the rose hips outside—won't just do the trick.

You see, you were never entirely out of our secret thoughts.

Reactions and repercussions. Doctor Chivers might have warned, but it was hardly his province, that this little thing, this mere trifle of a million here, a million there, can have its extraordinary behavioural consequences, its delayed and long-term side effects—and not really *side* effects at all.

Tim Harvey would never know just how perfect his timing was. If your dad hadn't been so—indisposed. Or do I really mean disposed? If Tim, with Uncle Eddie newly in his grave, hadn't made his approach rather like some dispossessed parent himself. Your dad took the job at *The Living World,* in any case. And I let him, God help me. A dead-end job as it seemed at the time, with more than a touch about it of the self-destructive. Not to mention the destruction of those snails. He said "twenty-seven," didn't he? He didn't hesitate in giving that answer. He'd just stuck, inside, at twenty-seven. There's part of me that's still twenty-seven too.

A dead-end job, that might have turned, in the fullness of time, into merely our embarrassing consolation. Merely! Look, we have no kids, but we have the Living World. And yet—isn't the story almost too good?—we've shared the treasure with you. The gift and the consolation too. There was a time when you were small, you'll perhaps remember, when we told you we have "two houses now." Meaning this one here and your dad's "other one" in town. Since that attic in Bloomsbury had expanded downwards, Living World

Publishing suddenly being on the up and up. The firm of architects who occupied the lower floors moved out—expanding, themselves—and your dad opportunely moved in. 12 Ormond Square. A very fine house too, a lovely fanlight over the front door, though we weren't suggesting, I hope, that your dad actually owned it and we certainly didn't want to give the impression that he might be going to *live* there.

But I'm jumping ahead again, years ahead, to when we were already taking those holidays in Cornwall. Gull Cottage, a third temporary little house. Come back—if you can do it—to life without you.

It was possible. It went on for several years. Don't be offended. Looking back now, it can even seem to me like some sweet and not unsunny and perfectly legitimate plateau. Just your dad and me. Don't hold it against us. Mike in his attic in Bloomsbury: at least it was a Georgian attic in a beautiful Georgian square, and not so far from me in St. James's. Lunches in Soho. I'd invariably pay. But we weren't so hard up, thanks to Walker's, even if these were the parsimonious Seventies. Your dad would sometimes say, as if in self-defence, that there simply wasn't the money around these days, even at Imperial, for pure research. I didn't argue.

Uncle Tim, breaking his own parsimonious habits (for a supposedly wealthy man), would sometimes treat us, like a forgetful guardian, to liberal lunches. I'd have the weird feeling, as he poured the Sancerre, that some legacy was under review, some announcement might be made over coffee. Or your Grandpa Dougie (without Margaret) would regale us at the Connaught, asking nothing in return, I sometimes felt, than that *I* should make it the occasion of a little announcement, which was never forthcoming.

He would be seventy-five soon. Perhaps I might make that little announcement, and how it would make his day, at his birthday party. He would divorce Margaret soon. Marry Georgina. Oh Daddy.

Our Brighton, our Sussex, our London—its gravity shifted from Earl's Court and the King's Road to the West End. And to unglamorous, unassuming, unexpectant Herne Hill. Count your blessings in life. Good, time-honoured counsel. Count your ample blessings. Stop counting sperm, that's been done. No one knew our little secret. We could even manage to ignore it, to forget it, ourselves—leaving just that space we never mentioned for miracles. What you never had, you can't miss, or fear to lose. More sound, homespun, reassuring advice.

And, anyway, one day, for no particular reason, we got a cat.

16

IT WAS MRS. LAMBERT at number twenty-three who put us up to it, or rather, who nobbled your father. In those days every quiet inner-suburban street had its complement of kindly, plucky old ladies, living all alone in their three-bedroomed houses as if they'd never done otherwise, but taking a beady-eyed interest in young couples like Mike and me. I wonder where they've gone.

Mrs. Lambert didn't live all alone, exactly. She had two cats, Toby and Nancy, and one day she cornered your father by her front gate and said that Mr. Nokes, the vet in Wells Road, had a lovely black cat going right now, a rescued stray, just a handsome black moggy. Who would want to abandon such a thing? She was just passing it on, but there'd be no harm, would there, in our going to have a look?

I don't think Mrs. Lambert's neighbourly wheedling would have worked so well on me. But there you are, when your dad was in his twenties he was a soft touch for little old ladies. And your dad might have ignored it, but he mentioned it to me, as if he had a duty to please Mrs. Lambert. He said that Mrs. Lambert had said that if it didn't find an owner soon, well, you know . . . And, put like that, it made us seem like callous murderers if we *didn't* go and take a look.

I said, "For God's sake, Mikey—a cat? A *cat*?" But we went along to take a look. And we were sold.

This is the simple truth that I don't think your father will mention tomorrow, though, arguably, he has even more invested in it than I do. Before there was you, there was a cat. But it goes a bit further, since it would be true enough to say that you owe your existence, your very genesis to a cat. You came from a black cat called Otis. A remarkable train of events, since Otis, like so many cats, had been well and truly neutered. But without Otis you might never have found your way into the world.

There, it's out of the bag. A secret that's never really needed to be a secret—I mean the existence of Otis—but we've kept it so, all the same. You've never heard us, at least till very recently, even mention his name. He died before you arrived. He was still there, at Davenport Road, not so very long at all before you were born and we left Davenport Road when you were still three. I'm always surprised you have any memories of the place at all. Perhaps tomorrow you'll try to dig up some more.

Otis. After Otis Redding, of course: the late-great Otis Redding, whose happy little paean, *My Girl*, had wafted over Brighton beach in the spring of 1966. And whose bitter-sweet but oddly buoyant ballad, *Dock of the Bay*, had later floated, one summer, over London—over Earl's Court, over our basement and its red bedspread, over Mike's snails in the lab at Imperial, where he sneaked in a transistor radio—and become, for some reason, *our* song, Mikey and Paulie's song, the song of our togetherness, our co-existence, our future.

There, another little secret. Why should a song of heartache and separation have become the song of our happiness and togetherness? I don't know, it just did. Perhaps it was because it was a seaside song and we'd first met in Brighton, or perhaps because of its unintended but gently meaningful resonance, even for us then in our early twenties. It was a swansong, after all, a posthumous hit. Otis himself was dead at twenty-six, that soulful voice imploring from the grave. Try a little tenderness . . .

Life is short, my darlings, or it can be. Seize it, treasure it, cradle it. But perhaps this has never occurred to you at sixteen.

There was never any question, anyway, once he'd entered our home and once we had to decide on a name, that Otis would be called Otis.

A cat. I know it's obvious—glaringly and perhaps even amusingly obvious—but we never presented it to ourselves in the way you're thinking. Otis was (as it would prove) before you, but not "instead" of you. We never spoke or even thought that thought. How could we have done when we didn't even know you? We just went along, rather awkwardly, to see Otis. And blessed the day. We even blessed Mrs. Lambert.

And we became, so we discovered, cat people. The world divides, they say: cat people and dog people. And some people, of course, who never find out. That's what our vet said, not Nokes, but the new one. "Some people, sadly," he said, "never find out"—dropping in that little "sadly" rather delicately. But I suppose he said it to everyone.

I didn't come from a family who kept pets, a home with an animal, nor did your dad—a strange thing, perhaps, for a future biologist. But I'd say my dad was a cat person, through and through. Perhaps I just mean he was a pussy-cat himself. And Fiona is a dog person. And perhaps in her case I just mean that there's another, more strictly correct word I still can't quite bring myself to use about my own mother. I'm harsh on her, I know. Perhaps it really stems from those days when I thought I'd never be a mother myself. I felt twice betrayed as a woman.

But we can all very definitely say that your Grandpa Pete was a dog person, since it's become a sort of family legend. When he died last year there was a dog with him, his black Labrador, Nelson. According to your father, there'd never been any sign of it in all the years he'd lived in Orpington, but when he moved with Grannie Helen to Coombe Cottage, it emerged like part of some prearranged formula. What would he do when he retired? He'd get a country cottage, he'd get a dog and he'd take it for long, bracing walks over the South Downs.

Which is exactly what he did. Mike used to say that it was such a rigorously carried through project that he wondered whether some weird replacement wasn't at work. First there'd been his dad, his mum and him: now there was the two of them and a dog. Uncle Eddie, living in the same place, had never had a dog, and he'd cycled rather than walked, but Grandpa Pete proved to be a dog person. And your dad proved to be a cat person (and a cyclist). It's just how it goes.

Why Nelson was called Nelson when Grandpa Pete was in the air force is just another of those odd things, but it's certainly true that Nelson was with Grandpa Pete, in all senses, right to the very end. Even beyond. Since, as you know, when poor Pete Hook dropped dead one crisp January morning in the middle of his regular walk, Nelson was not only with him at the time, but stayed with him patiently and dutifully for some time afterwards, till his body was found, perhaps under the impression that your grandfather would soon get up and they'd continue on their way.

It's a cruel irony, perhaps, that Grandpa Pete should have been struck down by a heart attack in such healthy circumstances and on a such a sparkling morning. On the other hand, if you're going to drop dead suddenly, there are worse ways of doing it. And a faithful dog remaining at your side, panting steadily into the frosty air, only completes the picture. It's the same as with that grave, among the other Hooks, in that archetypal churchyard, you could scarcely have ordered it better.

And maybe the irony isn't cruel at all. Once, when he was only twenty and only recently married, Grandpa Pete had had to jump into the night sky from a burning plane and must have thought he was more than likely going to die. There was no one to tell him he was wrong. No one to tell him that he'd die one day a retired businessman, walking his dog on the South Downs. Not even Grannie Helen could have guessed it.

Both of you always liked Nelson. You used to call him "Nellie," Kate, but it was very affectionately meant. All the same, I think you were cat children, and you're cat people.

A dog has all that trainable, loyal, best-friend stuff, which can sometimes even induce a tear. There's no record, is there, of a cat sitting staunchly by its dead master? Nonetheless, I think there's something servile, doltish even, about all that doggy doggedness (I'm sorry, Nelson, it's nothing personal). Sit. Heel. Stay. A cat knows better, a cat retains its animal integrity and comes and goes as it pleases. A cat will curl up in your lap, all kitten-softness, then do something you could never predict. A cat has a life you never see. But Otis shared our life—and rather more.

The secret nub of the matter (I promised I'd be frank): Otis was a party not just to our reaffirmed coupledom, but to our very coupling. We've never needed much spurring into action. And since that day when Doctor Chivers made his pronouncement we could abandon all precaution. We were free now any time. Look, no sperm. Sadness comes in sadder forms. Enough of that self-punishment and back-turning.

And Otis, if nothing more, was our witness.

This is how it would work. Stop listening, if you prefer. Otis had his basket and an old cushion, his designated sleeping quarters, down in a corner of the kitchen, but he frequently—usually—ignored them. We put a cat flap in the back door. He'd slip out at night, into his cat life, then, a little before dawn, he'd slip back in. Just occasionally he'd go for his basket, but more often than not he'd make his way straight upstairs to our bedroom (where the door was left always thoughtfully ajar) and, with a little soft leap, a delicious sudden tautening of the bedclothes and a switching-on of his purr, to top volume, declare himself to be with us.

By tradition, we'd groan and sigh, annoyed, half-awake. Must he? So early? Not again . . .

Of course, it was all an act, we loved it. The simple and undisguisable fact is that he got us going. It was an undeniable erotic addition, to have him sometimes furrily getting in the way, sometimes simply watching, sphinx-like and voyeuristically—neutered as he was. Don't neutered cats still have their inklings? It was as if his little gravelly purr, chugging into life like a miniature cement mixer, was actually saying: Come on, you two, do your stuff.

A catalyst. The untold story of cat ownership, perhaps. Dogs, they're about duty and service and the nobler virtues, but cats . . . No need, perhaps, to go into the nuances of fur, black and glossy in Otis's case, against naked skin. And take a look at Titian's Uffizi *Venus,* that most gloriously flagrant of nudes. Curled up on the bed, on the ruffled sheets, is a little lapdog, but it should have been a cat, it even *looks* more like a cat, and Titian must have put it there for a reason.

I think your father was a cat person even when he was principally a snail person. Close your ears if you wish, but once upon a time, when I was still working at Christie's, your dad used to phone me sometimes, from Imperial, just to say that he was thinking about me, he was thinking about me intensely. His mind wasn't on his snails. He was thinking about me so much, in fact, that would it be all right if he came round straight away, on the Mike-bike? And could Christie's meanwhile quickly find us some little niche, some cupboard somewhere, a space in one of the store rooms, among the artworks, where we could have immediate and urgent sexual congress?

I shan't tell you how these conversations continued, I've said too much already. But while I'm on this general theme, let me tell you that the early mornings have always been our favourite time for it. I mean, at home, in bed, not in store rooms, in the properly appointed parental or, as it once was, non-parental bedroom. Any time can be good, and once it used to be pretty well any place, including, as you now know, sand dunes. But, certainly since those days of Otis, we've always specially favoured—as if his ghost gets active around that time—the first pale hour of dawn when the light creeps in and the birds, even with a cat around, start to sing.

The very hour which is approaching now. But this rain perhaps (as if it knows) will hold it off a little longer, and delay and dampen all those little songs. It will eke out this fragile summer darkness. And I don't suppose we'll be making love this morning.

Life at Davenport Road. The two of us and a cat. Was it quite what Mrs. Lambert had intended? "You're looking well, you two, this morning." Had we been looking unwell? "You're looking full of the joys." Once we'd been students at Sussex University in the heady and joyous 1960s. Now look at us, this steady, settled married couple in their thirties, in their terraced house in Herne Hill. They even have a cat . . .

But all houses, perhaps, all couples, all families have a life you never see.

Sometimes, during or after our grey-lit lovemaking, we'd hear outside, a little like Otis's purr, the whirr of a milk float and that oddly satisfying and calming sound, the chink of a milk bottle being placed on the porch. How strange—and mystifying for you—to consider that the peace of those early mornings would one day be shattered (I'm not in the least complaining, I'm not in the least reproaching you) by your squallings and clamourings. You used to make me think, though you were several decibels louder, of those seagulls in Brighton. That was when you *let* me have a moment to think.

Or we'd hear, around the same time, that brisker, rougher but also pacifying sound, of the morning paper being thrust through the letter box. All's well with the world really, those two sounds seem to say, no matter what that newspaper actually has to tell you. Just count your blessings, just be thankful.

And all this went on for several years, until one black day Otis disappeared.

17

IT NEVER RAINS but it pours, they say. My father died in February, 1978. I call him your Grandpa Dougie, but he wasn't your grandfather when he died and I sometimes wonder, if he had been, if he'd ever have formed that ceremonious and masochistic notion of being buried at Invercullen. The dead, I suppose, can't be masochists. They can make it hard on the living.

I never saw my father in a kilt, the very idea would have made me giggle. But then I saw him that time in his red robes and wig, which was no laughing matter, and it seems that what counted for him at the end was the green, black and blue tartan of the Campbells. Black and blue, certainly. You never knew your Grandpa Dougie, but at least you were spared his funeral. Grandpa Pete's last year was an easy ride, in some ways, in comparison.

"There'll be a piper," I said to Mike, "be prepared. Someone's bound to arrange it, they have to." And so they did. And if you're going to have to hear that wailing sound, there's an argument that says let it be at a funeral, at a burial, when its keening and skirling will get to you. (It did.) And if the weather's wild and wet to go with it, then so much the better. Though there's a degree of wet, wild weather, you might think, that will defeat even the efforts of a bagpipe. Never mind the poor little birds, trying to sing in the rain.

My own deluge of grief couldn't quite drown out the suspicion that this was some last sly joke of my father's. He was smirking, somewhere, at the whole scene, he'd even whisked up the weather. And it was all my fault, perhaps. If, short of making him a grandfather, I'd at least levelled with him and told him the score—Dad, you're never going to *be* a grandfather—then my conscience would have been squared with him. But how would that have cheered him in his last remaining years? He cheered himself up, instead, with a third young wife, called Georgina York, who wasn't, as her name suggests, in the least bit Scottish.

I said to your dad, "You're going to have to meet a few Campbells. And I'm afraid you're going to have to meet Fiona."

But perhaps it was all just, simply, ancestral. All just the urging (is there any real basis for it in biology?) of the blood in his veins. My dad, the lambswool laird. Take me back, please, to where I came from. I felt, in any case, that little twist of treachery, mixed with a strange twist of pride: me, the daughter and only true child, the star, in one sense, of the show, alongside those three—let's use this word if I can't use the other one—witches.

In any case, I felt bereft.

My father travelled up in his coffin, in an undertaker's vehicle, before we did. We resisted all thoughts of travelling with him (he surely wouldn't have expected *that*) in grotesque, five-hundred-mile convoy. We drove up separately, deciding, in the painful circumstances, not to attempt the whole trip in one day, but overnighting en route—in a hotel overlooking Lake Windermere. Not one of our happiest hotel experiences. In the night the windows began to rattle. The bed felt like a raft. It was February, but until then greyly mild. The next day the choppy waters of the lake signalled worse to come, further north.

But before all this we'd had to arrange other, temporary, away-from-home accommodation. It's one of the guilty drawbacks of cat ownership and it's worst, the pang is sharpest, if you happen to be travelling, yourself, for sheer pleasure. But then again, if the reason is your father's funeral . . .

We used to take Otis to a place we'd found, in Carshalton, called, ridiculously, Felix Lodge, which traded on the notion that your cat too might really be enjoying a high-class, country-club-style break from it all. It was really just some rows of large wire cages set among trees, a few potted plants thrown in. Your dad told me—after Otis died—that it had always made him think of his father's wartime captivity.

And that occasion for depositing Otis was as wrenching as they'd ever been. I don't suppose Otis knew what was going on at all. But then I'm not so sure, given his subsequent behaviour. Who knows what animals know? Does Nelson miss Grandpa Pete? I know that when we left Otis that time—his green eyes staring at us from behind the wire—I couldn't hold back any more the flood of tears waiting inside me. My tears hadn't really happened yet, they hadn't found their moment. Felix Lodge was unhappily named.

But how our big feelings can get drawn out of us by small things. I don't mean to belittle Otis at all. I've often wondered just how much there was in his little green piercing stare. Your Grandpa Dougie's eyes, for the record, were a deep brown with just a touch, a hint of green. Like your eyes and mine. Your dad once looked into my eyes and called them "seaweedy eyes." It made my spine quiver. He would say things like that from time to time. He's not just a scientist. Or a publisher.

My eyes were pretty seaweedy that day, anyway. I cried salty tears all the way home to Herne Hill. Mike had to pull over at one point to comfort me. Poor Mikey, what times he let himself in for when he stayed that night at Osborne Street. He sat in the driver's seat, holding a box of Kleenex, while on the back seat Otis's empty white-wired travelling-cage was silently eloquent. I cried enough at my dad's funeral, in that wind and rain, but I don't believe I ever cried so wringingly as I cried once at the side of the road, somewhere between Beddington and Mitcham.

Your Grandma Fiona didn't cry at Invercullen. She was there, at least, and all the real water was long under the bridge. Nor did my stepfather, Alex, who had no particular reason to, dripping as he was with some kind of oil-derived, Texan–Aberdonian wealth. Twenty years my father's junior.

I suppose if my mother had cried I would have only hated her hypocrisy. Though I suppose there was another scenario: that the two of us might have cried together. Hugging and howling in some awful melting moment of reconciliation. In that freezing weather? So then you might have met her. And Mike, poor man, might have had to deal with her on an ongoing basis. He dealt with her bravely enough on that already challenging occasion.

"*The Living World*? A science journal? Well, how *interesting*, Michael . . ."

And if *you*'d been there—I mean, already there, or not even literally there but parked somewhere, like Otis, in deference to your tiny status—would that have made all the difference? Softened up her act and made Alex shift uncomfortably, perhaps, on his feet? We'll never know. It didn't happen. Your fairy grandmother. Thank God I never said to her, "And we have a cat."

Undoubtedly the best moment of that wretched start to the year was when we returned to Carshalton (a sunny, crocussy, even spring-like Carshalton, I'm glad to say) to collect Otis. But it was only the prelude to the worst. Some six weeks later, when I was just beginning to learn to live with the absence of my father, Otis went absent too. He went out one night, in his usual cat's way, but he didn't return to leap on our bed the next morning, or the next. Or the next after that.

I say "the worst." Worse than my father's death? I don't mean that literally, of course. The second absence was like an ill-timed, small-scale echo of the first? Yes, but I don't mean that exactly either. I mean that Otis's disappearance, his mere disappearance, was in itself like a grief. It shouldn't have been, but it was. And perhaps it would have been even if my father had still been alive. It was a separate grief and, yes—you may even begin to understand—perhaps it went a little further. When all is said, my dear, dear daddy was seventy-seven, and fathers do die at such an age.

You must judge us, my angels. You never saw him, but tomorrow you may need to borrow some of the spirit of your long dead grandfather. There'll be a lot for you to judge in a few hours' time.

It so happened that when Otis disappeared Walker's were handling some recently discovered studies of rustic subjects, including several animals, attributed to no less a figure than Jacopo Bassano. The art world partly lives for such unexpected finds, only then, of course, to become enmeshed in questions of authenticity. And even when the discoveries are judged authentic, there's the secondary, oddly unsettling thought: that they might have been lost for ever, that not so long ago, in fact, the art world, now giving these precious items its kid-glove treatment, was perfectly happy without them.

It's a different kind of thought, perhaps, but I had it: what do these little drawings matter beside the loss of a father? It's not a question a professional should voice, but I asked it (and I adore Bassano). It's a question I even took an absurd stage further. What do these mere drawings, of a lamb, a rabbit, a cockerel, matter beside a living cat? Would I have protested or lamented if, in order to guarantee the return of Otis, they'd been torn up and consigned to the oblivion they'd only recently come from? Or suppose Simon had said to me, if I can cast him in such an unlikely role: Paula, I'm afraid that Walker's temporary possession and the world's permanent ownership of these drawings depends on one little condition—that you sacrifice your cat. Would I have said, "No problem, Simon, leave it with me. No argument, no contest?"

Of course, Simon could never have made such an out-landish demand. (Or could he?) I'd never told him, in any case, about Otis. But he certainly knew that my father had died and he often glanced at me around this time with a real (and slightly paternal) concern—a rather heavier version of his look yesterday morning—as if for once he could shelve that jokey, brittle gambit of his: now, tell me all your troubles.

It's a question that can sometimes insidiously arise in a job that's all about putting a price on mere inanimate objects: what price a living human being? One Titian? Ten? And what price a cat? A small if exquisite study by some less illustrious old master? But do *cats* even come into it?

It's a question that gets harder if your job's also your passion. And it's a question that somehow wracked me after Otis vanished, even as I told myself, to no great effect, "For God's sake, pull yourself *together.*"

You yourselves may already be thinking, now you've been put in a certain picture, that in those years after we'd "decided against you," I'd have had, after all, my second love to fall back on. That second love that was then blooming under Simon's tutelage—or rather, you may even be surmising, taking needy root in the absence of you. Your mother had her pictures to console her. Or, more crudely, she had her career to think of (all the more so since your dad seemed not to have one). She was just like plenty of women, in fact, who have that blunt reason, anyway, for forgoing progeny. And how, indeed, with you around, could I have gone on those foreign art expeditions? Or found the time (or peace) to learn Italian?

Come on, Mum, you're even thinking, don't wrap it up in all that other stuff, you didn't get where you are in the art business without a little hard-nosed determination.

But not "fall back on." Or even "console." A love is a love. Don't turn me into half a woman. And would I swap you for twenty Titians? No. And hardly hard-nosed determination. Just imagine your mum for a moment, going into Walker's every day while really moping for a missing pet. Scarcely a brisk or an edifying picture.

But it's for you now to judge, to assess and to authenticate the double picture: your two parents in dismay for an absent cat. It will no doubt seem to you a very childish spectacle, one to bring out the latent, tutting, head-shaking adults in you. But don't be harsh on your own beginnings.

"He'll be back," Mike said. "Cats do these things. Lives of their own, he'll be back." Your dad, the biologist, the wise expert on animal behaviour. But the days passed, and your dad, I know, was thinking, *praying*, just as much as I was: please don't let him be dead, please don't let Otis be flattened somewhere, a gritty, bloody mess at the side of the road.

Reactions and repercussions. Nearly six years had passed since those bad enough days of the visits to Doctor Chivers, but now we found ourselves only re-enacting that earlier time—lying once more, I'm afraid, with even less evident psychosomatic cause, with our backs turned coldly on each other, our very bed yearning for that soft early morning thud. Not just dismay, but abstinence, and not just abstinence but blame. This *must* be someone's fault. If we'd never gone and got Otis in the first place . . . And wasn't *that* Mike's fault? (Mike, who'd been such a pillar when my dad died.) Mike, and that cat-woman, Mrs. Lambert.

Judge us, strictly if you must. What a pair of babies *we* must have been. But think it through. There's still a lot of explaining to do. Take it, perhaps, if you can, as a sobering piece of instruction. You're sixteen and now and then you must still feel the clutches of childhood pulling you back and making you feel, just when you don't want to, like mushy infants again. But your parents were twice-sixteen and more when a cat succeeded in turning their lives upside down.

Unless I'm wrong about you. Unless you really do live in that cool and shrugging, impervious world where tomorrow will be just a passing, absorbable jolt to you. And why should I be just as afraid of *that*? A tougher world, in some way I don't understand. Surely the argument should run that, in places like Putney at least—Putney, of all places— the living should only get softer and softer. Surely it has. But maybe you're part of some new steely generation whose future is going to require stern stuff of you, in ways that even you don't know yet. Though that waiting fact, I some-times sense it, is already being instilled into your little frames (I still think they're little). You're being geared and primed, even as you sleep right now.

Enough, it seems to me, that you have to face tomorrow. The future, right now, is simply tomorrow. By which, of course—I keep forgetting—I really mean today. We'll find out soon just what you're made of. And that's the very phrase, I think. Our ludicrous distress over a cat: what was *that* really made of ? I need to tell you more about Otis. But don't, at least, imagine that we've ever thought about you, as we once found ourselves thinking about him: that if you'd never come into our home, we'd never have suffered all the agonies of fearing we might lose you.

18

PICTURE US, ANYWAY—and mock us, if you will—in our bedroom in Herne Hill, in the first weak light of dawn, our backs grimly turned on each other, waiting, hoping for a little duvet-denting pounce. After the fifth or sixth day, even this pathetic scene would have looked more pitiful still. The fact is, Otis wouldn't have been there, but nor would your dad. You'd have seen your mother lying by herself with just a dip in the sheet where your dad had been.

I never urged him to it. On the other hand, I never told him not to. I never said: don't be a fool. Your dad, who could hardly blame himself for Otis's disappearance, nevertheless, after a certain while, saw it as his duty, his vaguely penitential mission to get Otis back. The days of his dawn patrols.

I'd pretend still to be asleep or at least I'd never acknowledge his slipping from the bed. I'd give the impression, perhaps, that this was behaviour I only expected and would even have demanded. There's a word, perhaps, for *my* behaviour. I'd be aware of him getting up and stepping carefully across the room. A little later, I'd hear the click of the front door being gently shut behind him. I wouldn't move.

It may be hard for you to imagine your father—though it may become tomorrow's presiding image—like some vagrant without a home. When these days he drives a top-of-the-range Saab, and in any case has the occasional services of a driver, in a dove-grey jacket and peaked cap, to pick him up, often me as well, and drive him hither and thither (I'm talking, of course, about Tony, in his black Mercedes, who's stopped threatening—I know it wouldn't look cool—also to drop you off at school). It may be hard to picture your father wandering like a lost soul round the streets of Herne Hill. But I still see him doing it and never without a pang.

I'm seeing him doing it now, though he's here beside me, as if the whole sorry phenomenon could be weirdly transposed, even now, to Putney. And I think Mike still dreams of it—those dreams we all have of impossible searches, unendable tasks. He may be dreaming of it this very minute. He's back there, tonight, in those dawn streets, looking for Otis again.

I didn't force him to do it, but once the pattern was established, it couldn't be abandoned. It became a kind of ritual, a superstition. Your scientific father, your hard-hearted mum. Our cat might already have perished, but if your father missed one of these sorties, then Otis was surely doomed.

I don't know what he actually *did*. But I suppose he did what anyone committed to such a desperate exercise would have done. He kept his eyes open, he scoured the gutters and kerbs. He looked under parked cars, among put-out dustbins. He stood listening intently, perhaps, beside plastic-sheeted skips. And, of course, he would have called out. Perhaps reluctantly and softly at first, feeling an idiot, not wishing neighbours stirring in their beds to hear what might sound like the cry of some lunatic, but then loudly, unashamedly: "Otis! Otis!" A cry we'd both got used to uttering, sometimes to the accompaniment of a rattled box of cat-crunchies, and to hearing fall, bleakly, on empty air.

The theory was that at dawn errant cats—or returning, limping-home cats—would be conspicuous, a reasonable enough theory. In the hour or so before human traffic starts, cats own the streets. And your dad must have seen them. He must have seen black cats and since, at a distance, one black cat can look much like another, your father's heart must sometimes have raced . . . But no, it wasn't Otis.

Picture your father in tracksuit and trainers. A rare sight now, though remember he was thirty-three then, and what else, at that time of the morning, should he have worn? At that hour, apart from cats, a sparse turn-out of dedicated joggers would have been the only other life around.

And I confess that your dad and I, as we passed thirty, had been seized by one of those keep-fit fevers that can strike couples at about that age, and nowadays even seem the norm. Don't assume, my shrimps, that you will be immune. Not that either of us, if I say it myself, was in poor shape. But in our case you might say it was something more than the regular malaise. I think our unspoken argument may have gone like this: if it's to be just us, then let us be a specimen pair, let us be trim and exemplary—adverts for non-issue. Forgive us. Though in your dad's case it wasn't so simple and even worked in reverse. I think your father (the qualified biologist) may actually have thought that if he exercised and sweated and generally pumped up the virility, then perhaps—who knows?—that slovenly sperm count of his . . .

When all's said, I started going to a gym—and, as you know, I still do. Your father, only getting what Tim Harvey paid him, started to jog (or to use his word, "run"). And his exertions lasted about a month. But he kept the tracksuit and trainers, still in almost-new condition, and now, for these Otis-searching forays, out they came again. A perfect alibi, in fact. He wasn't a suspicious and possibly demented loiterer, he was just an early-morning jogger. He just happened to be peering under a Volkswagen.

And, needless to say, he'd steal back home after these vain quests, a little like a cat himself, hoping, every time, that Otis would have beaten him to it and slipped in, in his old way, by the back door. That when he returned to the bedroom, unzipping his tracksuit, I'd be awake and smiling and saying: "Look who's here."

That was my wish too, believe me. But the truth is that when he crept back I'd be awake, but still rigorously pretending to sleep, as if unaware he'd ever gone. He'd take off the tracksuit and get back in beside me, I'd sense his cool skin appreciating the warmth, and I'd almost hear him contemplating the wisdom or total folly of sidling up to me and whispering in my ear some sweet lie: It's okay, I saw him, in Winterbourne Road. I couldn't catch him, but I saw him, he's okay. He'll be back in his own good time.

I still see him out there—your poor dad, I mean. In my vision the streets are mockingly peaceful, as they would be at that time. The houses are still slumbering, their curtains drawn. The sky is a rosy grey. Not such a bad time of day to be up and about in, once in a while. And it was spring. A green haze on the trees, a tingle in the air, even in Herne Hill. The birds would have been chirping. Not so peaceful in fact, and only more mocking: it was the mating season. Quite. And among the many, groping theories for Otis's decampment was precisely that. That he'd been searching for—he'd found—a mate. Though, in his sad anatomical condition, how could that have possibly worked?

Picture us both lying in bed again, back to back, like two curled-away-from-each-other foetuses, as if no strange expedition had just occurred.

But the truth is your dad used to do that little disappearing act *anyway.* He even still does it now and then. You may have noticed and you may have wondered—I hope not too much—what exactly is going on. On the other hand, both of you are usually far beyond consciousness in the early hours of the morning. I hope you are now.

Your dad would get up, I mean, and leave the bed—not to roam the streets, just to leave it and come back. Just for twenty minutes or so. He'd slip on his dressing gown. He'd pad around the house or sit quietly somewhere communing with it, listening to the little creaks and clicks and murmurs houses make when everything else is hushed. I suppose you'd have said, Kate, a few years back, that he was communing with Edward. At Davenport Road, who would it have been? Dave?

These days, of course, he has that expensively kitted-out study to retreat to—almost, I sometimes think, a kind of house within a house. He often goes there in the early hours (but not this morning, I fancy) to do a dawn stint of Living-World work, which you may think is as odd as his roaming the streets. It's the pressure of success, it's valuable time that has to be found. Except he still finds time (I'm glad to say) to come back a while to bed.

But this habit of your father's began long ago, before there was any pressure of success, when we first moved to Herne Hill and first acquired that novel but slightly sobering possession, a house. A habit or a game? He'd get up anyway, very early, just for "the sheer pleasure," he'd say, of coming back. Married life, how grown-up people behave. The game involved, if I was awake, my pretending to sleep while he tiptoed away. On the other hand, if I *was* asleep, his very absence, soundlessly accomplished though it was, would often be the cause of waking me, as if I knew something was wrong. I'd reach out a hand and find an empty space. I was alone! And if I wanted to, I could indulge the frisson of a panic, a terror, a desolation I knew wasn't real.

Easy enough in those days, not so easy now. A game, or not such a game? There are all those apparent "games" of animals which, as Professor Mike will tell you, look like play but are really serious training and preparation underneath. Was Otis playing a game with us?

A little benign dissembling, like the joy of finding a bad dream was only a dream. A little delicious feigned absence and desertion. It became our favourite time anyway, even before Otis was there to egg things along. Your dad would simply return from his bogus disappearance, some-where in the far reaches of the house. I'd pretend sometimes to be just waking up. Or I'd be staring at that indentation in the sheet.

He'd get in and nuzzle up. Here I am after all, I hadn't vanished, I hadn't gone. Here I am, it's me, all present and correct.

And it still happens, in the first light, to the first sound of birds. How wonderful life is.

19

IT'S GONE THREE A.M. It's getting closer. Not "tomorrow," I can't play that trick on myself for much longer. Today, today: the soft drumming of the rain seems to be saying it over and over.

Whatever else you're about to discover, I hope there's one thing you don't need to be told: that you came from happiness. Wherever else you came from, that's surely the main thing. I'm telling you about one of our worst times, but that's only to throw up the other thing, the truer thing. So— we had our patch of rough weather. Who doesn't? And in the grand scale, how does it rate? Our cat went missing. Hardly an earthquake.

And in the grand scale, how will this impending day rate, if you know that, underneath, you came from happiness? Happiness breeds happiness: it's as simple as that? It's not biology, but it's the best and the soundest system of reproduction. It's the best beginning and the best upbringing, all other circumstances aside, that anyone could ask for.

Though arguably, of course, it's also the worst, the very worst, and parents can never win, nor children. It only leaves you unprepared and unarmed for all the knocks and frights. Like tomorrow. Let's still call it that.

Look at Mike dreaming away here, as innocent as you are, right now, of what's to come. Don't wake yet, Mikey, sleep on. I swore to myself last night that I wouldn't let him wake up first, alone. He can still play that waking-first game—but he's here now already, and if I wasn't afraid of waking him, I'd be holding him tight. I have the shivery feeling that he won't be here any more, not after tomorrow.

There used to be a game, I suppose there still is though I don't think there's so much call for it now, called Happy Families. A simple, popular and platitudinous card game. Shuffle the pack, then put the families together: the smiling Mr. Baker with the smiling Mrs. Baker, and the two of them with the smiling little Bakers, so they all match up and beam. Not a popular game any more, and "happy families" these days, maybe, is a glaring misnomer, a contradiction in terms. Perhaps it always has been. Happiness, yes, families, yes—but the two together, forget it. The very idea is a fantasy from which we all have to wake up sooner or later. Would this Hook family, with its crooked name, have been a happy family *anyway*?

You got the one thing and not the other, and the rarer and the more important by far. Is that how you'll take it? A minor point, what we do with the fantasy. Family-shamilies, what do they really matter?

I've never had the Edward-fantasy, Kate. I've never thought any house I've lived in was like a person. Though I'm intrigued. Was this Edward (is he still?) like a friend? A father? A live-in lover? But I've often thought about the houses I've lived in, including this one, and wondered if the people who lived in it before were happy. Is there happiness in the fabric, in the bricks and walls, or is there still unevaporated sadness, a mildew of sorrow? That's just as daft, I'm sure, as dreaming up an Edward. How many here, before us—since this house was built? The people we bought Davenport Road from were called the Mallinsons, the people who sold us this place were called the Sutcliffes. Were they happy?

A "happy home": that's another inherent misnomer perhaps, another fantasy out of which we all have to be shaken, but in which, though you're sixteen, you're still carefully blanketed and cradled. Though you'll be woken abruptly enough soon.

For what it's worth, while you sleep on these last few hours of your sixteen-year sleep, let me tell you how I woke up long ago and came out of a dream (in more senses than one, you'll have to agree) when I was even younger than you. Don't worry, I haven't forgotten about poor Otis, or your poor dad, out there in the streets looking for him, I'll get back to them. And oh yes, your mother really *was,* once, if it's hard to picture, even younger than you.

Let me tell you the story which I once told your father, and never, till now, anyone else. As a matter of fact, I told him that time we went to Craiginish, the year we met: pillow-talking in the "croft," our skins all salty, that very first night, after he'd "proposed" to me and I'd said yes. You came from happiness, my darlings.

And this story can really be called a fairy tale, since your mother was not only younger than you at the time, but (unlike your Grandma Fiona) she was actually a fairy.

I was thirteen, though this was still, just, the nineteen-fifties when thirteen was younger than thirteen is now. But I didn't *want* to be a little fairy.

My all-girls boarding school was a posh sort of place in the Thames valley, as befitted the daughter of a judge. Every year in the summer they'd put on a Shakespeare play, outdoors, in a little natural grassy arena between the hockey field and the music rooms, in front of a clump of trees. And every other year, it seemed, it would be *A Midsummer Night's Dream*. Such a good play for the time of year and that setting and, of course, for girls. All those fairies.

I wanted to be Puck. Not a fairy, not Hermia or Helena (fairly soppy parts, in my view), not even Titania. When it comes to *A Midsummer Night's Dream*, Puck, if a girl may say so, is your only man: "I'll put a girdle round about the earth in forty minutes" (the word "girdle" producing a titter in a pack of schoolgirls, for reasons that, thankfully, you don't have to bother with). But my acting skills, I'll be honest, were rudimentary and Puck was a part for older girls. So I got Mustardseed: one of the fairies, number two or number three, it doesn't really matter. A couple of half-baked lines and a little flapping costume the colour of Colman's best.

It invariably turned grey and chilly, or it blew a gale. The arc lights, evoking moonlight, in among the trees, usually failed or crashed down. It was traditional, painful fun. But that year the weather was perfect: a serene and golden June evening turning to dusky purple even as the show progressed. The scent of newly mown grass. Not even a troupe of squeaking schoolgirls murdering Shakespeare could quite spoil the effect. Even the most long-suffering among the audience of stoical parents couldn't fail to be charmed.

As my father, I hope, was charmed. I hope it was at least some small, diverting consolation.

He was there, of course, to see me, his Mustardseed, to judge my performance. Just, as it happens, a little later that same year I'd go to see him, to judge his performance or at least just to witness it, from that secret but public gallery. He was there in the audience. I'd seen him secretly then too, from an off-stage spy-point, his bobbing, unostentatious panama visible among some fairly attention-seeking motherly hats. But the person I couldn't see (and her hat would have made its mark) was Fiona. Beside my father there was an empty space, an unoccupied brown-canvas and tubular-steel chair. It remained unoccupied, as the twilight gathered, throughout the evening.

This wasn't a matter of some temporary mishap or misunderstanding. My father wasn't looking at his watch, or appearing merely incidentally worried or annoyed. He kept looking at the "stage," at the magic transformations being enacted before him, including his daughter's temporary fairyhood, a vague but fixed smile on his face. I understood that something serious, not minor, had occurred, or perhaps had been occurring for some time, and this was my first, world-rearranging indication of it. My knees felt weak, though the show, of course, must go on. It was just as well I had that mere wisp of a role.

Afterwards, I could have simply asked him. I was thirteen. But thirteen was a still hesitant age. And best not to ask was my instinct. And not the best of times, patches of jaundice-like make-up still on my cheeks. Best just to listen to his obvious brave fib, and nod.

"Mummy's very sorry. She's feeling under the weather. Such *lovely* weather too, such a lovely evening . . . But you were wonderful, Paulie. A star! They really should have given you a bigger part."

That summer was the first year we didn't go to Craiginish. And that confirmed it. By then I knew there was a "situation," an ongoing situation. Ours was not any longer a happy home or a happy family, though it had been. And from now on I'd have to play a part and quite a big one, I'd have to polish and refine my acting skills, since the situation, if not carefully contained and managed, might be damaging to a judge's reputation.

Meanwhile, a former yellow fairy, I took a bus to the law courts to see a man in red robes.

There you are, I was a fairy once, in *A Midsummer Night's Dream*. Picture that. I had little wings. It's midsummer now, though it's raining, but all of you are dreaming. Your dad, when I told him, certainly tried to picture it. He said he wished he'd been there. He said he was jealous of my dad, even though my dad can't have been so happy that night. He said he wished he could have seen your mum when she was Mustardseed.

20

OTIS CAME BACK, he simply came back. That's the plain fact, and the mystery of the matter—as mysterious as his sudden departure.

It's easy to scoff at the pet-owners of this world, at the cooing Mrs. Lamberts, until you become one yourself. Sometimes you see, even in these hard-edged times, those poignant scatterings of notices, on trees, on lamp-posts, pleading for information, exuding despair. You never seem to see them being put up, as if that has to be done furtively in the dead of night. Nowadays they're run off on computers and copiers, there may even be an unhelpful inset photo, but once they always seemed to be hand-copied, a labour of love, in agonised blue biro.

"Have You Seen Our Budgie Archie?"

We scoffed once. Mike scoffed, with the full force of his biological schooling (but I think those snails of his had become his sort-of pets). He called it the anthropomorphic fallacy. An escaped budgerigar in Herne Hill, now which way would it fly—south, to Tulse Hill and Australia? And as if "Archie" would be written all over it, as if even a budgerigar was going to say, "Yes, I'm Archie."

"I don't rate Archie's chances," your dad said. In those

very streets which one day he'd comb at first light, in his cat-suit.

And we came preciously, repentingly close to preparing such a batch of plaintive notices ourselves, restrained only by the thought that it might already be too late. The mockery of all those "Missing"s if Otis was actually dead. And then what do you do? Go out again and solemnly, scrupulously take each little notice down?

But Otis came back. After nearly three weeks, he simply came back. We'll never know the story, we could hardly ask him. But then the story is perfect anyway in its barest summary: he disappeared, he came back. Has any better story ever been invented? But yes there has, since this is where your story *really* begins.

It was a Sunday morning, about ten o'clock. We were in the kitchen. The weather was damp and dull, a little threatening, but the back door was resolutely and hopefully half-open. And then there he suddenly was, like a precisely realised wish. A barely believable scuffling sound outside— more laboured and protracted, perhaps, than as we remembered it. But there he was, hesitantly pacing the kitchen floor, as if it might be a trick. As if *he* might be a trick. But he wasn't.

It was Otis, certainly, though it also wasn't Otis. He was thin and weak and bedraggled, his fur had lost its shine. He seemed as amazed to see us again as we were to see him. It was as if he'd wriggled free, only that morning and only in the nick of time, from some terrible sticky end. He couldn't explain. We'll never know.

But how little it takes to transform the world. Misery to

joy. Even the feeble flick of a cat's tail, even the shaky tread of four paws. We held him in our arms again. He weighed less, he weighed so much more. He managed a little reconnective purr.

"Straight to the vet's tomorrow morning," I said. A rather peremptory way of marking this miraculous moment—already the brisk, emotion-quashing mother. But Mike agreed. Both of us were oddly practical and bustling. Shouldn't we have just wept? But the fact is, now it was so wonderfully over, we half wanted to pretend that this nearly three-week desertion had never occurred. It was some weird and not very excusable aberration on our part, perhaps. We fed him. The tins were still there. There was his basket and cushion in the corner. Nothing had changed. We wanted the eclipsing illusion that he'd never been away and we'd never become, meanwhile, the bedraggled and diminished creatures we'd turned into.

But how little it takes. By the afternoon, the day had turned conspiringly, blissfully wet. Steady, set-in rain, like this rain falling now. How malign and bleak that rain would have seemed with Otis still gone. But we went back to bed. I almost said "all three of us." We hadn't done this for nearly three weeks, let alone on a wet Sunday afternoon. And Otis, it was not difficult to see, needed his bed too. He was with us again, if not quite with us as before. He curled up exhaustedly on one corner of the duvet, while we went thankfully, irresistibly about things. Even asleep, he worked his magic.

That was late April. Of course, we came to understand that things weren't, exactly, as they'd been. That Sunday afternoon was like a little separate island of reunion in the falling rain. Otis was back, but he was a shadow of himself and, even with loving care and feeding up, there was still a phantom absence. Again, I don't really mean my poor dad, barely two months dead as he was. Guess who I mean.

I went along to the vet's that Monday morning. I had work to do, I was still involved in the Bassano studies, among other things, but I called in and made excuses. I didn't say, "It's about my cat." We might both have gone, but these were the days when Tim Harvey had stepped aside. Your dad couldn't deputise for himself and an issue was being put to bed that week. There's a curious phrase, "being put to bed." Perhaps I felt, in any case, it was my particular duty, as—a mother. I've said it twice now, haven't I? The whole thing was suddenly pretty obvious, or it must have looked so to our vet.

Who wasn't Nokes, who'd moved on, but a new man, Fraser, whom we'd never had to deal with before. Nokes, it's true, I'd never much liked. He was like some jaded GP: mid-fifties, a gruff, conveyor-belt approach. No bedside manner. You wondered if he really liked animals. On the other hand, it needs to be said, we got Otis from Nokes, which is how we got you.

Fraser was around forty and reminded me a bit of Doctor Pope—without the psychedelic ties. But the most important thing was that Otis seemed to purr instantly, trustingly under his hand.

"I'm Alan," he said, having shaken my hand. "And this is . . . ?"

"Otis."

"Otis. Nice name. Hello, Otis. It looks as though Otis has been in the wars."

I explained.

"It happens," he said. "Cats do these things." I'd heard those words before. "Some go missing for months. But all's well that ends well. I'd say Otis is going to need some looking after."

His hands were feeling Otis for hidden injuries, and Otis went on purring.

"After the late-great, I assume?"

Of course, I had to tell him, with a little flutter of embarrassment and without further embellishment, that he was right. He said there weren't any rules that he knew of for naming cats.

He had the bedside manner. He had a touch of downright impudence too. Doctor Pope had a little of that, and it had worked, pretty infallibly, on nineteen-year-old girls. But I was thirty-two now.

Perhaps I had that age, and other things too, stamped on my forehead. The fact is that our vet, Alan Fraser, was the first person to utter, and with a casual, smiling directness, as if he'd just completed some easy diagnosis, the words—the thought—that your father and I had never uttered to each other. "Child substitute," he said.

Child substitute! No doubt as part of some long and reasonably delicate sentence, but it leapt out at me like some pronouncement in italics. Not even a question mark. How *dare* he?

But he seemed ready even for my flush of indignation. He smiled almost teasingly.

"It's nine o'clock. You're my first. I know that's because it's been counted as an emergency—which, incidentally, it isn't, strictly. But anyway, most young mothers usually come in a little later, after they've dropped the kids off at school."

It was true. In the waiting room there were two old biddies, one with a cat, one with a Scottie dog. Both of them had given me narrow looks when I was called in first.

I nearly walked out. I nearly grabbed Otis from under his hands and stormed out like a real matron. Except that, of course, would have made it obvious that a nerve had been touched, it would have made me look a fool. And in any case, he spoke with that unruffled smile, as if he'd hardly needed to explain his process of deduction, it didn't take a Sherlock Holmes. As if he'd been here many times before and always thought it best to get it out in the open.

"Don't be offended—you wouldn't be the only one. And no need to look apologetic. It's one of the virtues, one of the many virtues, of having a cat. I have two of my own. They're wonderful creatures, I don't have to tell you that." Otis still purred away. "He's a lovely cat—though not at his best right now. I'm sure it made your day when he came back. We'll need to do some tests, I think."

I'm getting very close to the nub of things now, to what your father is going to say to you. It seems to me, in fact, that he's going to have to speak to you a bit like a vet or a doctor, or some sort of knowledgeable and caring practitioner. You'll have your unexpected and worrying appointment.

I began to think, in those days when Otis required particular looking after, that another virtue of having a cat might actually be that of also having a vet. Someone, I mean, unlike Ian Nokes, you could actually talk to. God knows, you can't often do that so easily with your doctor, you always feel you're taking up *their* precious time. And that's when it's *you* who's under discussion. But vets can be people-doctors too, it seems. And Alan Fraser's surgery, with Otis there, like some guarantee, on the table, could be a strange little closeted confessional.

Speaking of doctors: when Doctor Chivers gave your dad the grim news, it was not really in his brief to do much further talking, along the what-happens-now lines. He was just a sperm man, really. He sketched in some possibilities, which would be matters for other professionals, but, of course, it would be up to your dad and me, as responsible adults, to weigh up for ourselves the available options. And, as you now know, though it must have sounded extremely odd to you, we settled on—childlessness.

But of the options we rejected (I really am telling you now only what your dad will elaborate tomorrow) the first to go was adoption. We both felt that that would be too much like theft. We wouldn't be there at the beginning. It would be too much—though we didn't have the comparison to assist us then—like going along to Mr. Nokes after a hint from Mrs. Lambert.

But a second option we gave more room to. For a while it actually dangled, if "dangled" is really the word I want. I mean artificial insemination. An ugly and chilling expression, even more upsetting, perhaps, than "child substitute," but a viable, and not so complicated alternative. Are you still listening?

In these days of IVF they speak more of "donor insemination," it makes it sound more personal perhaps. Back then, in the early Seventies, it was known officially as "artificial insemination by donor," though it was hastily switched around in the Eighties, after the arrival of AIDS, to "artificial donor insemination." But your dad and I once freely, if not exactly blithely, used the seemingly supportive acronym A.I.D.

But rejected it. For reasons which had more to do, perhaps, with your father than me, but which had to be respected. There are all sorts of things we can speculate about in comfortable theory. Certain primal sensitivities come into play in the actual situation, even for a rational scientist.

But I have to say that the reasons that mattered to your father certainly mattered to me too. The choice, as I boiled it down, was really between "How much did I want your father's child?" and "How much did I want a child?" It was the first question that counted more. Can I ask you to understand that? I wanted *this* man's child, for reasons that I hope are obvious. And neither of us could have it. Which left only one way of proceeding.

But six years later our vet, to whom I found I could talk in sympathetic confidence, to whom I found myself mentioning things I hadn't mentioned to my own mother who I no longer talked to, or to my own father who was dead, mentioned to me that very phrase, that acronym, that Mike and I had used, but only to each other, and then dispensed with, years before.

I had to go back several times with Otis, more times, in

fact, than expected, and if he'd broached that "child substitute" at that very first meeting, you could say that certain other things could hardly remain undiscussed. Do vets take oaths of professional secrecy? Otis kept purring away. Perhaps his ears were buzzing too.

He said, had we considered artificial insemination? On a vet's lips it didn't sound so unseemly. I said yes—and no. We'd rejected it, the whole matter was closed. It had always sounded, I said as a joke, like something that happened in a farmyard. He smiled and said he'd decided long ago against being an agricultural vet. He was more a domestic-animals man. But he said they'd made great strides in artificial insemination, the human kind, even in the last four or five years. "Strides," I remember thinking, was an unhappy choice of word.

"Maybe," I said, "but—no."

I'd already told him, and it was an immense thing to have said, that the "difficulty"—the reproductive difficulty—was with your dad. But, again, once the subject had been broached, how could these further levels of honesty be avoided? It wasn't like letting it slip over a dinner table and a glass too many to some mutual friend. But the fact is I'd *never*, in six years, said it to anyone else.

What else did I tell our trusty vet? My honest age: thirty-two, nearer thirty-three now. Married for eight years. That I was an only child. That my father had just died. That I hardly saw my mother. And he told me, as if reciprocation was only fair, that he had two kids, a boy and a girl, teenagers already, amazingly, but he saw them these days "by appointment only" (a little fragile smile), since last year he'd got divorced. "Family planning—in reverse," he said. Perhaps he wasn't, himself, he said, such a perfect domestic animal.

And, of course, he'd asked me what my husband did for a living. And I'd told him, with the usual circumspection I had with that information, and he'd sat back, truly impressed.

I have to say that after Otis's return I'd stopped my crying. Or I thought I had. I mean my seemingly incurable capacity to be sabotaged by tears at odd and inconvenient moments, at least to have to fight them back. Tears for my dead father, or for Otis who might be dead too. Tears for my father and for Otis hopelessly mixed. But when Otis came back, I went dry-eyed. I reset my sights.

What normally compensates for the loss of a parent? Not, really, a cat. To Mike's parents, to your Grandpa Pete and Grandma Helen, it must have looked, later that year, as if a perfectly understandable and not uncommon reaction had taken place. If, all the same, we'd left it a bit late.

I said to your dad, "I told him that you edit *The Living World*. He was bloody impressed, you know." And your dad looked pretty pleased, if he batted it off. "Well, that's *someone* who reads it," he said.

At that stage I didn't mention anything else.

"Well, there you are. You should meet him. You should take Otis in yourself one day and have a chat with him. He'd be pleased, I'm sure."

It was a little later that spring that I said, "Mikey, listen to me. I want us to think about it again. A.I.D. I want us to reconsider."

It wasn't an edict or an insistence or, certainly, a foregone conclusion. I wanted to reopen the debate. But I didn't get the impression, either, that it had struck your father like a bolt from the blue. He didn't say yes straight away, but it was different now, we both knew it. He looked sympathetic. Things had happened. And I was thirty-two.

And things, after that, actually happened quite fast. 1978 was quite a year. By midsummer, seventeen years ago this month, I was booked in for my first "procedure." As it turned out, it was the first of only two—which, I can tell you, is very good going. By mid-September I'd become pregnant. Though it's not that bit, you've always been able to work *that* out, that will be such news to you.

21

SO NOW YOU KNOW what awaits you, what your father will tell you in his own words. I don't know what precise words he'll use, if they're in his head right now, rehearsed and honed over sixteen years—if so, he's never let me hear them—or if he'll simply let the moment itself produce them. And, whatever they are, I can't be sure at all how you'll react to them.

Tonight you're like those two new babies again, back at Davenport Road, still deep in that time before you met your memory—or the one we gave you. I don't want you to be like that, I want you to be Nick and Kate, sixteen years old and as grown-up and as unimpededly advanced into your lives as sixteen can be. But tonight, though you don't know it and can't help it, you're like babies again. So, right now, is your father.

I'm in a house full of sleeping babies. Even this rain, like some second guardian, seems aware of it and is pressing a finger to its lips: *Sssshhhh* . . .

Whether he's learnt his lines or not, Mike must have played the scene so often in his mind that tomorrow will be like waking into a dream. He's dreaming now, poor man. But I really can't predict, I don't think I have the right to, how you'll react. I picture a bomb going off and this house falling to bits. I picture everything remaining oddly, precariously, ominously the same. An unexploded bomb. It still might go off—next week, the week after, any time.

Your father isn't your father. He's going to tell you himself. Who better? But what I hope he'll tell you too, after giving you all the necessary facts, is that if he could have chosen, if it worked like that and it were just a matter of choosing, then he simply couldn't have chosen better. And I hope you'll think, I hope you might always have thought, that it's the same for you, the other way round. Your dad.

There are plenty of "real" families (I have to use that expression) where it can seem, after all, that all the wrong choices got made. If only they could choose again, start again. And one day, perhaps not so far in the future, it will *all* be a matter of choice. Mike seems to think so. He has his peculiar, private reasons for thinking so, maybe, but then he's still technically a biologist and he's publisher of *Living World Magazine,* ear close to the scientific ground. Not that we all don't pick up the vibrations.

Mike thinks it's coming, even sooner than we might suppose. It's upon us. Give it thirty years, he says. Soon it will all be a matter of genetic engineering. Old-fashioned human biology will have had its day. Which means, when you think about it, though I don't want to think about it, least of all tonight, that you may at some point in your future be one of just a few, peculiar, old-style generations to see sprouting up around you the first generation of made-to-measure infants.

Or, as you'll discover tomorrow, you're already part of a gathering process. Since even sixteen years ago your dad and

I had our choices, our freedoms, which simply wouldn't have been there not so very long before. And what "strides" haven't been made since? We could specify, we could stipulate, up to a point—you should know this—before you were born. All down to science. We could even *see* you before you were born. That's a commonplace bit of magic now, I know, but your Grandpa Pete and Grannie Helen or Grandpa Dougie and Fiona were never able to see Mike and me.

And how wonderful it was, to see you.

We were born in the historic year of 1945, when a lot of big things happened, but your dad will tell you (he's told me enough times) that the biggest thing to have happened this century was a quiet little event that occurred in a laboratory: the discovery of the structure of DNA. Though, as your dad will be the first to admit, he didn't have a clue about it at the time. He was only eight years old, it was 1953. It was before he started spending those summers at Uncle Eddie's, learning about frogspawn and birds' eggs or whatever, a biologist in the making. But even when he was doing that, he hardly had a clue about DNA.

I'm not sure that Uncle Eddie, with all his old-fashioned natural-history books and mahogany collecting boxes, would have done either. Perhaps it was "Uncle" Tim, Tim Harvey—then sole editor of *The Living World*—who brought the momentous news, on one of those weekend visits to his old chum at Coombe Cottage. Have you heard, Eddie, have you *heard*? *The Living World* was about to devote a whole special issue to this extraordinary discovery . . .

I picture him and Uncle Eddie sitting up late into the night, Uncle Eddie puffing hard on his pipe, chewing it all over. And I picture them in subsequent years, when your dad would have been there too, a nipper of nine or ten sleeping upstairs, wondering: should they tell him, should they try to explain to the lad, or just let him get on with his "Nature Study"? A little like people must have said in that year that I was born: Have you heard? They've dropped an atom bomb, on Japan. Should we try explain it to the kids?

Your dad and I were born before DNA. Those innocent times. Of course, it had always existed, it was always *there*, it was just that nobody really understood it yet. And when they did, I can't say I was any the wiser. I've grown up with it all around me, but I can't say that I could tell you even now, and biologist's wife though I am, what it *is*. No doubt you could tell me, it's part of basic education these days.

In any case, tonight wouldn't be the right time to say you should ask your father.

For some reason, when I think of DNA I can't help thinking of my dad, cracking those codes in a sort of wartime laboratory, and blundering one day into the arms— and, oh Lord, the legs—of a pretty secretary called Fiona.

Your dad isn't your dad. It wasn't ever possible that he could be. But what I want you to know is that I *wanted* him to be. Oh, how I wanted him to be. I still wanted him to be even when that decision was taken that, though he wouldn't be, you would still have a father. I only wanted him to be, in a way, even more then. I still want him to be now.

That same year, that same busy, roller-coaster year of 1978, we went to Venice for a weekend. It was June. It was our anniversary, as it will be again very soon, but it wasn't a special anniversary. It was our eighth. Is there some humble metal for eighth anniversaries? Nickel? Steel? Zinc? And it was one of those several weekends of ours that were effectively subsidised by my employers, Walker and Fitch.

Simon had even said in his wrong-footing way, "Fancy a weekend in Venice?" All I'd have to do was meet someone from Montebello's—a convenient Friday lunch, say. It could all be done in a day, in fact. But Simon was clearly dangling a bait. A weekend for *two* possibly, I dared to ask, in my most insinuating mode. He went through an act of looking totally askance. But we came to a not unfamiliar deal: that we—*Mike* and I, that is—would find the extra air fare. A room for two was hardly any different from a room for one.

Though it didn't have to be the Rinaldi Palace. This really was a present from Simon. "Since it's your anniversary, Paula. I really didn't know. And since you've been with *us* for nearly as long."

I think he *did* know it was our anniversary coming up, though maybe he was simply thinking: she's had a tough year, she's still getting over her dad. Sweet Simon, I'd learnt it wasn't hard to be nice to him. And all I had to do was meet Signor Masi from Montebello's and be nice to *him* over a long lunch. Simon perhaps knew what he was doing—he might have gone himself.

I said to Mike, "You'll have to kick your heels, Mikey, while I go and meet this man." He looked scrutinisingly at me. "The things girls have to do," he said, "for the sake of art." It was Venice, I said, there'd be things he could do. I said he should go and look at the Tiepolos in the Scuola dei Carmini, one can't look enough.

A Thursday night to a Saturday night: our anniversary on the back of a business trip. But it was rather more than that. It was our way also of marking, confirming—"celebrating" isn't really the word—our decision: to go ahead, with "A.I.D.." My first appointment was booked, in fact, for the following week. It had all been fully resolved.

And yet. And yet we made love that weekend more busily and intensely, I believe, than we'd ever done in all our semi-wishful resortings to hotels. As if the opposite of the situation were really the case and this was our last chance, a desperate, last-ditch bid for the real thing. Maybe the unique magic of Venice . . . Maybe a room (last-ditch?) overlooking the Grand Canal . . .

And maybe *I* was the more intense. No, I know I definitely was. Mike had made his commitment. He wanted this weekend simply to endorse his assent—to reassure me. I think he was even bewildered by my intensity. He'd never known me quite this crazy for it.

And perhaps even Signor Masi registered, and possibly misinterpreted, that our long (altogether too long for me) lunch in one of Venice's finest restaurants was touched by a tingle of sexual impatience. Had it helped to swing the deal Walker's wanted? Did Mike even think, when we teamed up again in our hotel room in the late afternoon, that this Signor Masi had turned me on? He hadn't, actually. He was large and round and bald and (I have to say it) over fifty, though his name was, potentially, a turn-on. It was Sergio, Sergio Masi. I never mentioned that to your father.

For whom I was just crazy, anyway. What must you think of your mother? Shut your ears again if you wish.

It was late afternoon. We very quickly abandoned all possibility that we would simply change and go out for the evening. No, not yet. We pulled close the shutters onto our balcony, so the room had that faintly fiery glow. My linen dress was soon over the back of a chair. The hubbub from the Canal below was like something simmering in some magnificent kitchen. I'm not supposed to say these things to you, but I was very soon in a position on top of your father, though it went against all mechanistic wisdom about the best position to be in for getting pregnant. It went against, so to speak, the gravity of our situation.

Outside, the evening was just blooming and Venice was turning gold. All that treasure, all that glow. Camparis were being sipped at little sunset-catching tables. What setting could be richer, fuller? And yet I thought, even as I straddled your father, of all that wasn't there then, of all that was missing. What could possibly be missing?

Otis, for a start, wasn't there. He wasn't missing in that awful former sense, but he was consigned once again to Felix Lodge. How callous of us. And in his barely recovered condition. And how we'd suffered when he *had* been missing. This afternoon passion had nothing to do with him, with his purring, furry prompting. Or perhaps it had everything.

I thought of what can be missing even when you can seem to have everything—all of Venice lying at your feet. In a little while we ourselves would be sitting, showered and coolly dressed and mellow with recent lovemaking, at one of those little tables, in the even richer light. A good-looking couple, in their early thirties, on their anniversary. A glorious evening in Venice, let's not waste it. Seize it, treasure it.

Mike would have zipped up my dress, kissed my neck, grabbed the room keys, patted my bottom as he opened the door.

It was then that those dried-up tears came back for a brief unstaunchable while. It's a watery city, after all. That's what I said later, laughing it off, to your father. I cried in every sense that weekend. Cried out, as a woman will cry out, in the throes—audible, perhaps, even to those passing in the marbled corridor of the Rinaldi. I don't know where I stand on the volume scale, but I was louder, maybe, than I'd ever been, that weekend.

But I just cried too, in the other way, if the two cries can sometimes be hard to separate and though I tried to hide it. I stayed on top of your father—perhaps you really shouldn't be listening—even when I'd finished my crying out aloud and even when I'd begun to feel that warm stuff from him, that stuff that was the essence of the matter, beginning to trickle out of me. I was trying to stop it. And Mike, looking up, would have seen that my eyes were squeezed tight as well. I was trying but failing to stop them from trickling too.

22

I'VE GOT TO THE NUB, but there are harder things still to come, things your dad won't even touch on tomorrow. I think it's important that since you came into the world as you did you should know every twist and turn of the journey. I'm your mother, and now the truth is going to be uncovered, there should be no little residues of secrecy. A clean breast, as the saying goes, though it was my breast that fed you long ago and fed you from the beginning with the lie about your dad.

It was a factor from the very start, I mean even in those weeks before we went to Venice, it was a key part of the "debate": the question of lying. You can't get away from it. The biological necessities are plain, but the issue of dissimulation gets trickier and trickier, the more you think about it. *When* do you tell, how long do you leave it? Well, now you know our answer to that. But who else, if anyone, do you tell meanwhile? It was principally your Grandma Helen and your Grandpa Pete. Your Grandma Fiona was a more academic proposition.

To tell or not to tell. Suppose, having set out, for the best and most carefully considered reasons, on a course of pretence, your deception is suddenly rumbled? And how good, anyway, will you be at pretending? It's no easy ride. It's a little like being a secret agent and never being able to relax your cover story. What starts out as the simple task—which isn't simple at all—of acquiring offspring becomes a task of reconstructing the world.

And, as of tomorrow, I'm afraid it will become your task too. You'll have to take on your share of the lying—that is, of course, if you want to. Since it will very quickly become clear from what your father will tell you that we've told no one else, that we've lied, if you like, all round. Which sounds rather shocking. Though perhaps not as shocking as discovering that for sixteen years everyone else knew and you were the last to find out.

It's just within these walls, just the four of us. And Edward.

But then *that*'s clearly a lie too. I confess it. It goes without saying that, apart from your dad and me, there would have been certain people in the know for strictly clinical reasons, though they don't count, since they were bound by professional codes. But haven't I just said that I blurted it all out one day to our vet? Hardly a clinical disclosure. Or, more accurately, it was our vet, Alan Fraser, who was the first outsider to rumble our situation, still in its merely conceptual stage, and I had no choice but to own up. As I'm owning up to you.

Our vet knew, for one. And I think Otis knew, for another. I know that sounds preposterous. He could hardly have been listening, you're thinking, on that examination table, to what I said to our vet. Has your mum gone daft?

But I think he knew anyway, even before that. Cats can tell things, perhaps.

Why do people have pets? And why do they sometimes vanish? The simple, primal instinct of escape: Archie flying to the antipodes? Otis recovered, thanks to Alan Fraser, but it was a false recovery. Later that year he relapsed. I think he knew. He knew that the time was coming when his role in our lives would be over. He didn't need Alan Fraser to spell it out for him. He knew, perhaps, even from that time we'd left him in Carshalton and I'd cried my eyes out, but really for my father. He knew even better than I did.

But that's not all he'd have known if he'd truly been able to listen in to my conversations with our vet.

Biology's just a ruthless tyrant? It was all just to do with that famous biological clock ticking away inside me, at thirty-two a good deal more loudly than at twenty-six, so that even Otis could hear it and recognise it? If only it were as simple as that. I need to tell you that it wasn't nearly so simple, and I'm not going to pretend to you, anyway, that in her early thirties your mother had become a mere pawn of biology.

I still had my qualms—as I told our vet—about that little procedure so cheerfully called "artificial." It's artificial, and it's not artificial. A simple business, a few moments in a clinic, it doesn't even hurt, but it wasn't just Mike who flinched, believe me. It's clinical and detached and imper-sonal, but it's not, exactly. It's all done with a test tube, so to speak, but it's still done with someone else, and rather inti-mately. And you may start to worry rather seriously about these things tomorrow—from the other end, as it were. Sperm isn't just a general ingredient. It's not like self-raising flour.

It might seem that it's this man here beside me who's most in jeopardy. Poor Mike. Marching orders! You're no dad of ours. God forbid, my angels, God forbid. But is it so one-sided? You'll have to tell me. Why am I lying awake like this, stirring my conscience? Mike's the impostor—or just the hapless, innocent bystander? Of what was *he* the perpetrator?

You may look at it this way, though I don't want to put the formulation into your heads: I'm your *real* mother, of that there's no dispute or doubt, but I'm also the woman who, if by prior agreement and for the best of all possible reasons (I'm not sure you can quite escape being implicated yourselves), went and forsook your father and did it with another man.

Forgive me.

I'm getting to the really tough part now. It's just as well I've established the rules of this story. It's a bedtime story: exactly. I'm telling it, you're fast asleep. It's just as well Mike is too. The simple and hard truth is that, on my side of it, it wasn't just a matter of having qualms to work through, of reopening a debate. It was a matter, since I would be the actively engaged party, of—how can I put this?—prior experimentation.

Give me a while to explain.

It's possible that from tomorrow you will start to look at the whole world differently, not just this house in Rutherford Road. I've thought *this* through. You may start to look at complete strangers in a way you've never done before, but in a way, I assure you, I once started shiftily to do many years ago. And still do. It's even a fair bet that you may start to look at your own faces in the mirror in a way you never have before.

I know a lot of that goes on anyway—the mirror-gazing, I mean. You're teenagers, after all, the mirror's your daily obsession. Kate, you're already an experienced hand with the make-up, while oddly protesting (rightly as it happens) that you don't really need it. Nick, you're always looking for some *real* cause to use that razor. But you just look, anyway, at your faces. I've seen you. And though you both do it you like to catch each other at it, as if it's something vaguely shaming and damning—as if, I've sometimes thought, when either of you looks in the mirror, you're really gazing at each other.

Fundamentally (I know, I really do), you're each of you looking to see who you really *are*. You're looking to see that slow-about-it and fully separate creature actually, finally emerge. But now, from tomorrow, there's going to be a whole new dimension to your peering.

The fact is, isn't it: he's out there somewhere?

What I thought, as I deliberated, and still wavered, all those years ago (sometimes looking at my own face in the mirror, as if that would help) was this. Suppose it were *real*. It's tantamount to *being* real in the first place. Just because I'd never see *his* face—or, if it comes to it, any other part of him. Another man, who I'd never know. Another man, who wasn't Mike. It's why I'd balked that first time around, in the days when your dad talked to Doctor Chivers.

Maybe other women in my situation don't get caught on this hurdle. They're more desperate, perhaps, or more sensible. It's just something that happens in a clinic. But it's the union (can it be disputed in this age of DNA?) of two people. And the only way I could surmount this obstacle and know my own mind on the matter was to exorcise this ghost-in-advance, to do the real thing, in the flesh yet hypothetically, and see how it felt.

There, I've said it.

And after I've said a bit more, you may think it's all the most blatant twaddle. I didn't know my own mind then? I don't know it now. And wasn't I just talking about lying?

I was simply attracted, you may think, to our not unattractive vet, Alan Fraser. To his capable forearms, sleeves rolled up, as he handled Otis. To the way he made poor Otis purr, even in his poorliness. To his boldness and directness, even when—even because—it overstepped the mark. To the way he'd got so quickly under the skin of *my* "condition," all the time looking at me with sympathetic, forty-year-old, but (let me say it) ever so slightly boyish, ever so slightly unwise grey-blue eyes.

Not to mention the fact, I won't be coy about it, that he was attracted to me. One doesn't miss these things. Those dark-suited clients at Walker's, with their peeping red flames of breast-pocket handkerchiefs, not just looking at the pictures. Simon's own little low-burning flame. Thirty-two: but I knew I'd gained something—lost something, the first flush, but gained something. (You'll find out, Kate, how it works.)

Not to mention that safe, confessional, veterinary space in which all this occurred, under the chaperoneship of Otis. Now I'm confessing to you.

I even vicariously reversed the roles. That is, I pictured your poor dad—as a vet. Not such an unlikely job for a former biologist, nor such a bad one, and hardly a comedown, vets can make a decent living. Out of loyalty to your father (if I can say that), I didn't disabuse Alan Fraser of his evident respect for the editor of *The Living World.* I didn't say, it may be called *The Living World,* but it's run from a roof in Bloomsbury. But then I'd already given him, a complete stranger, the full low-down on my husband's spermatozoa.

Out of loyalty—and honesty too—to your father, I told Mike about these veterinary conversations, even about their non-veterinary element. I even told him he should make the acquaintance of Alan Fraser, and he did. They liked each other. And if the subject of families, of having them or not having them, came up between them, then, apparently, it didn't cause ructions. Your dad didn't feel obliged to hit Alan Fraser on the chin. Two scientists, two grown-up men.

Your dad would even say he was sorry, a few months later, when Fraser rather suddenly moved to a new practice, less than a year after he'd arrived.

I'm getting to the hard part. Now I've got there, there's no point in wrapping it up. Here we go. Alan Fraser and I went away together one weekend. That's even overstating it. It was a single night, a Friday night, you couldn't call it a weekend.

That trip to Venice wasn't the only business trip, or ostensible business trip, of mine in the first half of that year. I'd been to Paris, on my own, in January, and there'd been a second trip to Paris in May. Except it wasn't. May is a very nice time in Paris and this might have been another shameless opportunity for engineering a break for two, sponsored by W. and F. Especially as I was to be in Paris, apparently, on a Friday.

But this wasn't so very long after Otis's return and, though he was much on the mend, he was still in need of monitoring, still technically—under the vet. We could hardly cart him off to his cattery quite yet. And it was a time when we had things on our minds, our resurrected debate, that might only cloud the delights of a weekend in Paris. Your dad even said, "Another time. But stay over on the Saturday too, if you like." He saw me, perhaps, wandering broodily round Paris, clarifying my maternal position.

No, I said, I'd come straight back on the Saturday morning. I didn't want him to expect me to ring. Or vice versa. I wanted my own clean exit. But I gave your dad—it was a risk—the name and number of the hotel where I'd stayed before in January. He didn't ask to see my plane tickets. Why should he have done? I'd have said, anyway, they were for collection.

I wasn't in Paris at all. It wasn't a business trip. Alan (shall I call him just Alan?) wasn't offering Paris. I wasn't exactly in a position to specify, but, to be fair, nor did he want to be cheap or to make me feel that I was. Definitely not his flat in Stockwell.

For me it all involved considerable subterfuge and deception. That's not an excuse, but it makes me realise how much I needed to do it. He was unattached, a divorced man:

a pretty poor witness, you might say, for having a family, the very opposite of what, at this point, should have enticed me. Though enticement, I'm trying to explain, wasn't my only or chief motive.

He was on the lookout, of course, let's not pretend about that. *He* was experimenting too, and might even have used that convenient word himself. Where would a divorced vet first start to look? I don't know how many experiments he might already have conducted. But what I do know is that he was *my* only experiment, my only ever trial run.

And he didn't take me to Paris, though he was eager to impress. I took a morning train to Gatwick, as if to persuade myself I still might really be flying to Paris. He picked me up there in his car and we drove around for a bit, round Sussex, killing time, and had lunch in a pub.

Then he took me to the Gifford Park Hotel, five stars even in those days. Do you see my dilemma?

23

ODDLY, I SEE MYSELF now sleeping, alone, in the Hôtel Gustave, rue de Grenelle, Paris, where I truly did sleep and truly by myself, at the beginning of that eventful year, 1978. Not knowing then, of course, how eventful it would be and certainly not knowing that in a few months' time I would have pretended to have slept again in that same Paris hotel, while in fact I'd slept much nearer home and not by myself. If you're going to tell a lie, give it some dose of veracity.

And even when I slept with our vet, Alan Fraser, in Sussex in May, I thought about myself in Paris just four months before in January, but as if I might have been thinking of some other woman, some innocent me of long ago. It should have been the other way round, perhaps, I should have been innocent in spring, devious in winter. January and May: it's a proverbial motif, a not so uncommon subject for the painters of the past. As you know only too well, since among our Rutherford Road collection is a small depiction of just that personified theme by the Venetian artist Vareschi. *Gennaio e Maggio*. Vareschi, by any art-historical rating, can't claim to be much more than a very minor old master, but his work commands a price and it's a measure of something that we possess one at all.

There he sits, anyway, January, that is, scrawny and grey-bearded, contemplating an almost naked and extremely nubile May in some verdant enclave which could be the corner of an orchard or a fanciful wood. Fruit, in any case, of an indeterminate but vaguely testicular kind, hangs among the foliage—it seems to be autumn as well as those other months of the year—and there are some roses with particularly pointed thorns.

You may have wondered, in your strangely dainty way, how such a thing could have its place in our house, or ever have been put into a gilt frame at all. It's a dirty old man, isn't it, eyeing up young flesh? Except, of course, it's "art," which justifies all kinds of things, and it's pricey, it's that business of your mum's. And, incidentally—though what do you care, at sixteen?—it's a perennial and much-visited allegory, it's the whole sad tale of existence. The ageing male, his virile powers in decline, goes looking for some vision of lost youth. He picks up a young girl and takes her off to a hotel. For some curious, perennial reason, the young girl frequently obliges. January's also, if Vareschi makes no allusion to it, the double-headed, the two-faced one. The whole thing often involves cheating on a wife.

Hardly at all the situation of Alan Fraser and me: him at forty-one and divorced, and me at thirty-two and married.

But I thought about that woman of only that preceding January as if I might have been thinking of someone half my age.

The weather had been true January weather, cold and still and sparkling, the kind of winter weather that can make the stone of Paris radiate. I'd found time, then, to walk, not broodily but simply contentedly, by the icy Seine, the water and the white walls of the *quais* dazzling, my ears pinched by the air. And I'd wished Mike was with me, our vapour-breaths mingling. Was there any glad moment of my life he shouldn't share? All the same, I'd inhaled the strange pleasure of a separation that was hardly a separation at all—just a Wednesday night in Paris—and was almost over now anyway.

It would have been the same sort of morning in London perhaps, I thought, the same light teasing the charcoal grey of Bloomsbury and touching the windows of Mike's cramped attic-office, up among the gnarled and mottled branches of the plane trees that fill the centre of Ormond Square.

Now we have our own place in France.

It was just a week before your dad's birthday, and I'd even just bought him his present, in an antiques shop in the rue Bonaparte. It was one of those little brass calendar devices which you put on a desk, with a rotatable display of the day, the date and month: a particularly finely shaped and engineered example, elegantly scrolled and chased, with a pen-rest combined and with the pleasing distinction that the dates were, of course, in French. I saw myself, before I wrapped it, setting it to that all-important date for your father (and for me): "*le 20 Janvier.*"

Now it sits on his desk in that study-cum-office, the black numbers and letters on the white enamel regularly turned. And if you've ever wondered: well, I bought it in Paris in January, 1978. Not such an inexpensive whim for me then.

Now we can buy a Vareschi. I saw it in the shop window just as the shop was opening, went in and didn't hesitate. An electric fire blazed away while I counted out my francs. As I stood in that crystalline air on the Pont des Arts, taking in the classic view, my purchase waited for me, to be collected after my stroll, on my way back to my hotel. Then I'd check out and fly home to Mike.

Will he remember to turn on the date tomorrow? Or will he want it to stay always at yesterday? "*Le 16 Juin 1995.*"

There are points in our lives which, if we don't know it at the time, we look back on later and see ourselves as if suspended, poised on some mysterious fulcrum. What did I not have then to be thankful for? All of Paris scintillating before me. I simply didn't know what that year would bring, or take away, or what other hotel rooms I'd see, as well as that one at the Gustave, even before the year was half through. One by Lake Windermere, one in Venice. One, in between, at the Gifford Park. And that one in Paris, in a manner of speaking, twice.

An experiment. A practical, empirical (but top-secret) stage in our ongoing debate and, as it turned out, the decisive one. Your mother's just playing with you? She was really just up for it with this veterinary surgeon with his hands on her pussy cat? She really just felt, at thirty-two—not exactly young and foolish, though she's forty-nine now—like acting as if she was nineteen again at Sussex and screwing around? Here was another one to try. I don't think so.

What you don't have you can't lose. But then again, it's at least partly true that you don't really know what you have until you lose it, or risk doing so. You don't know the real things until you've sampled the false. At some point as the years gather, it's bound to come over us perhaps: the perverse and crazy, but oddly almost prudent wish to put the whole fabric of what we possess to the test.

Excuses? I just went to bed with this Alan. Alan! And Fraser, you may have been thinking, is a Scottish name. I let him pick me up in his Peugeot and carry me off to spend a Friday night in a country hotel. I had my reasons, but where did *he* think it might lead: just one night? It was just such a previous exercise, it turned out, that had landed him in divorce. He made the mistake (the serious mistake, I think) of telling me. It wasn't calculated to make me feel good. A little weekend escapade, he said, which shouldn't have been any more, but he'd tumbled further, so it seemed, and then, when it was too late, this other woman (unnamed) had ditched him. Punished at both ends, and at one of them by the upset of his whole domestic apple cart.

What was I supposed to say? "There, there?" Or "Tough?" Or even "The cow!?" And now, of course, with me, he was risking nothing, having already lost the lot.

I could be risking everything I had.

I think what people often want from these midlife episodes (and note how I speak from vast experience) is a rather unexciting thing: comparison. They haven't known it for a while, it's been one of the rules that they forgo it, but is it, anyway (and this is the real persuasion), such an outrageous thing? They want the reassurance, the instruction or perhaps the sheer surprise of comparison. Life cuts you off from comparison. It might have been someone else, not

Mike. I might never have met Mike. Poor me! And if not Mike, then it would have been someone else. Nothing's written in the stars.

But I, of course, had my quite specific and highly specialised reason to know what it was like, while still having a husband, to jump into bed with another man. Did he appreciate that he was a "test case?" Perhaps he did—after those conversations in his surgery, all that scurrilous talk of insemination. It might even have been a sort of card he played, an unusual but opportune seduction technique. And I was "seduced."

And he was a verifiable and practised father, if not the most shining example of paternity: two teenage kids. Just two cats now, apparently. What, incidentally, had he done with *them,* while we stole away to Sussex (Paris)? Just left them to fend for themselves?

Mike, back in Herne Hill, would have fixed himself a supper for one on a tray in front of the telly, then slept ignorantly alone—that is, if we don't count a still fragile Otis curled up on a corner of the duvet. But then, at this time, the very same proposition would have been going through Mike's head too: this primitive obstacle, this crude, unscientific bugbear to be overcome, that his wife, that Paula would have to do it, if not exactly at close-range or in hands-on fashion, with another man.

Oh lord. It rained that night too, though it had begun as a fine May day and finished with a balmy, hazy evening. Dinner in the "Akenhurst Room," candlelit and oak-panelled, while the first drops began to patter, apologetically, on the terrace outside. He just wanted female company, a woman to share his bed? It had been a while, perhaps, and he'd had to go, or felt he had to, to this considerable trouble and expense. It was rather touching. I should have been flattered. I'd become special to him? He saw me as some replacement Mrs. Fraser? He was falling in love with me? God forbid.

I listened to more snippets from his troubled family life, and considered what I might tell him of mine: my late father's divorces, for example, his three hapless marriages. And incidentally, he was a High Court judge. Switching subjects completely, I might have mentioned that Mike, whom by now, of course, Alan had met, used to work, before he worked on *The Living World,* on snails. Yes, snails. Perhaps Mike had mentioned them himself. But then if he had, surely Alan wouldn't have chosen them (another serious mistake)—to eat. *Escargots:* they were on the Gifford's distinctly Gallic menu, and Alan, as some Englishmen will, as a point almost of honour and bravado, went for them. Should I have said something?

To your dad and me, who'll eat most things, they've always been strictly taboo.

And—thinking of things French—I thought, later that night, about that woman, in January, in Paris, where I was supposed to be right then. "That girl" I nearly called her. And the fact is I wanted to reach out protectively to her, standing there on that bridge in the wonderful cold light and perfectly happy as she was, to pull her collar up and tuck her scarf a little more snugly round her chin.

But hold on, you'll be wondering: I had time to *think,* to contemplate, to conjure up such tender images, on this adventurous and plainly adulterous night, when thinking was hardly high on the agenda?

Yes, I had plenty. Without going into other details, my night with Alan Fraser ended up a little like now. I mean, absolutely not like now in one main respect, but in other respects, like it. It was even raining. The banal truth is that he fell asleep on me, and I stayed awake. There was dinner talk, there was preamble, there was even, I'm sure, during the thing itself, some gasping sex talk—but there was precious little pillow talk. I slept with him, I slept with our vet. I did all the things that that can mean. But, being strictly accurate, he slept with me before I slept with him, and I lay awake for a long while before I slept at all.

Perhaps I simply "satisfied" him. That's not to claim credit. He simply crashed, sated, as men quite often ungraciously do ("men": hark at me) into unconsciousness. He was the vet, but I put him to sleep. Not much pillow talk? Scarcely any, really—if I'd even wanted it.

I just lay awake, not particularly wishing to sleep, or even feeling ignored. Not even, I'll be honest, assailed by feelings of guilt and remorse. Just thinking steadily to myself, as if I actually needed this sleeping stranger at my side to set my thoughts in motion.

Not unlike now. It's an old and perennial situation, perhaps. You have it all to come, Kate. A woman does her best to be a lover, then, before she knows it, she becomes a mother, a sleeping charge beside her. But, of course, Mike here's not a stranger. And when I was lying there beside Alan Fraser, I was thinking mainly of your father. It's what I mean by comparison.

Oh how I love your father.

The room was on a first-floor corner, one of the best in the hotel. It actually had a four-poster bed. He'd forked out for the five-star Gifford Park and I'd been too polite or too amenable, if those are the right words, to protest. How much would it have cost him—just to fall asleep? I had the feeling that the place might have had some previous senti-mental significance for him and I didn't want to probe. And I was certainly too tactful or too compliant to broach its unsettling significance for me. Not so much the place itself (though now it has just such a significance), but the loca-tion. Did it have to be *Sussex,* and not so very far from the ancestral domains of the Hooks?

You see my dilemma? What am I to say, with barely a week now to go? "Cancel it?" Or, more preposterously: "Could it be some *other* hotel?" I have my excuse and my get-out, of course: *you.* You and my perfectly appropriate mother's instinct. How can we possibly even consider our anniversary, even if it is our twenty-fifth, at such a time as this? How can we just go off so soon and leave our bruised and shaken nestlings all by themselves?

Have I brought you now fully up to speed?

And yet I can see all your dad's reasons, all his needs and urgent contingency planning. It even makes sense: time for you to be alone, to think and talk it through. You're *not* helpless babies. And it is our twenty-fifth. I can see how the Sussex thing works now: *our* territory. Only six miles or so from Birle and at least, for him, there'll be *that* umbilical going off in that direction. And—with that direction in mind—what will Grannie Helen think if we don't do something special for our special anniversary?

Suppose it's the *same room.* Oh lord. Suppose (is it possible after seventeen years?) it's even the same bed. Mike would have gone for the best, of course he would, no expense spared. He'll have asked for *the* best—one of the reasons he booked so long in advance.

I can't get out of it. I'll just have to pretend, smile and pretend. Or treat it as some grotesque and appalling opportunity for confession. On top of everything else? Mikey, forgive me, forgive me. It was, believe me, all in a good cause.

The trouble is I know that he—which really means we—will put it to *you.* We'll ask you to judge us tomorrow in all kinds of ways, but we'll ask for your verdict on this tricky secondary matter. Namely whether you think it's right that, at this particular, traumatic point in your lives, we should swan off to a five-star hotel, leaving you here with the contents of the fridge.

But my hunch is that you will give us your "permission." I can't put myself in your shoes, but that's my hunch, or in one sense it's my earnest hope, since that will mean that what's about to occur tomorrow will have gone, so far as such a thing can, "well." But in one respect your letting us go off like reprieved offenders to celebrate our wedding anniversary won't help me at all.

I want it both ways. I want both to go and not to go to the Gifford Park. I want you to listen to these things I'm telling you and not to hear them at all. You see what I mean? Every twist and turn.

A corner room. I can't remember the number. It's just as well, perhaps. There were aquatints of Sussex scenes on the wall. A sepia photograph of some tweeded folk piled into a shooting brake. It had a fine view, through a latticed, wisteria-hung window, of those ever-suggestive Downs. And it had a chintz-hung four-poster bed with spiralled-oak pillars. Picture your mother in such a room, seventeen years ago, an unfamiliar man beside her, rain falling outside, drenching the wisteria leaves. Did it really happen, that curious little enterprise? It seems now both insignificant and far off, and flagrant as a just discovered crime. And yet it served its practical purpose, it's true to say that without that bizarre excursion, mysteriously involving a trip to Paris at the same time, there might never have been you.

Your dad's shown me the glossy brochure he was sent. I already knew: a Jacobean manor house, seat of the Aken-hurst family, grandly added to in the nineteenth century by the Giffords, who made a fortune in rubber. Our room—then, I mean, Alan's and mine—was in the Jacobean bit. There was a creaking, ancient staircase that made you feel, at once, that you were engaged in an act of stealth. Long-bearded, white-ruffed faces watched your every step. It's inconceivable that something so old and worthy of preservation can have been transformed beyond all uncomfortable recognition in less than twenty years. I can only hope.

Outside, there was, and must still be, a lovely garden: lawns, yew walks, fountains and some sets of just slightly vulgar statuary, a foible of the Giffords, depicting classical scenes. Diana and Actaeon inevitably, Narcissus bending over a pool. We'd done a tour of their half-clad forms before dinner. I thought of them out there in the rain, like creatures in some petrified zoo, the drops forming on the stone nipples and chins. The Giffords, with their rubbery new money, had gone for ancestry and myth.

His skin had its strange but distinct, personal-sweat smell: mine must have had, to him, its own smell too. An individual, yet generic scent. At thirty-two, I could just about remember it from earlier days: the animal tang of someone you've never been naked with before.

Or ever again, in this case. We didn't waste too much time over our departure the following morning. It was clear, bright weather again. Sunlight gleamed in the puddles on the terrace. The curves of the Downs were like a sure draughtsman's line. I'd slept eventually, and perfectly soundly. And my mind was crystal-sharp and made up. I knew it was all right now, I knew it was perfectly fine.

I asked Alan to drop me at East Croydon, so I could take the train from there. So I could muster again some token illusion that I'd returned from Paris, by a Gatwick flight which would have departed, allowing for the time difference, at around ten o'clock. Another train from Victoria to Herne Hill. I had only a light, one-night case. The rather slinky small black dress inside it would have been explained by the cocktail party I'd been required to attend.

I was ready to abide, scrupulously, by another pretence that in seventeen years your father has never even suspected, let alone uncovered. But he scarcely asked about my time in Paris, because very soon after I got back I changed the topic quickly and emphatically. Perhaps I'd overwhelmed him, anyway, in that still grief-shadowed spring, with the happy, glad-to-be-home light in my face, with the hug I gave him, pressing myself against him hard. It was a fine Saturday in May, not quite lunchtime. I said, "Let's go for a walk in Dulwich Park, Mikey. Let's have a look at the ducks. Let's have a drink in the Greyhound. I did some thinking while I was in Paris, and on the plane just now. A.I.D.: I'm absolutely sure. No problem, I want to go ahead."

24

LET ME MAKE ONE thing absolutely clear, in case any doubt has entered your minds: Alan Fraser (MRCVS) is not your father. Neither of you has grey-blue eyes. We—that is, he—took all due precautions, in a hotel once owned by rubber barons. I'd rather lost touch, you could say, with such things.

In any case, that wasn't the point of the exercise. The point of the exercise was—hypothetical. Alan Fraser isn't your father, any more than Otis was. It's just that without either of them, you might not be there at all.

But, of course, there must have been a *practical* exercise. It may not be wise to enquire too deeply into how we were brought about, but since the whole thing will be so calculatedly sprung on you tomorrow, since you're about to discover that you yourselves were the work of painstaking calculation, you'll at least want to know how the actual thing was done. Even if you don't ask, you're bound to wonder: you won't be able to avoid a certain—image of your mother.

But, for all I know, perhaps you *will* ask. Perhaps you'll both be uninhibitedly hungry for every graphic technical detail. Kids these days, they certainly don't hold back. I've tried so hard to anticipate every possible form your reaction might take, from outrage to laughter, that perhaps nothing will surprise me. Perhaps you'll even be *thrilled* to know that you were concocted in such a special way. You'll want a badge for it (I hope not: what would go on it?). And you won't feel at all like treading carefully. So, come on, Mum, spill it. We came out of a test tube?

No, not exactly. You came out of me—as I once explained, remember? When all's said, there's that wonderful fact and joy of my life, you came out of me. Have I ever told you how much I love you? Has your father?

It's hardly a secret, anyway, how it was done, how it has to be done. A little mechanical thinking will get you there. It's no more secret, mysterious or romantic, I'm afraid to say, than a visit to the dentist. To begin with, there was even a certain amount of dull bureaucracy, of form-filling and question-and-answer. First of all, we went along, the two of us, like responsible parents-to-be, to a place that dealt in such things and talked it over, in the strictest confidence of course.

We learnt the fundamental rule, which was the rule of anonymity. It's the same rule for you, my darlings, as for us, we'll need to make that clear tomorrow. There's no way of *knowing*, even for you. You were conceived anonymously— or semi-anonymously, let's more accurately say. Though, within the bounds of anonymity, it was possible to be selective, if not exactly fussy: skin, eye colour, hair colour. It was possible to attempt a kind of sketchy match. It was possible, I don't mean to be flippant, to place an order.

This was when your dad, with all his resolve and resignation, got a little uncomfortable. This was when "He" began to loom, to seem suddenly close and actual, like someone who might already have been told about *us* and put on standby.

But my own nerves were steady. I'd been to the Gifford Park with our vet.

Then we signed the forms. Then I had some standard tests and was given an appointment, relative to my menstrual cycle. A little while before it, when it happened to be our anniversary, we went to Venice. Then one fine and sunny morning at the very end of June, I went back to the clinic and to a special room. Your father came with me. He didn't have to—and I don't mean that he came as well into that special room—but he drove me to the clinic, as if I were some fragile out-patient about to undergo something potentially upsetting. We both joked about this misplaced analogy, but somehow couldn't shake it off.

I don't know what Mike did, while I was—busy. He read the paper? He drank coffee in a Styrofoam cup from a vending machine? He walked round the block? Or he just waited, not in the building, but in the car park, in the car. That's what he said: he'd be in the car, not in the building, where there were seats for waiting and magazines. Fair enough. When I came out through the glass doors he stepped from the car and walked towards me as if I might have needed help. Poor Mikey, what could he say: how did it go?

It doesn't take very long. The *real* thing, after all, needn't take very long. It all comes back to me now on this night: the ridiculous, bright-lit matter-of-factness. Like having an injection, a jab before you go on holiday. It had none of the momentousness of—tomorrow. I knew it might not even work. I didn't even know whether to treat it, in my mind, as special or as merely functional. Both options seemed somehow treacherous. I tried, in fact, not to think at all. That's the normal state of affairs, after all, with the real thing. It's called conception, but who's actually being conceptual?

It's like a simple vaginal examination. So far as I know, Kate, you've not had one of those: a treat in store. A sort of speculum. Except something *else,* of course, is introduced. A nurse did the honours, a straw-blonde nurse of roughly my age (that pleased me) who introduced herself as Becky. I still, strangely, see her face, in close, physiognomic detail: a slightly too sharp nose, a slightly too thin mouth. Was she a mother herself or single? And how exactly was I to think of her? A *nurse*? A midwife? Hardly. A mid-husband, perhaps, a helping hand . . . And should you joke or be serious? It seemed somehow understood that too much humour would be inappropriate. Smiles and friendly efficiency, yes, but this was not quite a laughing matter. If the real thing sometimes can be.

Clinical neutrality—definitely no sexy dim lighting or soft music in the background. And, beneath it all, banishing the jokes anyway, the vague feeling that you're doing something wrong, illicit or even, perhaps, harmful: you're really having an abortion. I'm sorry, I'm only being honest.

Afterwards they ask you just to lie down and "rest" for a bit. I don't know if it's to encourage the natural processes or because they actually think you might be tired. No cup of tea and a biscuit—though I didn't ask—and, of course, no post-coital cigarette. I did smoke a bit then too, as a matter of fact. I stopped, you'll be glad to know, when I became pregnant. I might have stirred my tea, taken a drag and made small talk with Becky. "I'm here because of a cat, you know. Called Otis."

So, not exactly a test tube. Though there would have been, I suppose, at some stage, a sort of test tube and someone, so to speak, would have been in it. A stranger slipped that day into our lives—an unfortunate phrase, since that's just what he didn't do, or not exactly, yes and no. When your dad saw me walk off to that special room I wasn't in anyone else's company, but when I walked out again through those glass doors you could say, in a manner of speaking, I was.

A stranger entered our lives—that's not quite a happy phrase either. And not a complete and absolute stranger anyway, because of that preliminary vetting. I don't seem to be able to get away from awkward puns.

In the "debating" stage, during those days and weeks after Otis's return, and again when we'd made up our minds and contacted the clinic, I used to ride the train up to work, the Tube from Victoria to Green Park, and look constantly, furtively, at men around me. Perhaps not as furtively as I thought, and perhaps if they caught my eye they might have got the wrong idea. This sort of thing, after all, goes on all the time. But they could hardly have guessed the nature of my interest. They could hardly have guessed that I wasn't just looking, but searching.

Even when I became pregnant I still looked. The truth is, I still look now sometimes. I've never stopped looking or searching, even though during the last sixteen years there have been long periods of time when I haven't caught myself doing it. But your mother, I'm afraid, has a fundamental and incurable habit of looking at other men. This year, these last few months, I've felt the need to look a lot. And even when I don't look, I still wonder. The more years that have gone by, in fact, the more reason there is to wonder. Suppose our paths have crossed, suppose we've actually looked, without knowing it, at each other. Suppose we've sat on the same train. What would be the chances? Beyond all reckoning? Sometimes, now, I have the strangely arresting thought: suppose he's no longer alive.

But, assuming he is, he's out there somewhere. Even now.

Do you see why I needed—I know it's the most exotic of excuses—my fling, if that's the word, with Alan Fraser? Not that it's actually stopped those supposings. Not that it's exorcised the ghost. And, of course, I can't prevent myself having the reverse notion, on *his*, the ghostly one's, behalf, though I know it's absurd: that he's interested in *me*. Or in *us*, I should say.

As if in this one case (how many other poor mums, after all, might he have serviced?) the iron rule has been broken and he's had the privilege of knowing who we are. He's been watching us all this time, unseen himself—from some special gallery. He even knows that tomorrow's the big day. He's been spying on us all these years, this happy family. Spying and perhaps waiting. He's been counting the "last times" too: the "last" Christmas, your dad's fiftieth—the last birthday of a so far successful impostor. He was outside that restaurant we took your dad to in January, peering in through the window at our table. He's out there right now, poor man, getting soaked in the rain and waiting for the dawn of this day: *his* big day, in a way. He'll be peering in at us tomorrow, perhaps, through the French windows, from behind the viburnum bush. Or—God help us—he might just crash through the French windows and make his sudden, dramatic, sopping-wet entrance.

Your real father, my demon lover.

I suppose Mike's had all these thoughts too. He must have done, I'm sure of it. And what would the two of them do if they should come face to face? What would *you* want them to do? Shake hands, hug each other? Take a swing at each other?

And, of course, when I've done my looking on the Tube, walking along Piccadilly, wherever, I've been consciously looking in a way—given that vetting process—for Mike's double, or something close to it. Another Mikey, a pseudo-Mikey, a quasi-Mikey, catching my eye for a fraction of a second, but not even recognizing me.

Isn't it astonishing that your dad's still asleep?

A third party entered our lives, a little before you did. Then he became, in due course, a sort of fifth party. Tomorrow he'll be officially recognised as such, like a christening. From tomorrow you'll know him about as well as we ever did, but it will be up to you, it has to be up to you, to decide how we should deal with him.

A third party entered your parents' lives. A fourth party, if you count Otis, who I haven't forgotten. And, just as with Otis, we had to find a name for him, a token, working name, since he came under that plain wrapping of anonymity. We didn't even have a number. Not that we wanted or needed, in those early days, to refer to him that much.

Except, perhaps, to thank him.

Yes, to thank him. Will you possibly look at it that way too tomorrow? Even consider it at all, that you might like to thank him? The trouble is, that only begs that other enormous but entirely understandable question: that you might like to meet him. That's impossible, though it may not stop you wishing it. It's impossible now as it was back then even to get a simple message of thanks through to him. There are no channels. And how do you thank someone, in any case, whose name you don't even know?

Tomorrow you may feel the need to give him a name of your own. It's not such a small matter. You'll have to use it for the rest of your lives. And perhaps we shouldn't even mention to you the name we've used. Or we should humbly and graciously trade it in for yours. We thought of calling him many things: "Mr. D.," for example, for "Mr. Donor." Though that was tricky because "D." might also stand for "Dad." *Your* dad (what a mountain there is in such a little word) came up with some inventive and truculent offerings of his own, which may not be so amusing to you. Such as "The Grand Inseminator" and "Spunky Jim." But in the end we settled on a formula that was neat and wholly to the point: Mr. S., short for Mr. Sperm.

25

AND, OF COURSE, I can see him in *you*. I don't have to look for him randomly in the street, on trains. He's there before my eyes, invisibly, every time I look at you. And from tomorrow, I'm sure, that mirror-gazing of yours will suddenly get rather serious.

You don't have grey-blue eyes. You have, as has often been innocently observed, your mother's dark brown, green-shot eyes, her nose, her cheekbones: but your father's mobile mouth, your father's expressions. Despite those specifications we made, it would seem that it was my genes, predominantly, that kicked in. Your dad has clear-blue eyes. We ordered *them* certainly, the same again, please. So you should know that Mr. Sperm, or whatever you choose to call him, has blue eyes too. But it didn't work out that way, you got my eyes. Which didn't stop people from saying, as if the other fifty per cent must be glowingly apparent somewhere else: Ah, but that's their dad's smile.

This is the strangest thing—how you've conspired, yourselves, in the conspiracy. People see what they expect to see, so why should they not have believed they were seeing Mike in you? Then again, from the start, you saw two faces looming over you that you took to be your parents, and why should you not have taken them as your model? And we did a lot of smiling over you, believe me. But perhaps it was Mike's smile that got imprinted, perhaps it was his you felt the greater obligation to.

If we've performed a part for sixteen years, then, without knowing it, so have you—and even more convincingly. There have definitely been times—whole lengths of time—when we ourselves have fallen totally for the illusion, when we've completely forgotten. You've been unwittingly such consummate actors, such consummate accomplices, that now it's like an extra cruelty that you'll have to undo it all.

And yet I've noticed already that it's started to slip, it's already started to look less plausible. You're sixteen, you want to be yourselves. The last thing you want to look like is your half-century-old parents. The last thing you want to do—it's perfectly natural at your age—is catch yourselves mimicking some fossilised gesture of ours. Will this help matters or just confuse them tomorrow?

These days, you don't even want to look like *each other*. But wasn't that, from the start, the little unexpected marvel that helped fool everyone? We couldn't have bargained for it, and certainly couldn't have specified it when we put in our request list. But people simply, perhaps, mistook the one thing for the other, or the one thing distracted from the other. Of course there was consistency and resemblance here, of course you must look like us, because you looked so much like each other.

When we took those holidays down in Cornwall, you were perhaps at the very peak of your symbiosis, your two-peas-in-a-podness: a little team of two acting as one, wanting no other company. It's what everyone else would notice, your happy, frolicking duality. And so, by a simple process of completing the square, they'd acknowledge our immaculateness as a family.

But I would notice your differences, your imbalances. A mother sees things. I would often see how you *were* like your father (Mike, of course, I mean), or I would see how the illusion was achieved. Nick, you were always that fraction behind your sister, you waited on her initiative, her shelter. When the two of you ran across the beach, your feet making little sand-puffs, her shoulder was always just ahead of yours, you were tucked in her slipstream, like birds in formation. She learnt to swim first, but as soon as she did, so did you. The same with bicycles.

It seemed to me, Nick, though it's a big thing to say, I know, that you always relied on Kate to hold your world together. And that while Kate was simply happy and though you might be happy too, a small voice inside you was always saying: please, Kate, don't let this stop, please don't let this come to an end. The world was always a question for you, and a possible disaster, hingeing on your sister. Was this my imagination?

But this all had more than one source, I could see that too. You had a special frown, just a tiny knot, a question mark in the middle of your brow, which could appear sometimes, oddly, just when everything else was sunny. But then it wasn't your frown. It was your father's. I mean Mike's. It was the special frown he'd have, and had never had before

you were born, whenever he'd remind himself of the *fact,*
whenever he'd stop forgetting and say to himself: but this
isn't what it seems, this can't go on for ever.

Which way round did it work, Nick? You borrowed it
from him? He took it from you? But there it was, on both of
you, a father-and-son resemblance: both of you disturbed by
happiness. Not your father's smile, actually, but his frown.
I'd see Mike sometimes reach out and for no apparent reason, Nick, put his hand on your brow, as if feeling for a
fever. How *my* pulse would rush. But you must surely
remember this yourself. I could see him wanting to smooth
away that little obstinate pucker, to take it away in his palm.
How could he not be your father when he wanted to touch
and reclaim that little mark of himself in you?

Those holidays in Cornwall, midway through this sixteen-
year period, when for whole days, weeks long we'd all be so
close, were like some almost believable high point for me,
the very sun and sea and air colluding, like some annual
process of kindly weathering, to mould and fuse us together.
By the same token, I think Mike always thought they threat-
ened to expose us. All of us there in just our swimming
things. It will be on one of these holidays, I think he thought,
in the middle of our August happiness, that the whole thing
will somehow come apart, get dashed to bits, like a Cornish
shipwreck. That cottage where we regularly stayed, Gull
Cottage, with its hollyhocks and lavender bushes and its
ship's-steering-wheel mirror and sand getting everywhere,
reminded him, too, of Craiginish Croft (that trapped
essence inside): another paradise waiting to be lost.

And on that terrible day when something even *worse* (there could be) than those fears of his nearly happened, perhaps you noticed, if you were able to notice, that his relief, his joy, his sheer emotion when it was over, was even greater than mine. If we were both of us off the scale.

I don't mean that I didn't feel exactly the same: the worst thing that could ever happen and it *hadn't*. Oh, my angels. But I didn't, I couldn't have the second thought that he was having, even as he struggled to get back his breath. That you were saved, you were still there and it was beyond words, but—one day—he was going to lose you anyway.

Perhaps tomorrow in fact.

Perhaps tomorrow you'll simply relive that day again. It will come back to you—has it ever gone away?—and it will be your answer. The worst day, until this one that's coming, of your lives. You'll see him again swimming towards you. I wasn't able to see his face then as it would have looked to you, as it came towards you. I wasn't able to see the expression on it. But how could that man not have been your father?

Or perhaps you'll remember how that day began: with *your* pretence, your foolish meddling with our terror and joy. And you didn't know the half of it. Perhaps tomorrow, on top of that cold returning memory, you'll have the sudden freezing thought that if the very worst had happened that day and you'd disappeared for ever, then, of course, you'd never have known what you must know now. The lie would have had no end.

I don't want to think about it either.

Mike's going to be the outcast tomorrow? Or simply the one, now, you'll have to rescue?

But spare a thought for your mother. Why do people have children? Why did Grannie Helen get herself pregnant in all that haste? In one sense the haste wasn't necessary. After the war Grandpa Pete was still there, and there too, luckily for me, was Mike. But now, of course—there has to come a time *some* time—Grandpa Pete isn't there.

If Grandma Helen still wants to see Grandpa Pete, or see a living bit of him, there's only one thing she can do. She can look (not now, of course) at this man lying next to me. I can't hold that against her, but it's one of the reasons I'm afraid of her, and it's one of the reasons, but not the main one—a secondary worry sprouting from a secondary worry—why I'm afraid of the Gifford Park. If your dad should really get it into his head to go traipsing off those few miles to see her, for Sunday morning coffee, to take her to lunch, even, at the Star in Birle, it will be the first time we see her since we'll have told you. Are you with me?

But this is something that never occurred to your dad and me—though, God knows, we tried to think of everything— when we went along to discuss it all at the clinic. We were simply younger then. When you look at yourselves in the mirror tomorrow you'll be doing for the first time something that I've done, over and over again, when I've looked at you. That is, there'll be someone, when you look, who you *won't* see, and now you'll know it. When I look at you, I don't see, I can't see your father. What does that matter? I can just look at *him*. But think again, though you're only sixteen. Think of that day in Cornwall.

When your dad looks at you, it's a simple, patent fact: he can see *me*. In you, Kate, of course, especially. I'm not trying to flatter myself. He can even see me when I was younger than I am now, though your dad never knew me when I was sixteen.

I'm the one who's alone in this respect. I ask you to consider it, and I won't skirt around it any longer. If Mike were suddenly not to be here, I wouldn't have anywhere to look. I wouldn't be like Grannie Helen. I wouldn't have that age-old shred of consolation of looking at you and knowing that you were his too.

Think of it: as a couple gets older there's only one, unspoken question. But perhaps the two of you, being what you are, have known this all your lives and from the very start. Who will go first? Who will it be? And how *can* it be?

Don't worry, we've no intention. We're only forty-nine and fifty. These days, that's still young, isn't it? We're spring chickens. But I can't see him in you. I want you to remember it: all I have and ever will have of this man here I call your father—and it's more than I can ever say—is bound up in this sleeping body next to me now. Understand that tomorrow.

26

TO COME BACK to that time when he was sitting in the car park and I was inside having congress with—Mr. S. Your father must have wondered how many more times he might have to do this, to go through this weird, supportive but extraneous ritual, waiting for me to emerge through the glass doors. But I was lucky second time around, which is lucky indeed. The frozen and preserved stuff, they rather tactlessly tell you, simply isn't as reliable as the fresh. But I only needed two goes—two goes, I've sometimes thought, for the two of you, but, of course, it doesn't work like that.

I learnt I was pregnant that October. But even before that Otis had entered his slow and final decline. Perhaps he'd never truly recovered, though under Alan Fraser's care it had seemed that he had and one explanation (though it was mainly your father's) for his eventual deterioration was that when Fraser moved to his new practice, Otis was simply left without proper veterinary care. The new incumbent, Myers, according to your dad at least, was frankly not up to much.

All this pains me, of course. Your dad genuinely got on with Fraser. He would vie with me to be the one to take Otis along for his check-ups and injections—and for the friendly chats. I admit that after my night at the Gifford Park I was quite happy for your dad to take on that role exclusively. It was hardly likely that Fraser (I'll call him that now) was going to own up to your father. On the other hand, I can see that he might constantly have feared that your dad, having had *my* confession, might one day turn up, with or without Otis, and deliver some unpleasant comeuppance. So he made his exit that July.

That's all rather far-fetched, I know. It puts me at the root of it all—the sly bitch pitting one man's ignorance against another man's guesswork. That was hardly my position. I'm not even sure if I cared that much. Remember, I was now concentrating on becoming your mother. That was my position. I'd put myself, with all the guesswork that can entail, in the hands of a fertility clinic.

It's entirely possible that Fraser's sudden departure had nothing to do with Mr. and Mrs. Hook. Though I wasn't sorry, by then, to see him go. The plain truth is he'd served his non-veterinary purpose. Am I now sounding even a little vicious? But I was clearing the path towards your birth. And so far as Otis's relapse and decline went, I'll always believe that something similar was going on. I mean that Otis knew he'd served *his* purpose too. Even Fraser, if he'd stuck around, wouldn't have been able to save him.

He understood, even before there was any physical sign, that our house was being prepared for a presence other than his. His mysterious disappearance—who knows?—might even have been some clairvoyant protest at the prospect, which didn't work, which even redounded against him. He imagined, purring under Alan Fraser's hands, that all might be as it was again, we'd learnt a lesson. Then, when we went

to Venice perhaps and he was interned once more in Carshalton, he realised he was wrong.

Call me unscientific. There's a feline logic. Your father
never subscribed to this theory, he was even rather rattled by
its fantasticality. How could Otis *know* he was being side-
lined? In any case, Otis gradually declined. If there was a
scientific explanation, Myers couldn't come up with it or
provide an antidote. It wasn't for want of trying. Unlike
your father, I don't think Myers was such a bad vet—if he
lacked the bedside manner. Perhaps I'd developed a general
charity towards vets. Otis wasn't a young cat any more. Since
we'd acquired him as a kind of orphan, we'd never known
exactly how old he might be. Anyway, cats, it seems, for all
their nine lives, sometimes simply fade away.

And the plain truth is that, meanwhile, something wonderful was happening. Otis dwindled while I got bigger.

By the later stages of my pregnancy—by the spring of
1979—it was clear that Otis's condition was mortal: it was
only a matter of time. But I couldn't share your father's
heaviness of heart, his grief-in-readiness, yet again, for a cat.
Nor his remarkable ability, even if I was the mother-in-
readiness, to nurse Otis, tenderly and patiently, through all
his last frailties. If anyone could have saved Otis, I think
it was your father. I was inside some immune and happy
bubble—a bit like you. I was eight months gone when, in
early May, Otis died. It will sound heartless of me to say I
accepted his death dry-eyed, that I barely mourned, I who'd
once been abject at his mere absence, who'd wept just to
leave him at a cattery. I couldn't weep for his death.

I can think of him now, and my eyes go watery. I can

picture him now, as if *he* might be out there, too, his fur getting saturated in this rain. I can recall with an extra thud of my heart that little thud on our bed. But when he died there were no tears. I was full of *you*. How could I weep? It even seemed like a small forfeit to have paid to fortune. A cat.

It was your dad who wept—and you'll know he's capable of that. I'm not so sure that when he shed those tears at his father's funeral he wasn't remembering another ceremony at which he did the burying himself. Tears can work like that.

Will it help you at all, tomorrow, to imagine your father weeping for a cat?

He dug a large hole under the lilac tree. Apparently you remember that lilac at Davenport Road, or you do, Nick. It was a true, cat-sized grave. Your father expended great labour and care over it, a once-only job. He made sure it was deep enough so that Otis's bones would never be disturbed. For a while, as he dug, I thought his mood was simply workmanlike and practical: how to dispose efficiently of a cat. I remembered his snails.

Even your dad could see, if he didn't accept it as an explanation, that a death was being exchanged for a birth. It was May, the air was warm, the soil was yeasty, our little garden was bursting. On the other hand, it was your dad who, almost exactly a year before, had gone out on those mad patrols in the spring dawns, fearing then that Otis might already be a corpse.

There's no better way, perhaps, of absorbing and deflecting emotion—perhaps it's been so arranged—than to dig, to attack the earth with a spade. The lilac was in bloom. It seemed the right, the obvious spot. In my condition, of course, there was no way I was going to assist your dad with his excavating, but I stood there with him after he'd carried out Otis very gently, in some sacking, as if he still might be alive, and put him in his place. He shovelled earth back on top and patted it firmly down. It was only then, with nothing else to do except say, "Goodbye, Otis," that he leant on his spade and wept.

Your father, who is a scientist by training and has shown himself in recent years to have quite a canny head for business, is an emotional man. When we walked back from our lunch in St. James's Park, before he took that taxi, I half expected him to clasp me like some soldier leaving for the front. Perhaps he'll weep tomorrow and get very emotional indeed. Perhaps he'll go for scientific rigour. Perhaps he'll try to be businesslike. My father was a perpetual soft touch, soft as they come, at least to me—but he was that iron judge. We all have more than one creature inside us perhaps. And there are some moments in our lives that make us ripe for metamorphosis. Tomorrow you'll start a new life. And you'll have to choose between your fathers, if you see what I mean. You'll have to give judgement on who that man is.

I won't be the one on trial, but in any case I'm giving you now my testimony in advance. What would your judgement be of me? A bit of a vixen when it comes to it, a touch of my own mother, the seldom-sighted Fiona McKay? I think if your dad knew the truth, had all the facts of *my* behaviour before him, the twists and turns and mood-swings of that pivotal year before you were born, he might, in the end, just stoically shrug and say that it was all just biology working through me, it was just the old, eternal, ever-crafty maternal instinct, using me as its tool. What a good excuse.

But, anyway, what he'd also say, I know it, is: don't we have two beautiful kids?

We decided on no marker, no silly, cat-proportioned memorial. Just the lilac itself. In both our heads, perhaps, was the unavoidable funeral music, incongruous as the sound of waves in Herne Hill: "*Sit-ting on the dock of the bay . . .*"

We planted lily-of-the-valley and grape hyacinth over the grave. We were already thinking, perhaps, that *you* should never know. Otis belonged, firmly, to a world before you. But it seems, Nick, that you might have guessed. In any case, it occurs to me that, as a matter of simple, incontestable fact, you were *there*, both of you were there, even as we buried Otis. You were there, inside me. You couldn't see a thing, but both of you were undoubtedly present and in attendance at Otis's funeral.

Both of you. And that was simply the most wonderful, crowning fact of all, that had made me impervious to sorrow and tears, and would make even your father very soon forget his grief for Otis—as they say, if I wasn't quite ready yet to put it to the test, a mother's birth-pains are instantly forgotten once birth occurs.

If we'd ever doubted this thing that we'd done—I mean, that I'd done, with your father's assent and cooperation—if we'd ever questioned, even after the point of no return, the strange bypassing path we'd taken, then didn't nature, in the end, simply reward and approve and exonerate and congratulate us? Nature—and science. Including that wonderful and still young then science of sonography, which enabled us to *see you,* even before you were "there," even before that day by the lilac tree.

If we'd had no doubts at all, there still might have been an awkward follow-up. Suppose all went well and, yes, we acquired a child. Then suppose we wanted *another one.* What exactly would have been the procedure then? To go back and ask for the same "Mr. S.," to ask him to oblige once again? But that delicate question would never require an answer, and all doubts, quandaries and compunctions were resolved. One November day we both looked at a strange, blurry, magical screen and saw two little pulsating blobs. Forgive me, but the image stuck: two little floating shrimps. The whole complete and entrancing set all in one go and, as it proved, a boy and a girl. A nuclear family. Twins.

27

GEMINI. On the tenth of June, 1979. And, as we have told you, without any fraudulent invention, at more or less two in the morning. Something we certainly couldn't specify, but it was what we got. What an extraordinary, world-transforming little word it suddenly seemed to be: two.

And how did your father feel, even months before—when he looked with me at that wobbly screen? Doubly excluded, doubly dismissed? It's important for you to know, it's of the utmost relevance for tomorrow. I was there—I had to be—to see you for the first time, but I also looked at your father. And what I saw, for the first time, was that it was *real* for him. Whatever he may have expected, whatever reactions he may even have prepared, he was smitten from that moment on, as smitten as I was, by you. Quite simply, I saw your father swoon, I saw him tip into love all over again—excuse me for saying so, but I think I could recognise the spectacle. I could almost see the train of thought in his head. Not his? No—not really? Mine, certainly. But none of that was the point. Ours, *ours*.

A strange, rather chilly contraption (but thank heaven for it) was resting on my belly and I was trying to keep as still as possible, but I wondered if the rush of emotion passing through me, and, for all I know, through you, was making that little screen wobble and judder—"dance" perhaps I mean—so much the more.

On the way back in the car I was genuinely worried your dad's mind might not be on the road. "Mikey, the lights have turned green."

Truly, we'd never supposed, in all our suppositions and imaginings, that you might be two—if I can put it like that. Was that thoroughly short-sighted of us? In all our calculations, and how absurd it seems, we'd used only basic arithmetic, we'd never got beyond the simple addition of one. But for sixteen years now, whatever else they may amount to, we've been living in the binary system. This strange equilibrium: a family of two couples. There's always been that bond and that division between us. I don't honestly know how it will affect tomorrow. Suppose there were just one of you now to inform. Poor thing. Suppose there were two of you, but with the usual sort of gap. How would that have affected our sixteenth-birthday principle?

You'll sit side by side on the sofa. You'll have each other.

And as for your twinness in itself: I bow to it. I don't pretend to fathom it, even if I am your mother. You're well aware by now that your parents, this other couple here, consist of two "onlies." A completely different route into life, a completely different grounding. When we first knew you were two, we had only the usual jumble of uneducated notions. We know a bit more now. But in sixteen years of being the mother of twins and of observing you even more closely perhaps than the average mother, I can't say I've got beyond the conclusion that only twins themselves know what it's like.

They say you're a race apart, a separate lore. You're not like the rest of us, either in your dealings with the world or in your dealings with each other. Do you think that's all hokum? A special understanding surely gets formed in that double confinement in the womb. It's not, at least, like the standard experience when there's only room for one and our arrival on the scene is a big, bawling solo act. Me! Me! Me!

They say you're less selfish, you've learnt to share. They say you're the opposite: you're selfishness times two. There's nothing you won't do for each other in the eternal struggle with non-twins. Or, then again, behind your interchangeable smiles (but I've never thought your smiles were identical), you're really at war with each other: sibling rivalry without limits.

We've seen you slip in and out of almost every version, every interpretation of twinness, play it up, play it down, play against it. Oh you know how to perform. But the truth is, and you both must know it, you were living proof of the harmony principle. You tug against each other now, as if you know that life, for you, will mean the difficult art of separation, but underneath there's still that sweet solidarity, that glue that you came with. Will tomorrow just bring you together again? Bind you? Thwart you? Delay you?

Nick and Kate; two little balancing sounds. We just liked them. It works the longer way too: Nicholas and Katherine. Apart from that wonderful wobbly image on the screen,

I've always had the picture in my head of a seesaw. Nick-and-Kate, Nick-and-Kate, a seesaw, your two monosyllables riding up and down. A seesaw can be a grim confrontation: one can give the other a hell of a ride. Or it can be an instrument of swaying delight. And that's how it's mostly been, with the occasional rhythmic agitation: swaying delight—in you yourselves, and swaying delight in us, your almost jealous beholders.

What had we done to deserve you? But we knew *exactly* what we'd done or, in Mike's case, not done. Was it in some weird way *because* of that? Or was the trick of it that you were boy and girl? It's only with boy-twins or girl-twins that the trouble starts? But a boy and girl born together is like a perfect piece of matchmaking. You even used to say (deny it though you will) that you wanted to marry. So in that way too you took after your parents. A seesaw for four—boy-girl, boy-girl—that's rocked and swayed away for sixteen years.

And that little discrepancy between you only seemed to enhance the balance. Even with twins, there's priority—one of you had to be born first. And that was you, Kate, by a length. It's known among the four of us, but it's stamped upon you anyway: that edge, that lead you've always had. But I never saw it as the sign of some race between you—quite the opposite, in fact.

It's absurd, when I was *there*, trying my utmost (I assure you) to make the whole astonishing thing happen, that I sometimes picture your birth as if I had nothing to do with it. All your own mutual work. As if you were in some hidey-hole together, waiting your chance, two would-be escapers, and it was you, Kate, who had the courage to poke your head out first and see if all was clear. And the first thing you did was not to make your own quick, brave bolt for it, but to turn back and reach out your hand: "Come on, Nick. It's okay. Let's go!"

At two o'clock in the morning, in these small hours, sixteen years ago. I wouldn't have known if it was raining then, the weather was my last concern.

You helped your brother into the world, Kate. Isn't that the truth of it? And that's meant something that I could never have foreseen and that's occasionally upset the happy motion of the seesaw, if it's also added, strangely, to its balance. We recognise it between us, I think, don't we, if it's never been uttered? That you and I are rival mothers, so far as Nick is concerned. If you both have rival fathers—who will be introduced to you, so to speak, tomorrow—Nick has always had his rival mums.

I think that little pucker was really in his brow at birth, Kate, don't you? Help me! Wait for me! But since both your faces were such a mass of puckers and creases at that time, I can never be sure. Two little shrimps? Two little livid dumplings! "His father's frown"—that's how we say it, that way round. But why shouldn't we just as well say of a father, why shouldn't it be just as natural: "Oh, he has his son's way of knotting his brow?"

Your lungs announced their presence, Nick, seven minutes after your sister. I think your father also gasped.

What will happen tomorrow? But what's the worst fear of any parent anyway? It starts in the delivery suite. Don't mix them up with *anyone else's*. Having got you, and in such an elaborate way, how frightened we were of losing you. I'm not thinking now, at all, of tomorrow. Of losing you *anyway*. Your precious little arrived-together selves. Someone should have told us about this perfectly normal parental terror. But didn't having it prove that we *were* normal parents?

You can't have the one thing (or indeed the two) without the other, the possession without the dread: it's the fundamental contract. Don't think for one moment that our peculiar contract in any way diminished that. And don't doubt when you learn what you'll learn tomorrow that there's ever been any difference in that respect between the two of us. *We*'re perfect twins, that way, too. Both of us, either of us would lay down our lives in an instant if it meant not losing either or both of you.

But you know this. You've even borne witness to it— or almost. You know, of course, what I'm coming to. What shocked me and paralysed me, that terrible day in Cornwall—what added, I mean, to my multiple shock, panic, terror, utter distraction—was your father's own terrifying insistence. He *screamed* it at me, he *ordered* me: "No! Me! Wait there!" As if, amid everything else, he saw this as his moment of opportunity.

He was the stronger, of course, but I was the better swimmer. He knew this: he'd seen me at Craiginish, he'd seen me in Brighton. He'd seen me, for goodness' sake, right there in Cornwall. But he dived in almost at the same time as he let out that yell to me. How was he to know that that current that was pulling you out and away from the rocks wouldn't be as defeating for an adult as for your own nine-year-old frames?

It swept him out to you quickly enough at least. To *both* of you. I'd already, for the second time in my life, taken overpowering and indelible note of your both-ness. That is, that you were being drawn away from dry land by some force that neither of you could resist and you, Nick, even less than your sister, but you weren't going to be separated from each other. Your two bobbing heads, like linked, swirling buoys—another image of you that's with me for ever.

Mike moved rapidly towards you, almost too rapidly. I could only see the back of his own bobbing head. I had the unthinkable thought that in the next few gliding moments you would *all* be lost, all pulled away from me, all that mattered to me, and I would have to watch. I saw myself standing alone on bare rock, wishing to turn to rock myself.

Everything in my memory of that day is like some evil blend of the benign and the horrific. It was a beautiful day, it was hot, it was more like a day in the Mediterranean than in Cornwall. It was the third summer we'd spent by that little safe, sandy cove and we thought we could trust you now if you scampered off a bit further. You'd learnt to swim two years before. You were good and confident at it, like me. The sea was blue and wallowy and lazy, the tide was coming in. On the other side of the headland, when we got there, there was a touch of breeze and a bit of swell and slap to the waves, but no one would have called that sea dangerous.

There were other happy people on the beach. The two of us had been swimming not so long before and we were lying, drying, becoming sweetly drowsy. It sends a terror through me, even now, that we might have just fallen asleep. But we both had the sudden simultaneous alarm: *where are they?* It makes me quiver still—I can't explain our decision— that we might have gone in the *other* direction first.

Even as I stood there, looking at the three of you, about to leave me, I had the mocking, the split-second dream of a thought: that this would be a nice spot to be in, just to stand here or to sit, on this warm, basking shelf of rock, with these beautiful dark-blue waves now and then sending up pleasing spouts of spray, with the cliffs and the blue sky and the whole hazy, summery coastline curving away. I think I even saw myself flipped safely, inviolately back: a girl again, aged nine myself, on the beach at Craiginish, where none of this could possibly be happening.

But I saw something wonderful enough. I saw your father reach you, and I saw some commotion between you: sounds, words that I couldn't hear. Perhaps he just barked at you too. But I saw that your father was sizing up the situation, he wasn't just *struggling*. I saw—oh God, this was the vital, the crucial factor—that when he turned, the current was only of infant-threatening significance, he could make his way, with effort, against it. On the other hand, he had to make his way with the two of you.

The wonderful thing is that you acted, all of you, like a team. That is, you took decisions, you made pacts among yourselves, all of which might have been risky, but which turned out in every case to be the right ones. It was almost as if you'd practised it. He couldn't ferry you *both* in, that might have been disastrous. It had to be Nick first, and that meant that you, Kate (I won't forget it), had to put yourself at lonely, terrible risk. It stopped me being too angry later. How brave you were, how on your own. I could see there was not much more you could do than hold your own against the current, perhaps make the very tiniest headway. You were thinking of the distance your father would have to cover a second time: you were losing strength and you had to think of how it might be used or wasted.

Meanwhile *your* strength, Nick, as your dad towed you in, had almost vanished. I still see your white, drained face, lolling against the blue. Somehow you managed to hang on to his shoulder and kick a bit yourself, while he managed to swim, with one arm and your weight, and still outswim the current.

Please don't let go, Nick. And please don't drown your dad.

He got you to a low ledge of rock, where I was waiting for you. You were already like some piece of limp delivered cargo. He was thinking of Kate. He spluttered out, in that same uncontradictable voice, "Wrists! Quick! Pull!"—the last word almost lost in a watery glug. With a strength I never knew I had I got you by both wrists and pulled you out before the downward suck of the wave made you twice as heavy. But I think, even if it had, I would have *made* you unheavy. I would have *made* you eject. Up you shot anyway, like a cork from a bottle, into my arms, and I screamed at you, with your dad's fierce force, "Breathe, Nick! Breathe!" I don't think you needed telling.

On the way up, you scraped your knee against the rock (you complained like crazy later). Blood ran down your shin. It didn't matter. Blood was good, it was somehow very good. On your way up too, I noticed, with another strange little intensity of mere observation, that under the lip of the ledge, just beneath the glinting waterline, there were clusters of barnacles, little clenched, packed shells, tresses and twirls of swaying seaweed, a whole world of gripping life.

Mike was already swimming out again. When I could look, I saw that you, Kate, had hardly anything left now, but you managed to hold on to your father in a slightly more efficient way than Nick. And Mike said later that on that second journey back, even in the moments (but they seemed like hours) that had passed, the current had actually lessened. It must have been some trick of just that stage of the tide. And that was just as well. It was a longer journey this time: your dad's strength was going. But there was a point when I *knew*, even before it had actually quite happened, like a sudden flooding current itself, fighting back a dreadful anti-current of "ifs" and "might have beens" and eternal anguish for ever after, that my wonderful and adorable family, my incomparable family, every precious member of it, was going to be restored to me. It would be there at the end of this summer's day, just as it had been at the start.

There we were on that warm slab of firm rock, like miniature people on some giant's dry, magic, outspread palm. Or rather, there were the three of us. Your dad was still clinging to its edge, still in the water, too exhausted yet to heave himself out, breathing furiously, his wet forearms clear, his head bowed, not even looking at us. What was he thinking?

28

YOU WERE NINE years old. You were too young then to understand that the great wave of anger that heaved up inside me, like nausea, only moments later wasn't what it seemed. It was its opposite. It was a venting, it wasn't a punishing. Punish you? For being *saved*?

"What on earth were you *doing*?! Just what were you *doing*?!"

I surprised even myself, I surprised Mike, with my uncontrollable rage. And you were too young not to think that that current itself hadn't been like some punishment prepared specially for you—never mind your mother's fury. But you didn't have to confess, Kate, to the extent that you did. You might just have said it had been a dare, an adventure, to swim back round the headland, and it had all gone wrong. And, yes, you should never have gone off like that out of sight in the first place.

You didn't have the art yet of concealment. We'd been practising it for nine whole years. It all poured out of you, like water might so nearly have poured that day out of your lifeless lungs. And *you* did all the confessing. Nick was silent. So was Mike. He'd got himself out now and was sitting hunched and exhausted and (I noticed) shaking just a little.

He might have been another guilty party. It had all been your idea, your fault, you said. Nick had just tagged along. Oh Kate. And I'd just seen you swimming frantically round your brother like a duck round a distressed duckling.

And it had all been *about* concealment. You'd wanted to hide. You'd found a little cave, you said, a cranny at the end of that channel between the rocks—you even pointed, as if the cave itself might have been to blame—just big enough for the two of you and just reachable by scrambling down on foot and wading through what was then just a long, safe pool. And you'd got the idea—*your* idea—of just sitting there and waiting, till you saw us coming over the rocks, looking for you and calling. When, of course, you'd burst out and surprise us. Woo-hoo! Here we are!

We hadn't come. You'd waited. We weren't cooperating, it seemed, in your game of hide and seek. And you hadn't reckoned on how quickly the tide would turn and how the waves would start to run in along the pool and to fill the cave itself. You couldn't stay where you were, but you couldn't get back now onto the steep rocks you'd come down by. The only thing was to swim for it, to go further out along the headland where the rocks were flat (to where we were standing, and I was glowering at you, right then). But there was that unexpected current.

Then the pretend-thing had turned real. This is the bit you didn't have to say. That it wasn't just a game. You'd *wanted* us to think, if only for a while, you were lost, you were gone. You'd wanted to see and hear our panic—"Nick! Kate!"—to measure it. How *long* before we came? That's why you'd stayed so long yourselves, too long, in that cave.

Right then and there on that sunny, happy, warm plate of rock I could have hit you, Kate. It was the nearest I've ever got, and I think you saw it, to a full-blooded, maternal, non-maternal clout. You'd wanted to *test* us, our love, how much we cared, how much you mattered to us. Suppose, you'd thought, they were suddenly without us, suppose we weren't here any more. How would they look? How would they behave?

Well, now you knew. The results of your experiment. Look at your mother, on the point of hitting you, with all the force of her love. Look at your dad there, who's just saved your lives, his face a strange picture of misery.

You started to splutter, the full-scale, bleating confession, though you didn't have to say it. You could have just said you were sorry, and that you were glad, incidentally, to be alive. Suppose we'd decided to go that other way first?

And yet I *admired* you, Kate. I was even in awe of you, even as you blubbed and I wanted to hit you. There was so much else that you *didn't* say. Am I wrong? That it would have been you, whether it was your fault or not, who would have made that last-minute decision, while the water gushed in and Nick panicked or just froze. "Come on! Let's go!" Your little wriggling bodies launching out, breasting the waves, yours just that fraction ahead.

And just a few moments later—am I wrong?—it would have been you who made another, terrifying decision: that you weren't going to leave your brother, even though it might still have been in your power. Even as we came over the crest of the rocks and saw your two bobbing heads (They're there! It's all right! No, it's not!), *that* had already become the most important thing. I saw it, Mike saw it, though it's never been spoken of between us. You already knew that you wouldn't make it, not the *two* of you. Your only task now was to make Nick believe that you would and, when the moment came, to go down with him.

And I know for certain too, Nick, that if it had turned out the other way round, if you'd suddenly found a boy's strength that your sister didn't have, it would have been just the same, you'd have gone down with her. She'd have led, you'd have followed.

I didn't hit you, Kate, I hugged you. You must have seen my anger drop from me like something dropping through water. I hugged you so tightly that you must have thought, after nearly being drowned, that now your mum was going to smother you.

Among all the "what-ifs" of that day, there's one that's even more unthinkable than all the others, that's even more unthinkable—can it even be said?—than the thought that we might have lost you both. That we might have lost, Mike might have saved, just one of you. That there might have been, even now, even on this night, Nick without Kate, or Kate without Nick.

This family would have had its irretrievable history.

I'm only your mother. What do I know about how it really works between you? You're a mystery, you're a joy, you're an anguish. Is it a blessing or a curse being what you are: wedded, if that's how it is, from birth? You have it easy, you have it made? You won't ever need to find, either of you, that other one in life who'll make you complete? Or being what you are will just make it harder? You're a little afraid, even now, of beginning? None of those *other* ones will ever be good enough or come as close. You'll never have your Brighton beach.

You've known from the start the cruel rule of coupledom: one day there has to be only one. But *that* day, at least, you would have defied it.

I'm afraid that tomorrow's only going to pull you back to that day. Not that you will ever get away from it. I'm afraid that tomorrow's only going to be like that invisible rope already being stretched and strained between you (who's going to cut it first?) but which then might have pulled you swiftly, surely, one after the other, under those waves.

At Grandpa Pete's funeral you must have had your teenage pangs, so far as it's possible, for Grannie Helen. Poor Grannie Helen. And then, perhaps, a premonitory pang for Mike and me: one day, one of them too. And then, perhaps, with that day in Cornwall behind you, a pang, a double pang, for yourselves.

Your first taste of death? Of course it wasn't. You carried yourselves with such dignity, such seeming seasonedness and wisdom. Look, Dad's trying not to cry, Mum's holding his arm. A cold clamminess hung over the churchyard. Every tree dripped. An early frost had melted to a sticky dew, the grass under our feet was wet and chewed. A day like cattle's breath. The tops of the Downs, where Grandpa Pete had died, were hidden in a sort of steam.

I gripped your father's arm, remembering his hand on my arm at Invercullen. If Grannie Helen had broken down and wept then I'd have had to yield, to step aside, to be the tactful, deferring daughter-in-law. But it was your dad who wept. Grannie Helen stood dry-eyed on that sopping grass. And I'd had the sudden thought (since *that* secret was out now): she's standing where one day she'll *be*. And then I'd had the extra thought, coming from nowhere: are there graveyards, are there instances (I suppose there must be) where twins get laid side by side?

With twins it's somehow insupportable, as if the second heart must simply stop beating too.

I fear for you sometimes. I fear for your future. Your future? Your futures? I don't even know which is best to say. I want each one of you to have, to know something at least as good as Mike and I have known. And still know. Is your mother just becoming a heavy mother—a clinging, burdensome, smothering mother? Well, your dad, you'll soon discover, could hardly be lighter, or more disengaged.

I think you're still a virgin, Kate, and I think your brother won't make a move before you do. What's new in that? But then, for all I really know, each of you may already have had your string of episodes, you may even compare notes frankly with each other. I'm seldom around at what must be the witching hour, immediately after school, and perhaps you find it inconvenient these days that your dad sometimes is—working at home in his study. But then again, perhaps for each of you it's the other one's presence that's the real, inhibiting factor. Compare notes? Hardly.

In any case, I've been looking for the telltale signs and I don't think either of you yet has some special friend, some really special friend, to whom you might just go and blab everything you're about to learn. Or find it hard not to. Perhaps Mike and I should be grateful. You're late and cautious beginners, it seems, for whatever reason. Though tomorrow, for all we know, may deliver you a pretty hefty kick-start. If your mum could do it with a test tube—what's keeping you?

I fear for both of you. Mothers fret and wonder and lie awake at three in the morning. Tell me I'm foolish. I fear for you in ways that have nothing to do with tomorrow. As if tomorrow won't be enough for you, anyway, to be getting on with.

29

YOUR DAD'S TURNING in his sleep. Don't wake yet, Mikey, not yet. For a little while yet he can still be that: "your dad." He's snuffling softly like some rooting animal. How I want to hold him tight, but I'm afraid to wake him. In a few hours he'll be in your hands. I'll have to hand him over to you.

And it'll be up to you then what you call him. It seems to me that he's going to speak to you, one last time, more like a father than he's ever done, a big, stern, serious daddy. Listen to your father, he's got something important to say. And then he'll be nobody, he'll be what you make of him. If you want, you can even tell him to leave.

But I hope you know that if he goes, I go too. That's how it is. I'm your mother, he's not your father, but we go together anyway, just as surely as the two of you. Have I made that clear? When push comes to shove, that's how it is. I'm your mother, but you're sixteen now, and how much longer will you even need me around? That indefatigable maternal instinct eventually found its way from me to you, but I'm not sure if biology rules. Is that heresy? Your dad was never your biological father. That disqualifies him? How many real fathers are qualified biologists?

Tomorrow—if you decide in his favour—you'll agree to *make* him, artificially, your father, as we once agreed to make you artificially (according to that ugly phrase) our children. But then, you'll quickly discover, the artifice doesn't stop there. It's not just the truth you'll be getting tomorrow, it's that whole issue of pretence.

That little side-question of *next* weekend, of the Gifford Park Hotel, to let us go or not, will seem small stuff in comparison. Though I've already imagined how it might be—should it work this way—your neat means of revenge. Forgive me. I see you, *next* Saturday morning, after a remarkably calm and uncatastrophic week (but one in which you've had time to plan), standing at the front door to wave us off on our silver weekend—with all the ceremonial good grace, in fact, that you displayed at Grandpa Pete's funeral. I even imagine Mike and I feeling for a moment like the spoilt (but humbled) children, while you stand there like the magnanimous householders of 14 Rutherford Road.

Except that when we come back next Sunday evening, you'll have gone. The house will be ransacked, wrecked. Could you be so cunning? Pretence and dissimulation all round. My little pretence with your father in a five-star hotel, in a four-poster bed in Sussex will have been the least of my worries.

But that larger dissimulation—assuming we *are* all here, one way or another, under this roof after next weekend—where does it stop? Think about it. Your dad's right, you might need next weekend just to think. We might have told Grandpa Pete and Grannie Helen, years ago—think about it—and, of course, that would have been honest. But it would have robbed them, if you see what I mean, of two little grandchildren and burdened them with a share in our dishonesty. Now you'll have to decide whether to be honest or not.

Children are brought up not to tell lies. Were we ever so big on that with you? Consider one little mitigating factor, at least. Everyone else's ignorance—and surprising credulity—only made it easier to perpetrate the lie. Everyone else's unwitting collusion only made it easier for us to feel (have a little mercy) that the lie might be the truth.

The rain's getting harder, I think. You'll have the option—the perfect right—if you wish, to tell the whole world. Starting on Monday, with all your friends at school. Though why wait till then? A few phone calls tomorrow afternoon. Pass it around. We're in no position to stop you. Think what ripples you could set in motion in just a few moments, after sixteen years. But at least consider how far those ripples could spread, and that you won't be able, should you feel like it later, to turn them around.

Here's a thought for you that you may not even have this weekend or for some time to come, but I've certainly thought it for you. Suppose, one day, *you* have children. I mean (enough of that old childhood joke) that *each* of you or either of you one day has children. Will you be happy for them to think that this man lying here is their grandfather? If he isn't, who is? Will that be a simple decision for you, hardly needing a moment's thought, or will you think that one day, when *they've* grown up, they'll need to know? That they'll have to be told a story too, like the one I'm telling you now, involving, of course, a rainy weekend in June, once upon a time when you were sixteen?

Grandpa Mikey! Spare us, the poor man's only fifty. He doesn't look like a grandpa to me. But that's not the point. It goes off into the future, you see. And it begs the simple question: *will* you, one day, have children—each of you, either of you—of your own? I don't suppose that's even a flicker of a question in your heads yet. But it's one of the things you may suddenly find yourselves, as from tomorrow, having to think about intently: that line going off into the future, with more little Hooks on it, perhaps.

And that only begs another, bigger question, which may simply swallow up the first. Why have children at all? Clearly, I must have asked myself that big question once, and once I must have come up with an answer which, as you now know, lasted only so long. Life was possible without them. Without *you* two though—now that's a different matter.

But then I don't remember, even to bolster my rather peculiar position, ever putting the question like this: why bring children into the world? Is it such a good, safe world to bring them into? Is it going to be? I don't remember Mike employing that argument either, though for him it must have been an even more tempting fall-back. Was it such a sweet, safe world then, in 1972, when Doctor Chivers gave him the news? I was afraid for *our* future perhaps, not the world's.

Your dad likes to joke these days, when he can afford to, that it ought to be called *The Perishing World.* The magazine,

I mean, though the same is true of the books. More and more of its pages seem to deal with declines and depletions, not to say outright extinctions, things going wrong with nature, harm being done to it, disasters in store. There even seems to be a readership that relishes this dire-warning stuff. Though there's also still a dependable readership that, as your dad puts it, just wants to know about frogs.

The bulk of Living World Books are still just "nature books": lovely to look at, brightly designed, modern-day equivalents of Uncle Edward's book of molluscs. Your dad sometimes worries about this. It's a sort of thorn in the side that he seems to need. He worries about the "just nature" books. He worries that the "just nature" stuff is really heads-in-the-sand stuff, it's not even good science. Those dire warnings aren't made up, the planet's in serious trouble. I think he worries about being a "just nature" man himself. Still running around Sussex in short trousers, not even knowing about the existence of DNA. Or me.

But look at your mother. The planet's in serious trouble, and she's still dealing in art. Part of her's still in the Renaissance.

Was it a better world in 1972 when, as you now know, you were never really on the cards at all? Perhaps you've sometimes thought that, like your parents, you were pretty well timed, two little cold-war babies, emerging, just when you were ready to emerge, into a world that was no longer cold: a happier, sweeter climate all round. Now, just a few years on, it's not looking so good. We're even told the climate's getting too warm.

Your futures? Your future? What will the world be like in just five years' time, in the year 2000, when you'll be twenty-one? What will it be like in another sixteen, when you're thirty-two, the same age I was when I decided to become a mother? What will it be like when *you're* fifty, your dad's age? You won't thank me for sometimes being prey to this sort of arithmetic (especially tonight), or for sometimes concluding that your dad and I, born neatly in 1945, may have been set down in the *best slot history has ever put on offer.* But maybe every generation thinks that.

The planet's in serious trouble? It's 1995, a millennium's ending, we're all about to go over the edge? I don't know if the planet's in serious trouble, listening to this rain doing the garden good. I think number fourteen Rutherford Road might be in serious trouble. These might be just the early hours of Doomsday. Is that what we'll call it when we look back? "Doomsday." "Bombshell Day?" Will it just find its regular place, one day, in our calendar, in our private annals? *That* day, that day in June. We'll refer to it frankly and calmly—though, of course, just among ourselves—with a touch of respect and solidarity, even a touch of humour. "Bombshell Day," as a joke, because no bomb, really, ever went off. "Doomsday," because it wasn't the end of the world, just a wet Saturday in June. Another special day, a week after your birthday, that every year will be discreetly but smilingly observed?

I see everything in this house in just a few hours' time looking the same as it always was. I see everything—every item, every picture on the wall, every little memento, every

gathered-together token of our good life and good fortune—
looking hollow and false. But then none of that stuff (as you
so sensitively call it) would matter anyway, believe us, not in
the balance with you. I've told Mike so many times that,
surely, I must believe it myself: that he has nothing to fear,
not about the fundamental thing. "Have they had any better
dad?" (Well, *have* you?) So many times that I must have
finally convinced him. Look at him here, sound asleep. But
in any case you must simply believe me that your dad, who
in recent years—whatever he gets called tomorrow—has
taken on the unexpected sobriquet "Mr. Living World,"
would gladly give up everything, would give the living
world, if you could *really* be his.

If it wasn't for this rain, I think by now there'd be the first
streaks of light. It's no longer pattering and trickling. It's
started to beat down as if from some motionless, massing
cloud. Centred on Putney. Just a wet Saturday in June, or
time to build an ark?

Among all the possessions and artworks in this house is,
still, if you don't know it, a small and precious selection of
the paintings you both did at primary school when you were
six or seven. They're in that special box of mine. But they
would have been displayed once, if you remember, on our
kitchen wall. For a period of your life there was a constantly
changing show. You knew then, just about, that I worked
with "art," I bought and sold pictures, and when your pictures got taken down to be replaced by your latest produc-
tions, you used to think I went off and sold them. You were
nobly contributing to your mother's livelihood. You never
enquired further and never seemed to mind that you weren't

getting a percentage of your own. What a grasping dealer your mother was. But I didn't throw them all away, you'll be pleased to know, I kept some of the best. And if I'd had to give a top prize, there's little doubt I'd have given it to your Noah's Arks.

There was a strict kitchen-gallery policy of not favouring one of you over the other, and I'd never have let on anyway, even with my professional eye, which one of you I thought was the better watercolourist (though, actually, I think it was you, Nick, one way in which you could pip your sister). But since you both went to the same primary school and were in the same class, you both very often painted the same subject. There was equality, at least, in that.

Noah's Ark must be a sure winner, anyway, the all-time favourite for primary-school painting sessions. Is there a child who's never been asked? A rainy afternoon in the class-room, the lights are on, out come the paints. The teacher tells the story first, then the brushes get to work. For both of *you*, of course, it was that memorable phrase "two by two" that struck an inspirational chord. The animals went in two by two and they did so, you were given to understand, so that the world would be saved. Whether or not you knew what that really meant, you clearly thought that being what you were meant your own salvation was guaranteed. In those days you used to get called "the Hook twins," something you'd loathe now.

But there was clearly also some confusion in your minds as to whether the Ark and the Flood were things that *had* happened or that might or would. This was shown by the fact that both of you, with connivance or not, included yourselves among the elephants, camels, inevitable towering giraffes and, in your case, Nick, a couple of surprising (since they can swim) but really rather charming polar bears.

But there, in both cases, are both of you. You're not readily recognisable, but Kate's the one with the longer hair and the stiffly triangular skirt. Your place on Noah's Ark has been emphatically reserved. In fact, in both cases again, neither Noah or his wife are visible at all and it rather looks as though the two of you have assumed those venerable roles and are not just among the lucky passengers, but have taken charge of the ship.

We didn't flummox you by asking if there was a chance your dad and I might be saved too and be given our place on board, and you were too young for the joke that it was your dad, surely, who ought to be Noah, being in command as he already was of *The Living World*. But those pictures certainly got saved. They're in this house now, in my box. Remarkable thick blue ribbons of rain fall down in each of them, though in your case, Nick, out of a convincing enough thundery-black sky. And that box, you'll now understand, with its hoard of items, a surprising number of which are in sets of two, has come to seem itself like a miniature ark, waiting for some particularly rainy day.

30

BUT I THINK I can really see it now, round the edges of the curtains, the first grey hint of light. It's today now, not tomorrow, I can't pretend any more: the first day of your second life.

Your dad told me once about a time when Grannie Helen told him about the time before he was born. Here I am, doing the same for the two of you. But I know, Kate, that only last Christmas he told you about that very same thing, about another Christmas long ago when his mother had talked to him. And you must have worked out that he was talking about the year he and I first met, that year when, as far as I'm concerned, *my* second life began. It was another little piece, perhaps, in that jigsaw you'd tried to put together ever since I told you about the word "propose." Though perhaps you'd long stopped caring about seeing the whole picture, and you no longer had a little girl's notion that something similar (even with Nick) ought to happen to you.

But you would have worked out that he was talking about Christmas 1966. Maybe he just told you anyway, made a thing of it, even: "It was the year your mother and I first met."

He was at home for Christmas, in Orpington. I was in Kensington. By then, I would have met your dad's parents only a couple of times and that business of the sand dune was definitely just a secret between Mike and me. But I think his mum knew. Not about the sand dune, I mean. I think she knew that Mike and I weren't a temporary thing. Mothers can tell things. She'd have known too, without needing to know any details, that the way Mike and I had got together was a lot different from the way she and Grandpa Pete had once set out to share their lives. It was 1966, it was a different world. She probably even thought: kids, these days, they have it on a plate. But anyway she decided to tell Mike—and he decided to tell you, Kate, all those Christmases later—about that time when his dad wasn't around.

And, of course, he wasn't around then, last Christmas. The first Christmas without him and the first anniversary coming up, in January, not to mention your dad's fiftieth barely a week later. A tricky time of year all round. Your dad said to you, "Come on, Katesy, let's do the washing-up." Or rather he whispered it. Grannie Helen had fallen asleep. Perhaps she was dreaming of Grandpa Pete. But there was something in his voice, in that whisper, I don't know if you felt it too, that was the same as if he might have said, "Let's have a private word, Kate, let's have a heart-to-heart."

And I had one of those wobbly moments. You know what I mean now. I thought he might be going to *tell you*, to jump the gun, so to speak, and, for some reason, over the washing-up and, for some reason, just you and not Nick. It was a sign of how edgy things were (it was "next year" now, after all, and next year was close) that I could actually have thought this. It would have been a strange way of going about it. The truth is, ever since Grandpa Pete's death, part of me had been on alert. I thought your dad might just blurt it now, any time.

It turned out he just wanted to remember that other Christmas with you. Though, come tomorrow, Kate, you may think, looking back, that he'd been nudging pretty close to the other thing. It was a little preparation.

Back in 1966, it had been Grandpa Pete who'd fallen asleep, full of Christmas dinner, by the fire. And it was Grannie Helen, as you know, Kate, who'd said to him then, not let's do the washing-up, but let's go for a walk, while your dad sleeps it off. The strange thing is that last Christmas I said almost exactly the same to you, Nick. I said, "Well, if they're going to do the washing-up, let's take a walk round the block." It didn't occur to me I was echoing Grannie Helen. I was trying to put aside that feeling that Mike was about to do some blurting—surely not—but I was also simply thinking of Nelson.

We had that reason to take a walk too. The first Christmas after Grandpa Pete's death: it could hardly be at Coombe Cottage. Grannie Helen came to us, and that meant Nelson came too. And she was the one fast asleep now, in our living room. And, being fast asleep, she can't have known anything of what your dad was telling you, Kate, in the kitchen. But then I'm not so sure. She's a canny woman. She must have felt, when she walked round the block with Mike, all those years ago, that it was the right time to speak.

Anyway, she told him about yet another Christmas—Christmas 1944—when his dad hadn't been there because he was having Christmas in a prisoner-of-war camp. At least he wasn't just "missing" any more. Grannie Helen was spending Christmas at home in Dartford. And *your* dad wasn't there either—not quite. Or perhaps you could say that, in a way, he was. She was in her last month and he was keeping her company.

But what your grandmother really wanted to offer your father was a sort of apology. She'd kept it to herself long enough and she might have just gone on doing so, but Mike was twenty-one and that was another thing, perhaps, that had prodded her. He was the same age as his dad had been, back then. What she wanted to make clear was that when Mike was born and Grandpa Pete was still a prisoner, she'd never mentioned him to Mike. She'd never mentioned his own dad.

Of course, Mike was just a tiny baby, so what would he have understood? But then most mothers with a father missing like that who'd one day be coming home would have talked about him, perhaps quite a lot, to make up for his absence. They'd have talked him *up*. They'd have prattled on about him to this new little pair of ears, if only to keep their own spirits up. And who knows what even a tiny baby, by some instinctual process, might not have picked up?

But then what do I know about such a situation? Nobody could have known when Mike was born that the war would be over inside six months. Grandma Helen had taken another, tougher view of things. She didn't want to say anything to your dad that she might just find foolish and regrettable later. She didn't want to spin him some fairy-tale yarn—even if he didn't understand a word—that she'd only have to unspin. I'm a mother too, I can understand that. There's a way in which Grannie Helen and I see eye to eye. Though it doesn't stop me being afraid of her.

The fact is, though Grannie Helen knew that Grandpa Pete was alive and a prisoner, there was no guarantee that she'd see him again. I suppose that was only realistic, and I suppose you could say she'd been well trained in that way of thinking. The only training I've ever had in that sort of thing is when your dad gets up early in the morning (but not this morning, I think) and, just for a while, leaves that bit of empty, cooling sheet beside me.

But Grannie Helen would have got into a much sterner habit of guarding her feelings against the worst. When she'd first heard that Grandpa Pete had gone missing, she'd worked on the assumption that he was dead. That's what she told your dad. She wanted to say that too. She hadn't nursed fragile hopes. It sounded harsh, but there'd seemed less pain that way, she'd told him, in the long run.

If she hadn't had a child inside her, it might have been different. But this was one of the reasons, after all, why she—why they—had *wanted* that child inside her. It's just your mother's hunch, but I think it may have been one reason too why Mike remained an only child. Anyway, given that she *had* a child inside her, she had to be pretty practical and hard-headed.

All this she told your dad. She even told him that when she'd been pregnant and his dad was missing, she'd seriously considered finding someone else—to be Mike's daddy. It was only how a lot of women in such situations had had to think then, let alone the ones who actually *knew* their husbands were dead. In any case, now, after all these years, she wanted to say she was sorry. Sorry that she'd had to take that attitude and that she'd kept him in the dark, so to speak, even after he was born. Even if he was in the dark anyway.

Your dad told me that when his mum told him all this he'd had the fleeting thought that she'd actually *had* some other man lined up, as it were, or more than lined up, and this was what it was all building up to. But she'd read that thought and put him straight. She'd said, "Don't worry, Mikey, I wasn't planning on marrying your Uncle Eddie."

She just needed to apologise, it seemed, after all that time, just for the *thoughts* she'd had, as if even they had been a form of betrayal. Perhaps she was just glad—a little jealous, maybe—that things were so easy for Mike and me, lucky little war babies. Perhaps she just wanted to tell her son, in some sentimental Christmassy way, brought on by the fact that he seemed to have had this "steady girlfriend" now for most of a year (I don't know what she knew about all the other girlfriends), how much she loved his father, how much she'd once missed him and feared for him—the man who was sleeping right then, safe and sound in Orpington, his belly full, by a Christmas fire.

Perhaps, if you turn it round, it was all a kind of early training itself, if she didn't know it then—for when *she*'d be sleeping by a Christmas fire and Grandpa Pete would really have gone missing for good. Maybe that's what occurred to your dad, Kate, last Christmas.

Anyway, she told your dad that it wasn't until the war was

over and even a little while after that, that she dared to begin to tell him—and he may or may not have got the message—that, yes, he had a daddy, and, yes, he'd be coming home soon. Very soon now he was going to see him.

I don't know quite how much of this he actually passed on to you, Kate, what slant he might have put on it. He told me too, later, that he'd told you over the washing-up about that time with his mum, and I thought it best not to probe. But while he was talking to you, Nick and I were having our own little Christmas heart-to-heart.

You and me, Nick, and of course Nelson. Nelson could have been listening in, if he'd wanted to. What do dogs know? He didn't seemed to mind much that these were the streets of Putney, not the South Downs, or even to be thinking that there was something different and strange and sad about this Christmas. But I think *we* both had the same thought, Nick—that we were really taking Grandpa Pete for a walk.

Anyway, you suddenly said, looking at Nelson padding on ahead, "Did you and dad ever have a dog?"

And I said, "No." And then I took a few silent paces. Then I said, "But we used to have a cat."

And you said, after a bit of a pause too, "Yes, I know."

You can be a dark horse, Nick. You're not such a wary, cagey little brother these days.

"You *know*? But it was before you were born. It was at Davenport Road."

"Yes. There was a lilac tree there, wasn't there? Kate told me once that Dad had said there was a cat under the lilac, and she'd kept looking and she'd never seen it. She'd thought Dad was playing a game. Kate can be pretty dumb, can't she?"

"She can't have been more than three, Nick. I'm amazed she remembered."

"Yeah, but it was a real cat, right? It was a *dead* cat. You'd buried it under the lilac tree."

"You worked that out? When you were three?"

"Later. That's not the point. The thing is, why didn't you ever tell us? Why didn't you just tell us you'd had a cat?"

"I just have, Nick."

"Yeah, after all these years."

"Is it so important?"

I was holding your arm. The streets were deserted and curfew-quiet, as they only ever are at Christmas. Other people's fairy lights twinkled at us in the dark. For the first time in my life I thought: I'm a mother, leaning on my son.

"What was its name?" you said.

"Otis. He was called Otis."

Nelson padded on ahead.

"As in Otis Redding?"

"Yes, Nick. I'm surprised you've even heard of Otis Redding."

"I haven't heard of any other Otis. Till now. You and Dad had some thing about Otis Redding?"

"He was a lovely cat, Nick, a lovely black cat. He died the month before you and Kate were born. I think that's why we've never told you."

Your dad and Grandpa Pete always did the washing-up at Christmas, a tradition. They did it for the last time barely two weeks before Grandpa Pete died. It was the last father-and-son chat they ever had. You must have been thinking that, Kate, as Mike was talking to you.

I dare say Nick told you about Otis, though you've never brought it up. But I dare say that you remembered that thing about the lilac tree, and tomorrow—today—you'll be thinking: well, now that cat's finally jumped out.

But I don't know if Mike told you the last bit of what his mum said to him all those Christmases ago. Maybe not. Or maybe the turkey carcass, sitting there amid all the wreckage on the kitchen table, would only have prompted him. She'd said that even when she knew Grandpa Pete was coming back, even when he *did* come back, she'd thought it might have been a mistake, to have talked up the event beforehand.

The thing is, prisoners of war didn't just sit around in their camps cheerfully waiting to be liberated—any more than they all tried to escape. He'd been force-marched, in midwinter, along with thousands of others, a lot of whom died. Your Grandpa Pete had been at death's door for a while, in a hospital, still in Germany. So had Charlie Dean. They never talked about it. I think they helped each other survive.

And even when he was well enough to be returned home he was hardly like the man Grannie Helen had last seen over a year before. This was in late June 1945, almost exactly fifty years ago. What a crowded month June is. Grandpa Pete was just a shadow of himself. He was home at last, but as Grannie Helen put it to your father that Christmas in Orpington, "My God, Mikey, there wasn't much of him. He needed some feeding up. He was all skin and bone."

31

NOW YOU'RE ABOUT to learn he was never your grandfather anyway, something he never had to learn himself. You see how far the ripples can go? Back in those days when you were about to be born we had to play a little at being god. What will the world be like in sixteen years' time? It will be 1995. Pete and Helen will have turned seventy . . .

Once, over sixteen years ago, your dad had to make another big announcement that you could say was the opposite of the one he'll make today. Perhaps today you may even find yourselves wondering about it. He had to phone *his* mum and dad to give them a simple, happy message— and by then they must have been wondering if it was ever going to come. I was sitting listening while your dad made that call. He wanted me to be there. And Otis was there too, curled in my lap.

It follows, of course, that you were present too, if not exactly listening, though that call was very much about you. And Otis may already have known what else was in my lap, because though I was stroking him, he wasn't purring. There'd come a time soon when Otis would get very poorly and wouldn't sit in my lap at all. But you should know that though you never saw him, you were sometimes very close to Otis, very close indeed, close enough to have heard—if he'd been so inclined—his muffled purr.

But perhaps he wasn't purring that day because he was listening, like me, to what your dad was saying into the phone.

"Paula's pregnant" is what he said, the formula he chose. It wasn't a lie, and why not give all credit to the mother? But what your dad never said, to his own parents, as someone making such a call might very understandably have said, was: "I'm going to be a dad." Or: "You're going to be grandparents." He was very careful not to use—though he'd get to use them later, even without thinking—the words "grandparents" or "grandchildren."

This would have been in the autumn of 1978. It was a false call he was making, you could say, a fraudulent call, though not in fact, in any word I heard uttered, untruthful. And what you should certainly know is that when your dad was making it he was genuinely, plainly excited. No one at the other end would have had cause for doubt or suspicion, and why on earth should they? Does anyone say or even think after such an opening statement: "Oh—and who is the father?"

Your dad put on a remarkably convincing act, but at the same time it wasn't an act at all. It was like that moment when we first "saw" you. He didn't act then. The truth is that though I'd worried about how he would handle that phone call, when it came to it, I actually felt jealous. I mean I felt jealous that I'd never be able to make one like it myself.

Since it was Grandpa Pete who answered (and your Grannie Fiona was already lost in fairyland). The first words your dad said were, "Hello Dad." Your Grandpa Pete got the news first. Of course, sitting close by though I was, I couldn't hear his side of the conversation, let alone see how he reacted—my situation was a bit like yours with Otis—but I can definitely vouch that he was very excited too. He was not only taken by surprise by what his son had to say, he was also rather overcome. There was quite a long pause, in fact, in which I think I could detect, just as surely as Mike could with his ear pressed to the receiver, the sound of a man being changed into a grandfather. It's a distinctive sound, perhaps. It was as if Grandpa Pete, at the other end, had had to put down his receiver, turn around, take a few deep breaths, then come back as that transformed figure.

And that only made me doubly jealous. Although what I also felt was: well, that's really done it now, Mikey, no going back. That's the seal on it. You can hardly say now, "Actually—there's something you should know."

But the jealousy bit didn't stop there. Because some while later your dad had to make another call and then, too, it was Grandpa Pete who answered.

"I've got something else to tell you, Dad. Even better. Twins."

Then too he avoided the word "grandchildren." But I was doubly-doubly jealous.

When Grannie Helen first knew she was pregnant, neither she nor Grandpa Pete would have had any special reason to think: what will the world be like when our child's sixteen? What sort of world will it grow up into? Their world was pressing enough at the time—and could it get any worse? And when, just a little later, Grandpa Pete was shot down over Germany and taken prisoner, it must have been a comfort for him to know he had a child now on its way. It must have been quite something. And it must have meant a lot to him, if he had no idea when or if he'd see his home again, when the message at last got through to him in his prisoner-of-war camp, that his child had safely arrived and it was a son.

Perhaps during, or very soon after, that first phone call Mike made, Grandpa Pete would have shed a tear or two. Perhaps some pretty terrible memories would have flashed through his head. When he jumped from that burning plane he can't possibly have supposed that one day he'd send that unborn son of his, when *he*'d be twenty-one, a case of champagne, let alone that one day that same son would phone him to inform him, if not in so many words, that he was a grandfather. Biology's a strange thing (but ask your father), it squanders millions of sperm as if the numbers don't matter, but now and then, it seems, it can seize any single one of us and shake us to the core.

Now you'll know that those tears you saw your father shed at his father's funeral weren't the simple tears you thought they were, if tears for a father are ever that simple. Now you'll know that this man lying here is really the last of the Hooks, the very end of the line, the last of the Hooks of Sussex. Just as your Grandpa Dougie—your *real* grandfather—turned out to be, despite his three marriages, the last of the Campbells, or of his particular strand of them, a point he seemed eager to drive home at *his* funeral.

The last of the Hooks, the last of the Campbells. Does it really matter? The last of the Mohicans . . . It sounds all rather grand and heroic—and just a bit masculine, don't you think, Kate? The last dodo . . . The last coelacanth . . . When everything's done by cloning-to-order and genetic engineering, will it be the men who'll miss more keenly the old torch-passing stuff of fatherhood or women who'll miss the authentic taste of maternity?

It's light, it's really getting light.

"Uncle" Charlie and "Auntie" Grace were also at Grandpa Pete's funeral. You always knew, of course, they were never a *real* aunt or uncle. All the same, they had to be there. They'd flown in from Spain as soon as they'd got the news and, standing there with their tanned faces in that January churchyard, they looked like some holiday couple who'd somehow boarded the wrong flight.

When Charlie jumped out of that same burning plane in 1944 he can't have supposed, either, that one day, after a profitable career in light industry, he'd retire to a villa with a swimming pool near Málaga—the "Villa Sidcup" as he'd waggishly name it. But he must surely have been thinking as he stood there among those gravestones that *he* was the last one left now, the very last one of that old crew, the crew that must have been, if only briefly—if just for the space of a night—a bit like some specially put together family.

You both know the story. Grandpa Pete the navigator and Charlie ("What else, with my name?") the tail gunner, the only two out of seven who'd survived, and then met up again in the same prison camp. It would form a bond, a lasting bond, and so it did. "Dean and Hook." Now it was just "Dean." The frost had melted, but his head had its own frosting of close-cropped, almost white hair.

Charlie, of course, had Grace standing beside him,

holding his arm: a whole other partnership. But, however it comes about, to be the last one left, the only one left of just two, isn't that the worst thing ever? Worse than being the end of any line?

But Charlie didn't just have Grace, you'll remember, he had Nelson. Given the circumstances of Grandpa Pete's death, Nelson absolutely had to be there too. And, given those circumstances and Nelson's manifest capacity for loyalty, you might have thought he would have attached himself now to Grannie Helen, or to Mike. But he attached himself, to everyone's surprise and vague embarrassment, to Charlie. Charlie stood by his old pal's grave with Grace on one side and on the other a dog devotedly squatting on its haunches.

Did you miss your grandfather, were you grieving for him? Will you grieve for him now? You didn't weep. You were fourteen. Nor did Charlie weep, even with Nelson there to induce him, he just stood very still. Only your father wept. Even Grannie Helen controlled her tears, as you would have noticed, though she had most cause to weep, and her son was weeping beside her. A tougher generation? And she'd had all that early training.

Would I like to be a grandmother? Don't worry, that's a rhetorical question. Though it's a legitimate one, as legitimate as for a woman to ask, at thirty-two: am I going to be a mother? Though, for goodness' sake, I'm only forty-nine—I still have a whole *decade* on your father. And "Grannie Paulie," that's just plain *ghastly*.

And the short answer, anyway, is that even the word sends a chill through me, the word itself scares me. As if the next word can only be "widow." I'll settle for being a mother. Mike's wife and a mother: my complete and exact position in life.

But does Grannie Helen, now in her second year of widowhood, draw comfort and strength from being a grandmother, and from knowing that Grandpa Pete died a grandfather? You see what confronts you? You'll understand now how, despite our sixteen-year rule, both Mike and I, after his dad's funeral, went through a fever of feeling that *this* might be the right time, the best time even, never mind empty embargoes. You'd behaved in such a grown-up way, after all, and what could be more appropriate: after the death of *one* father?

But it would have been too sudden, too cruel, at such a time. And Mike simply wanted to keep you—can I put it like that, and will you blame him?—that year and a half longer. He wanted to "keep you." And, anyway, suppose that at that already trying time, and through whatever chain of unfortunate reactions, it should have found its way to his mother? What a further blow. And what an injustice: that Mike's father would have gone to his grave a self-believing grandparent and his mother would have the whole double burden of knowledge. You see what faces you? There was still that official margin of another eighteen months.

And that's passed now anyway, or has only hours left to run. It's dawn on the seventeenth of June, a wet and murky dawn, a reluctant sort of dawn. So it should be. And this man lying here, snoring gently, his familiar features reassembling out of the dark, is still sound asleep—how amazing—as if he's determined to remain so. "This man": is he no more than that now? I was once Mustardseed, my darlings, Titania's little helper. O, how I love thee! How I dote on thee!

And—how amazing: that's a bird out there, singing clearly, despite the falling rain, doing what birds must do at dawn in June. It's not a blackbird, I think. A thrush? A robin? Mike would know, he knows these things. I could wake him, ask him.

I'm afraid of Grannie Helen. I was afraid of her at that funeral. Were you a bit afraid, too, to look her closely in the eye? I didn't know how to comfort her. My own mother's example didn't help me. But Grannie Helen certainly looked, intently and often, at *you*. Did you notice that? As if perhaps *you* were really her best comfort on that day, or she was just, perhaps, full of admiration for you. How big you were now, how you'd shot up, not those two infants any more. And it's one of the features of these sixteen years, which may seem to you to have been immeasurably long—they're your whole life, after all—that they've sometimes seemed to us to rush you along, as if every month has produced some new version of you. There's been a sort of wild comfort in it, even as it's frightened us: all that amazing room for change.

But I'm afraid of Grannie Helen, who at seventy-two, we can fairly say, has stopped growing and changing and is just who she is. I'm afraid of that word "widow." I think she's probably awake now too, at Coombe Cottage—I feel sure she is—watching the grey light loom and listening to the thrum of the rain. I'm so simply afraid of Mike here no longer being here, it's the fear of my life. And I know this isn't the time for me to think of myself and I know it's up to you, but please don't take him from me today.

But I'm afraid of Grannie Helen in another way. I have to say this to you too. I've seen her look at you intently before. Fair enough, she's your grandmother—or she doesn't know she isn't. I've seen her look at you and then at Mike, then back again at you. Fair enough, she's a mother too. But mothers know things, they can just tell.

I think at that funeral, at which she didn't cry, she might have been thinking of how successfully she'd protected your Grandpa Pete. Now it might be her own son she's protecting, if not quite in the same way. Mothers only want the best for their children. It could be that as from today she'll be protecting you too, from the lie that you'll think you'll be keeping from her. If that's how it's to be, if that's how you choose.

Mike wants us to go to the Gifford Park, just those few miles from Birle. A coincidence? A coincidence on top of another coincidence, known only to me. There'll have to be some first time, anyway, when Mike and I see Grannie Helen, knowing that, now, you know. There'll have to be a first time for you. And when that time comes for me I'll have to look at her, knowing that you know, but thinking also that she might have guessed all along. Are you with me? And what kind of double-double dissimulation and treading on eggs is that going to entail? I could do without that, too, next weekend.

Perhaps I'm wrong, perhaps it's all just the stress of this situation and all in my overstretched imagination. It's dawn, one week after your sixteenth birthday. It's raining, it's teeming. Some little bedraggled bird I can't identify, which no doubt has a nest somewhere which is getting drenched too, is singing its heart out. Perhaps I'm wrong, but sometimes mothers can just tell things. In any case, they only want the best for their children.

THE LIGHT OF DAY

On the anniversary of a life-shattering event, George Webb, a former policeman turned private detective, revisits the catastrophes of his past and reaffirms the extraordinary direction of his future. Two years before, an assignment to follow a strayed husband and his mistress appeared simple enough, but this routine job left George a transformed man. Suspenseful, moving, and hailed by critics as a detective story unlike any other, *The Light of Day* is a gripping tale of murder and redemption, as well as a bold exploration of love and self-discovery.

Fiction/Literature/978-1-4000-3221-1

LAST ORDERS

Four men—friends, most of them, for half a lifetime—gather in a London pub. They have taken it upon themselves to carry out the last orders of Jack Dodds, master butcher, and deliver his ashes to the sea. As they drive toward the fulfillment of their mission, their errand becomes an extraordinary journey into their collective and individual pasts. Braiding these men's voices—and that of Jack's mysteriously absent widow—into a choir of secret sorrow and resentment, passion and regret, Graham Swift creates a testament to a changing England and to enduring mortality.

Fiction/Literature/978-0-679-76662-9

THE SWEET-SHOP OWNER

This flawlessly constructed and deeply compassionate novel is set during a single June day in the life of an outwardly unremarkable man whose inner world proves to be exceptionally resonant. As he tends to his customers, Willy Chapman, the sweet-shop owner, confronts the specters of his beautiful and distant wife and his clever, angry daughter, the history through which he has passed, and the great, unrequited passion that has tormented and redeemed him for forty years.

Fiction/Literature/978-0-679-73980-7

EVER AFTER

Dazzling in its structure and shattering in its emotional force, *Ever After* spans two centuries and settings from the adulterous bedrooms of postwar Paris to contemporary entanglements in the groves of academe. It is the story of Bill Unwin, a man haunted by the death of his beautiful wife and a survivor himself of a recent brush with mortality. And although it touches on Darwin and dinosaurs, bees and bridge builders, the true subject of *Ever After* is nothing less than the eternal question, "Why should things matter?" as pondered by both Bill Unwin and his Victorian ancestor, whose private notebooks reveal a quest for truth that bears eerie—and ultimately heartbreaking—parallels to Unwin's own.

Fiction/Literature/978-0-679-74026-1

OUT OF THIS WORLD

Out of This World interweaves the history of a blighted family with the tragic and ludicrous history of the twentieth century. Its alternating narrators are a father and daughter—each obsessed with the other and irrevocably estranged—surveying their losses and grievances on opposite sides of the Atlantic. Their voices are unforgettable, their hurts terribly moving, and their vision of our era, like Swift's itself, shocking and terribly persuasive.

Fiction/Literature/978-0-679-74032-2

SHUTTLECOCK

Prentis, the narrator of this nightmarish masterpiece, catalogs "dead crimes" for a branch of the London Police Department and suspects that he is going crazy. His files keep vanishing. His boss subjects him to cryptic taunts. His family despises him. And as Prentis desperately tries to hold on to the scraps of his sanity, he uncovers a conspiracy of blackmail and betrayal that extends from his department and into the buried past of his father, a war hero codenamed "Shuttlecock"—and, lately, a resident of a hospital for the insane. At once a fiendishly devious mystery and a profound reckoning of the debts that bind sons to fathers, *Shuttlecock* is a brilliantly accomplished work of fiction.

Fiction/Literature/978-0-679-73933-3